Novels by Elizabeth Savage

Toward
the End

Toward the End

A NOVEL BY

Elizabeth Savage

Little, Brown and Company   Boston Toronto

Second Printing

LIBRARY OF CONGRESS CATALOGING IN PUBLICATION DATA

Savage, Elizabeth.
  Toward the end.

  I. Title.
PZ4.S263To.   [PS3569.A823] 813'.54   79-27364
ISBN 0-316-77156-2

BP

Designed by D. Christine Benders

*Published simultaneously in Canada
by Little, Brown & Company (Canada) Limited*

PRINTED IN THE UNITED STATES OF AMERICA

This book is for Billie and Sewall Webster,
   who were there in every sense of the word,
And for Gene Youngken,
   who helped mop up.

Toward
the End

1

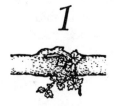

THOSE OF THEM who in that fateful year decided to winter were (except for Jessie) very proud and very thoughtful.

At the post office people asked, "How come?"

No one had ever wintered on Crow Point.

All of them said the same thing and meant it: Maine was the good place, Jacataqua Island the good part of Maine and Crow Point the good part of Jacataqua Island. But that did not explain why, at this particular time, they had decided to hole up in their summer homes. Their answers, had they given answers, would have been as complicated as their personalities and not entirely honest.

But Jessie Thorne had an honest answer.

She snapped shut the glass door of her post office box, twirled the lock, flung her short wheat-colored hair from her eyes and said, "Because I'm being divorced."

3

Jessie had great smoke-colored eyes smudged with black lashes; she was outspoken and they gave her credit for not having changed. Way back when she was five there had been that fire down on the Point and when the Volunteers tried to find out what started it, Jessie had stood there in her busted sneakers and had said, "I did."

She had been a sturdy and a sunny child.

Those who knew Jessie (one or two knew Jessie) could tell now that she was distressed: her forehead whitened and all the little hairs about her face dampened and curled like a hot baby's. Those who did not know her saw only the same tall, direct young woman who had been around forever. People like people who do not change.

But Jessie had changed, and not for the better. During that final bitter week with Howard she had turned dangerous and was so appalled by her own rage and venom that she decided to isolate herself before somebody had to isolate her. She thought in terms of blood. His. Hers. Anyone's.

When he first said that he wanted out, Jessie had slashed at her own innards like a wounded shark. Her mediocrity. Her lack of allure.

"After eight years," he said, "allure has nothing to do with it."

That should have been comforting, but wasn't.

He was a handsome man, which had been her undoing, and was a little older than she was, which had accustomed her to instant obedience.

He was Black Irish and wanted everyone to forget it. He turned on her the blue electric look that was so persuasive to his clients and, having promised her protection, took it away from her.

That was the first night.

Later he said, "Make a life of your own. Do something. Be somebody."

But she had married him so that she wouldn't have to be any-body. And this was that very man who had inveighed against the new women and had called them neutered.

4

Now he said, "Go be a new woman, because you can't live my life."

But Jessie was not a new woman. She was an old, old woman. She wanted to bear a child (which had not yet proved convenient) and to fight with the male who would fight for the child.

"Why don't you get some friends of your own?" he asked.

She had thought that his friends were her friends. But apparently not.

During the brief time that it took the marriage to dissolve, he went to the office in the daytime and thought about other things. But Jessie stayed home and wondered why she had been badly educated. Her grandmother had brought her up; her grandmother was a stern and sterling woman with a granite mind which (Jessie saw now) was imbedded in another century. She had taught Jessie that a wife is gentle and faithful and, in recompense, the man gets out of the house and makes a living. She had not taught Jessie what to do if the man does not particularly care if you are faithful or how, in that event, you yourself can make a living. By this Jessie did not mean how you go on writing checks but how you go on living.

Thinking about these things that she had not thought to think about, Jessie, who had been open as a child, grew closed and cynical and began to see the world as through the cold walls of an aquarium. Urged to be a new woman, she felt like a porpoise, caught in an evolutionary net. The creature who looked in on her was not, she saw, the creature she had taken him to be.

That being so, she should have swum away in silence. It was a mistake, on that last bad night, to say what she had said.

She said, "There's someone else."

He said, "No, there isn't."

She believed him. Howard was honest to a fault.

But if there were no one else it meant that Jessie was rejected rather than he besotted. It also meant he was more ruthless than she had recognized and perhaps weaker. So there would soon be

5

someone else, someone as unlike Jessie as possible, which meant somebody dark, short, adoring and adorable.

Thoughtfully, she said, "And maybe male."

So naturally he hit her, one sharp blow with his open hand that was designed for her cheek. Unfortunately, instead of wincing away, at that very moment Jessie turned on him and he struck her squarely on the nose. Oddly enough, in the morning her face was unmarked, but when she used the Waterpik her mouth filled with blood.

There could be no living with one another after that.

First he moved out and then she moved out and just as soon as it was warm enough she went back to Maine.

First and for eons the ancient seas rained down shells. Then earthquakes and volcanoes pushed the new land high; twelve times the ranges rose and weathered and the seas rose and fell. Glaciers, like cold bulldozers, pushed rock to the water's edge until the weak ground sank beneath the weight and the sea rushed in, leaving the drowned peaks islanded. Storms shook the shore. Then came the Red Paint People and then the Indians and after them the farmers and fighters and fishermen.

Then came the summer people.

Jessie Thorne was a summer person; Charley Pratt was not. Jessie was young and Charley Pratt was ninety, but they had been friends for a good long time.

Charley thought that she looked peaked.

In his time Charley had kept the store, been postmaster and first selectman and town moderator and was still the only notary public on the island. Some were afraid of him, not because he was unkind, because he wasn't unkind, but because he had been around so long that he knew everything about everyone, which is not comfortable. And it is true that Charley had decided as a sharp-featured child that people were a shabby lot, and had had little reason since to alter that decision.

But he liked Jessie. Her small sins were open ones. She was fierce, stubborn and competitive but no backbiter, and if she

6

was notional, her notions threatened no one but herself. He saw no reason now to give the town something to cluck about. So he whacked at a fly for the looks of the thing and then glanced up at the Seth Thomas clock and said, "She'll be waiting. She'll want to see you."

He meant Mrs. Charley.

It would be nice if nothing ever changed, but things do change and every year something is different. Up the road a piece, a new small house was painted Canadian blue; the owners thought flowerpots would prove attractive and preferred those which hang from an object which resembles the bare ribs of an umbrella. A handwritten sign on the town pump said not to drink the water or if you were going to drink it, it might be good to boil it first. Albert Walters had died during the winter and in his yard weeds leaned against the FOR SALE sign, which made Jessie sad. Albert had always kept his yard so nice. But the blue waters still shimmered in the cove and before the Atterburys' white salt-box the flag still striped the sky and snapped.

This year Jessie had missed out on the mayflowers, but she had missed little else. It had been a long, cold spring. Well, spring comes late to Maine, and every year folks fret for fear the lilacs won't be out in time for the graves. But now, ten days into June, everything was out all together: forsythia, lilacs purple and white and the hot pink of wild crab. On the downside of Charley Pratt's house apple blossoms were pale in the aging orchard. The green velvet lawns were still buttoned with dandelions.

Charley said, "Climate's changing."

Most took what he said for gospel, but not Jessie. He was a fine old fake and not even a real Pratt, but had been adopted over New Hampshire way, though there were few to remember it and they had long lost interest. Jessie slipped her arm through his and they were halfway across the road when this motorcycle burned over the brow of the hill and hurtled down on them roaring an imperious gangway.

Jessie shoved Charley back and then she stepped forward into the path of the machine and watched with cold amusement while the motorcycle bucked on its back wheel and banged back, scoured a screaming curve across the road and stopped too close to a burly tree. The cyclist got his boots to the ground. His knees, on either side the saddle, shook.

"Jesus Christ, lady," he said.

"Pissant," Jessie said to Charley.

On the safe side of the road Charley Pratt said to her, "You've soured." It wasn't a reprimand; it was a comment. "That's Roger Prescott's kid," he said. "He's not much but there's no need to kill him."

She hadn't meant to kill Roger Prescott's kid. Yes, she had. Jessie didn't take Charley's arm again. He was a friend but he was one of them: a man. If she had soured on men, she had reason. She'd been a good wife to Howard — jim-dandy. Cheerful, uncomplaining, sometimes amusing and often considerate. Look how he paid her back. What's more, when she was not going to have the child, where was he? Off trying to amuse himself. Since when they parted she hadn't told him she was pregnant because he didn't deserve to know, it was probably unfair to hold this against him, but she did. Men walk away, but women have to tidy up.

They went in through the ell because that way you don't track up the floors. Mrs. Charley put out her arms and Jessie went right into them. It seemed to Charley that a drink might help and it so happened he had one to offer. Summer people liked to think of Charley as the grand old man, to point him out to visiting friends and to put gifts before him. Most were useless: Scotch sweaters, Greek fishing caps, Irish whisky. But every summer one of them brought him rum from Jamaica, and the Pratts liked it in their tea.

Charley Pratt knew that it was a long time since there had been a grand old man. Communities outgrow traditions and the authority of the old men dwindles as the population waxes and wanes with the widened highways. Still, it was nice to have the rum.

8

They thought that what Jessie proposed to do was crazy but would not discourage her because that just makes folks more sot. She meant to block off the fireplace and put in a woodstove; everybody does, these days. If the pipes froze she could haul water from the well. Nobody had ever got around to taking the old outhouse out. People used to live that way all the time.

"What do you think, Charley? Can I do it?"

"Oh, you can *do* it. Cost you something."

Because the town wouldn't plow beyond the Bombing Gate. It wasn't town road past the Bombing Gate.

"I'll get an old truck and a snow-blade."

No need of that. Road commissioner would plow her. So as she understood it would be at her expense and when he got around to it.

When Mrs. Charley wished to protest she knotted her hands beneath her apron. She knew how fast larders empty and she also knew the road commissioner. There wasn't a nicer man in town, but he tired easily of plowing.

"What if you run out of things?" she asked.

"She won't run out of things," said Charley.

The rum was a hundred and fifty proof and Charley's friend said that in Jamaica they chased it with Red Stripe beer. Jessie had recently found that you can't trust liquor; sometimes it's an upper and sometimes it is not.

"What you said in the post office," Charley said. "That was a funny way to put it. Most would say because *I'm* getting a divorce."

"Not me," Jessie said bitterly. "If he wants it, he can get it."

Charley said, "I always wondered if he suited."

Jessie had always thought that Howard suited. But to be struck is shameful and it is unfair that it is the stricken and not the striker who is shamed. Long after the discolored tissue mends, the ego throbs: it may well sicken and destroy its host.

Howard had thought her unreasonably irate, since he had not intended to draw blood. However, it was not he who had been slapped but she. It is never he who is slapped, but she. Nature has seen fit to bestow on only one-half of the race the sinew and the clout. And then, she had been carrying his child.

Charley crossed one long leg above the other. Mrs. Charley knew that this meant he would soon excuse himself, and so she waited. Certain things Jessie and Mrs. Charley would not discuss until he retreated to the bathroom; from their point of view it was felicitous that as he grew older he went oftener.

Mrs. Charley said, "How did you feel about it?"

"Rotten," Jessie said.

The Pratts were childless. Mrs. Charley said, "It's so much easier these days. I wish I'd had the option."

Jessie said, "So do I."

The teaspoons clicked.

"Mother always used to say if you can hear the spoons click, someone needs more." They listened for the flush. Mrs. Charley poured. "It looks like regular tea," she said.

After a moment Jessie said, "There's nothing to it. That's the bad part, that there's nothing much to it."

Mrs. Charley said, "If you can afford."

Something about the conversation suddenly made Jessie uneasy, as if she were speaking in Spanish to someone listening in Portuguese.

Mrs. Charley said, "Do you remember Rose Ella Rodgers?"

Jessie remembered Rose Ella well, a pleasant, witless girl well liked in town who couldn't get the knack of not getting pregnant. Some of the kids she kept and some she couldn't see her way clear to.

"Last time they did that thing that they do now with salt."

Jessie pushed the damp hair from her brow and asked, "Who paid?"

"I did," Mrs. Charley said. "I knew her mother."

The trouble with some older people is that they're not easily shocked. Jessie saw that Mrs. Charley thought that she had had her child aborted, but she would not have done that and was about to say so when Charley came back fighting up his fly. His spectacles had somehow managed to slide over the high hump of his nose. He put his gnarled hand on the rum bottle and raised his brows and Jessie nodded.

Later she rose with what she thought considerable grace.

"I thank you very much," she said. "That tea certainly hit the spot."

Mrs. Charley said, "We like it."

At the door Jessie turned. She said, "I'd just as soon it didn't get around."

They knew she didn't mean the divorce but the wintering. Summer people say that the town talks a lot, but the town knows who it is who talks a lot. Nobody likes to think that everybody thinks that you have lost your mind.

"And besides, I can do it," Jessie said. A moment later she returned and poked her shining head around the door. She said, "Is the climate really changing?"

"How would I know?" asked Charley.

They watched her cross the yard with her head held like a banner. Mrs. Charley had her own way of handling Charley.

She said, "I thought it good in you not to say anything about Tom Elder."

"They never did get along all that well," he said, pleased, "and Jessie always wants to be the first. Least said, soonest mended." Then he turned from the window to his wife.

"Is she going to be all right?" he asked.

Some things Mrs. Charley didn't tell Charley because it was none of his business.

"I don't know," Mrs. Charley said.

2

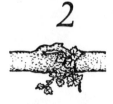

NO ONE WHO SUMMERED on Crow Point hadn't wistfully thought it would be nice to throw up one's hands and stay.

They were all tired of Baltimore and of Boston and of Fairfield and they felt that with a little forethought they could keep comfortable enough. Why, the driftwood alone! Nobody told them not to burn driftwood, not in a stove: it makes for rust. One day the bottom of the stove goes out and there's your fire on the floor.

There was no telephone down there, but they were tired of telephones. Sometimes the message is pleasant but usually not. And they were tired of not trusting anyone. When was the last time you walked on a street? It looks funny. You must be drunk, or poor. There are no sidewalks anymore. Where do the kids roller-skate?

What they would all prefer was immaculate air and silence.

Blue spruce shadows on the snow. Good hot simple soups. And chowders.

They were tired of the mailman with his daily demands. On Crow Point, if you really had to have your mail, someone else was always going into town, and the postmistress took a certain amount of welcome latitude.

"Oh, they won't want that," she said, and then she threw it out. They trusted her. Personal letters and honest bills went into the boxes, but there just wasn't enough room for catalogues and magazines and political pleas, so if you wanted those you leafed through the common pile and took what you required. Who would have thought that the Cavanaghs subscribed to *Commentary?*

The men tired of their jobs and of commuting with madmen; on Route 128 the cars spin out ahead of you as if it is a racetrack. The women tired of their houses, which were colorless as their cars.

And all this time in the background, there was Maine.

It even might make sense. Every year they rented their camps for enough to pay the local taxes; three hundred dollars a week isn't chicken feed. But it wasn't enough to keep up with their city properties, and the last time the taxes went up again in Baltimore and Boston they had about had it with the split-level and the gracious old brick and the built-in mortgage and the explosive costs for the New Math and the Black Studies. However, some of them had children.

If you had children, it wasn't practical to winter on Crow Point. You couldn't expect the town to send the bus down there, and Lily Butts, who drove the school bus, would have resigned first anyway: nobody would have blamed her. It would be an adventure to be snowed in, but not with children. One does not wish even to be rained in, not with children.

Women seem to remember the third grade better than men. Lydia Pullen spoke of "the frolic architecture of the snow."

"John Greenleaf Whittier," her husband said, pleased.

Lydia said, "Ralph Waldo Emerson."

" 'Snow-Bound.' "

" 'The Snow-Storm.' "

Her husband said that he could have sworn.

Lydia said, "Get the *Bartlett's*." Lydia was in the habit of being right.

No, there was not one of them who wouldn't like to be snow-bound and of the world forgetting, by the world forgot. But they couldn't do it this year and probably not next. They were all prosperous and in debt, they couldn't pass up the promotion and they had to think about the retirement funds.

And then, none of them yet had seen a winter storm.

Tom Elder had come closest, because he showed up every year for Town Meeting, which was easy enough for him. Teachers get time off for Christmas and Chanukkah and everything but the month of Ramadan and it looks as if that may be coming.

Somebody said, "He isn't a teacher anymore."

"Oh?"

"Now he just stays home and paints. The aunt died."

No one was much impressed. On Jacataqua Island the woods are filled with painters. On Jacataqua there is one post office, one central school, one firehouse and altogether too many creative people.

From the beginning there had been a peppering of painters and sculptors and musicians, all pleasant people and some of them eminent. They worked hard, kept to themselves and in the fall went home to wherever they were eminent. William Zorach lived here and Gaston Lachaise and Marsden Hartley. If you ever get as far as New York you can see them at the Metropolitan. Seguin Light!

But there were those, and Charley Pratt was among them, who felt that things were getting out of hand. Where there had once been two writers there were ten, and curious skills were proliferating. Young people made pottery and harpsichords and custom cabinets or carved amusing bottle-stoppers and made little boxes. For the most part the young people were from off-island; this did not mean that native gifts did not abound. The local ladies knit and quilt and make beach bags out of fishing nets; there is a brisk demand for miniature lobster buoys. Jim Lincoln, who runs the store, paints seascapes and advertises CHEESE, FILMS and OIL PAINTINGS; he sells a surprising amount of all.

But there is too much of it going on and, moreover, many of these talented persons do not get along in complete accord. Set aside individual resentments: composers don't think much of the manual arts and writers don't like the fact that painters are not sued for recognizable likenesses. Professionals look with suspicion on those who do not appear to work, and lobstermen and shipyard workers take a dim view of all.

So when Tom Elder showed up on the first Saturday of every March, with no vote but opinions about everything and two pies for the Pot Luck Supper, it did not make him as popular as he thought.

The town is not flattered by the sustained interest of a summer resident. Summer people are summer people and the town is the town and that's that. Summer people always think you can do something about the dump. You can't do anything about the dump. The gulls come and the rats come and that is the way it is. If you tried to bulldoze the way you are supposed to do, Perry couldn't handle it, and then there would be the problem about what to do with Perry.

Perry is very tall and excessively thin and simple and he is old and faithful. Rain or shine he is there every Saturday to see that the fire doesn't get away, and male or female, he calls you "dear." But of course that is not surprising. Everyone in these parts calls you "dear." Some of the latecomers are startled, because you don't expect it from the grocery boy or, for that matter, from the sheriff. And if you are not male Perry lugs your bottles, which is more than the kids will do.

Perry is well connected. His mother was a Stroud and oddly enough his father was a Stroud too, but they were ever so far removed, so that has nothing to do with his simplicity. At one point the state offered to be responsible for him, but nobody wanted that. During the summertime he berries and all year around he accepts your trash and is never curious about what it is in it. One does not forget that he is a Stroud, and a pleasant man, to boot.

Nobody wants to have anything to do with the state.

Rats are not popular, but gulls are nice.

Later (quite a lot later) Tom Elder had to admit that he had been carried away. The first Saturday in March was radiant; along the roads the snow was piled like egg-whites and the sun was moving north; before his cottage it would rise now over East Brown Cow instead of Ragged Island and briefly now, at noon, it stroked your shoulders like a trusted hand. But when it slanted, which it still did quickly, you knew the wind was going to nip your nape, and all those puddles which dazzled like turquoise in the light would search and find that place where the sole of your boot should have been stitched.

Nobody in Maine gives advice. If they like you, they may suggest alternatives. Charley Pratt had never much taken to Tom Elder. In spite of what anyone might think, Charley was not a lovable old curmudgeon with a secret love for children. It depends on the child. Charley had known Tom since Tom was a sprout and he always thought he was a show-off and a know-it-all.

So when Tom Elder asked if he could get down to Crow Point with his car, Charley Pratt said, "I'm sure I don't know."

Edna Joy Lincoln was the janitor: her mother was a Popham. She had greased the hall like glass, not so that people would see that she did a good job — everyone knew that Edna Joy did a good job — but so that the little kids could slide and stay out of their parents' way.

Article six, section five, was coming up.

To see if the town will publish the names of the town poor.

16

Certainly not!

Nobody was going to shame Mary Elizabeth Powers because her grandson hadn't turned out well. So everyone lined up when Charley Pratt said, "Bring your ballots in."

It wasn't easy, either, because although they had taken the partition out that separated the fourth grade from the fifth, and had borrowed all those folding chairs from the New Bristol YMCA, there wasn't really room and they had to go out one door and in the other just to get in line.

About some articles nobody cared much; the men went to smoke and the women stretched their legs on the porch steps and said, "Let me know when next."

One thing that made Tom Elder furious (and did every year) was that as the offices came up the candidates stood just this side of the ballot box and passed out ballots. Some were shrewd enough to accept slips from everyone, but most only winked and took one from their friend. Call that a secret ballot?

For any irregularity, the town clerk tried to make up. You might have known her forever and have seen her yesterday, but she said, "Name, please?" and then laboriously her finger moved upon the list until she found you. Then she looked up quickly to make sure.

There was a momentary rumpus when Eleanor Tradgett (the most beautiful child you have ever seen and her ears pierced already) butted Joey Pope in the belly. Both mothers rushed to castigate their own. Charley Pratt moderated.

Tom Elder demanded, "When are they going to get to the clam flats?"

Charley Pratt lifted his tempestuous brows. He said, "Don't know, I'm sure."

The Crow Point road proved to be plowed past the Whittakers', which was reasonable, because they had been coming for so many seasons that their position was ambiguous: not quite town and not quite from away. They had been known to hold Christmas in their big handsome house on the cove that looked across to the little palisades and to the woods which (thank God) had been willed to the Audubon Society. The Whittakers could hardly be called from away. What was not so reasonable was that the road had been plowed a half-mile- beyond the Whittakers', in order to accommodate the terrible trailer.

If of the five points on Jacataqua Crow Point was the most desirable (and it was), it was because up until now it had not been defiled by the battered trucks, car carcasses and piled lobster pots of those real residents whose patched-up houses shouldered the summer cottages. Those who had built those cottages had erroneously assumed that their neighbors would, in good time, die out; instead, their multiplying descendants filled the nights with the roar of their motorcycles and shattered Maine Public Broadcasting with their C.B.'s.

Now here on the Crow Point road there was this trailer. Trailers accumulate a lot of broken chairs (some of them over-stuffed) and old refrigerators. One supposes that from the nature of the thing, there is no room in the trailer for the refrigerator. None of the summer people knew who the young man was; surprisingly, they leaped to the conclusion that he was a member of the Mafia. Who knows how these things get about? It is established that the Mafia is very strong in Waterville, God knows why.

Anyway, there the young man was, strong, handsome and black-haired, with a pretty wife, and a lovely little girl, six German shepherds and the refrigerators. But if he was a member of the Mafia he was not high in the hierarchy. As we understand, the Mafia may well go in for German shepherds but are not much for trailers.

The town could have told Crow Point who he was. He was Leota Sellar's stepson and had always been very good to Leota. He hoped to get started lobstering and in the meantime did odd jobs (some of them very odd indeed) and had married that nice girl from Cundy's Harbor. Even the summer people (summer people are not beasts) got to like him very much because he came when he said he was going to come, and when the lovely child cut her foot rather badly on a mussel shell, at the sight of his darling's blood, he fainted. One can live with a man like that.

Tom Elder had a fine, fretful face which he averted as he passed the trailer, rather quickly because the shepherds had a habit of leaping at your car. They probably couldn't get in, but it is unsettling. When the trailer first appeared everyone from Crow Point had turned up at Town Meeting, filled with rage and armed with their old tax receipts. To their surprise, the town agreed: no more trailers. Except for those already sanctioned by the grandfather clause, a bit of jugglery that was to prove more comforting to them all than at that time they had any way of knowing.

All right. First you go by the trailer and then you go by the marsh, where every one of them has seen a deer startle. One of them has claimed to have seen a moose, but he has never been reliable. You do see porcupines — that outré animal — and little red fox and woodchucks and blue heron in their ungainly flight. And squirrels and skunks and chipmunks and all like that.

Past the marsh the land is posted: Private Property. No trespassing. No hunting. Of course everyone hunts. Who cares? Only Massachusetts hunters get drunk and throw their bottles through your windows, but Massachusetts hunters don't much come up this time of year, perhaps because so much is going on in Massachusetts. And then, people from Massachusetts worry about legal licenses, which is tomfool now that everyone has a freezer and an honest need to keep it filled. Some of us wonder who it is who stops for hunting and fishing licenses at L. L. Bean's in the middle of the night. Probably he would have had his last drink in Kittery.

Tom had to leave his car at the Bombing Gate because after that it was all uphill and old cold mean and crusted snow, the kind that has sullenly settled in. The Bombing Gate dates back to one of those World Wars when it had seemed expedient to teach the young men how to bomb. At that time, no one was to pass the gate for fear of being bombed. This meant that the clam-diggers couldn't get to the clam flats and that the Raffertys, a popular old couple, couldn't cross at low tide and walk on Higgins' Head. Naturally they were sore because they weren't used to having anyone tell them anything, let alone that they couldn't walk on Higgins' Head.

But after a while they all had a lot of fun. The soldier boys could cross at low tide and swim back if they had to. The boys brought the Raffertys cigarettes and butter and the Raffertys laid in more beer. But the fun ended one afternoon when four of the fellows drove an amphibious truck out toward the Black Rocks. It wasn't that amphibious.

On Jacataqua Island you have your annual accidents. Someone flips off Route 27 into a tree or a telephone pole or into the Round Pond, where, from time to time, they drown. But for the most part when people drown it is because they *will* go down after a storm to watch the combers and they *will* go out on the rocks in order to see them better and then that one rogue wave comes along and goodbye voyeur. That is a lot of water out there and don't you forget it.

The Bombing Gate long ago rotted out, along with several individual liberties. The clam-diggers still couldn't get to the clam flats because the town had voted to reseed the clam flats; perhaps they shouldn't have taken the state's advice. Even when the flats were reopened, the diggers weren't going to be able to drive down there through the salt meadow as they had done since Hannah was a pup, because there was now a Crow Point Association and the association had put a chain across the road. The old families wouldn't have done that; it would have embarrassed them, they liked the clam-diggers and anyway, they wouldn't have Associated. These new people knew perfectly well that they couldn't control the clam flats, which were public lands, but they wished passionately to control the access to the public lands. If diggers or picnickers or Canadians wanted to come in by boat, very well.

However, Crow Point was not to get off scot-free. For when the flats were opened again the owners of contiguous properties (and only contiguous properties) were to be limited to a peck of clams a day. That is more clams than anybody wants but the principle annoys, and in those cottages where the clam hoe and the clam hod had long been treasured, they hung now as a mute reminder that they could not be used without collusive and contiguous friends. And even that at the risk of fines and the laughter of the town.

From where he had to leave the car, Tom Elder felt a familiar clutch of tension as he mounted the short steep hill, so heavily wooded that one lost the glint of the sea and the taupe of the sand; a tension magnified because he was not used to going up (as he did now) upon his hands and knees. It was a position he would not ordinarily assume, but the surface of the old snow was so hard that he could not smash his boots into it, and it did cross his mind that it was a foolhardy place to snap an ankle. The hard clean snow was stenciled by a thin fall of needles over a pattern of bird prints, caught in the sudden freezing of an earlier day.

Then he looked down on his own house, which seemed to teeter upon the very verge of the Atlantic Ocean, although Tom knew it to be a good ten feet above turf-line and a tumbling forty feet above high water; of this his father had made sure. His father had often pointed with pride and pleasure to the continuous ledge of solid rock that ran across their own frontage and made it safe to build.

There the camp was. Safe, sound, and well — there. Steam rose from the sun-warmed roof. Crystal dropped from the quaking-aspen tree.

Tom was never sure what dread thing he anticipated. After the first snowfall there was no fear of forest fires, but someone who broke in might have been careless with the stove. Kids might have burned it down for the hell of it. Maybe the wind took off the roof. From freeze-up until after mudding, no disaster would have been reported.

But there it was again. All his life it had been a summer refuge from harassment and from whatever he felt ill equipped or disinclined to do. To Jacataqua, where he had wandered anonymous as a tern, Tom credited his success.

Well, *success*. Brigid had once told him that his dependency upon the island was sickly, but at the time she had just been playing the married game. His name was not well known and his paintings hung in no important galleries, but that was because he had been netted by the necessity of making a little living. It had prevented him from the private vision that was — he knew — the difference between mediocrity and recognition. Now he was freed from the importunities of students since his aunt, bless her heart, had succumbed to a massive insult to the brain. She had not left as much as he had been given to believe, but what she had, he got, and with it he intended to become famous. He was a lucky man.

Moreover, he had had the good judgment to marry a blithe young woman who could support herself, since she was accomplished at her own (less distinguished) métier. She was a stockbroker.

Brokeress?

Brigid freely admitted that she herself was a town girl, but she had been good about his summers in the country and willing to join him there on many weekends. She was a fine wife and a good friend, and looking down now on the walls of his own house he thought it would be nice to go to bed with her. One could light a small fire. She always liked to go to bed as long as it was in a bed, but had not proved cooperative about what he had always wanted to do, which was to lie down in the woods.

"Didn't you ever?" he had asked her once.

"Well," she said. "But I didn't like it."

When she finally consented it was with the stipulation that it be after dark: she had tricked him. She knew very well that after it was decent to have the first drink, no one was going to get him out into the woods.

Nobody's perfect.

Looking down the long cluttered slope to his house, Tom remembered another time when her taste had lapsed. Some of the latecomers, with no appreciation of the natural beauty of windfalls and puckerbrush, had put in lawns.

Brigid said, "We could have a gorgeous lawn."

"Perhaps," he said icily, "you would like flamingoes?"

She was aware of her mistake at once and said she had been thinking of keeping the mosquitoes down, but he knew and she knew this was subterfuge. Besides, a lawn meant truckloads of what in these parts is known as *loom*, and it meant reseeding every year where your friends drove down too far and later spun their wheels trying to get out, and it meant not only buying a power mower but operating it, too. No, thank you.

Tom's father, he felt, had built wisely. There were no frills to the house at all, but there was a long living room with a north light that made a dandy studio, a woodstove, a sink, a bedroom and a small serviceable bath and, what's more, water for it. What money there was (his father had never had much money) had bought the land and sunk the deep well. The former had gone up tenfold in value and because of the latter, the Elders were not dependent on summer surface pipes, which meant that — theoretically — they could come down out of season. Actually, they would have to lug their water like everybody else, because the pipes had to be drained in the fall and kerosene poured down lest one of the unpleasant surprises Tom anticipated should be burst pipes.

Nevertheless, he thought now, he could manage through a winter if he chose, and he might just so choose. Brigid had not taken with a whole heart to Tom's staying home all day long and painting. In fact, she would not permit it in the living room of the apartment on Arlington Street. Brigid was neat and painters are not known for neatness, and though he kept the door to the guest room closed, he knew she did not like what she knew was going on behind it.

And then, she liked a rather more active social life than he felt conducive to becoming great and famous, and she felt that the best social life ensues when the wife (with cut flowers) and the husband (with the wine) arrive home simultaneously and right after the cleaning woman has left. At these small galas Jessie and Howard Thorne were often guests, a fact that Tom was sure had not pleased Jessie any more than it had pleased him. A mutual dislike as children does not ensure adult compatibility, and while Brigid and Howard were much at ease in one another's company, these city dinners Tom could do without. He thought instead of cold and sunny days with the smell of woodsmoke and of long lonely evenings loud with music, and his eyes narrowed reflectively.

You would have to keep in a lot of supplies. There might be days when you would have to use snowshoes. The pipe from the well would have to be covered deeper than it was; it could be wrapped in electric tape. If you lost the power you might have to drain everything. So?

Whistling, he started down.

Every year the yard filled up with the debris of winter. Branches went flying, the shallow-rooted spruce blew over; certain bushes would be uprooted, though never the tenacious sumac with its rust-colored candelabra that were so decorative and avaricious. For the most part nature sort of cleaned it up. Most of the stuff eventually would rot away or be covered up when the wild raspberry burst into a green foam.

Nature did nothing about down timber. Man had to clear it from his path. This year a big maple had gone down and Tom had to fling one leg across it and then swing the other one. It was too big for him with his own ax and was a job for the Williams boys and their power saws. Some of the summer people had their own power saws and boasted that they cut their own firewood, and others, with Tom, agreed that the soft wood didn't burn well and that the savage saws could take a hand off at the wrist and had best be left to the Williams boys, who knew what they were doing.

He dropped heavily down into the snow. Now came the best part, which brought the annual excitement of Christmas.

Almost without exception the houses on the sea side of Crow Point were pitched upon stilt legs, to let the high winter tides slide under. As the years went by and their caution quieted, many owners covered the open spaces with crisscross lathing: they thought it looked better. Tom Elder thought it looked like Revere Beach. He enjoyed being perched on those high legs and he enjoyed seeing what the winter sea had brought him.

Because of the savage indentations of the coast, the running of the tides and the way the channels lay, some places were more protected and some less so, and Tom's house got a better catch than most. Whereas against his neighbor's latticework the tall winter seas nudged plastic detergent bottles, oil cans and scraps of Styrofoam, under his own house he found pieces of twisted driftwood that could be used as lamp-bases, and small bottles that the summer sun had purpled. Bright colored lobster buoys — his was the best collection on the Point. Once in a while an entire lobster trap, though always with the slats kicked in by the winter water. A child's boat that had traveled unknown leagues. Once a note in a bottle, but it proved to have been launched only from Gin Beach.

In the beginning the town had frightened the beginners with dubious glances and downright warnings against trying to build down there. The water had been known to cut through the road in two crucial places, temporarily islanding the whole Point; waves had broken over the building sites, great portions of the cliffs had been knocked away. Nonsense. The first house had been finished in '32, and nothing like that had ever happened since.

The anxiety of the women crested and subsided. They suspected a little malice on the part of the town.

Certainly there had been hard feelings when the Private Property signs went up. There were many, still active and robust, who all their lives had liked to hike the single footpath that threaded the wooded Point and then the first road, that was not much more than a wagon track with high grass sprouting in the middle. From here they could crash through the underbrush to the beaches with their picnic baskets and their hats and bathing shoes.

The present generation was used to being unwelcome but was not supposed to take it personally because since the Association, no one was welcome. Owners were requested to carry stickers on their cars, which was ridiculous: they all knew each others' cars. They were also requested to see that their legitimate guests did the same, which was even sillier. Who is going to ask his guest to do that? And for that matter, who can put his hand upon that little bunch of stickers?

This inhospitable attitude which the majority deemed necessary to their privacy ensured that the young people of the town sped around by night throwing out their beer cans and that in the fall the hunters headed first for Crow Point and shot up the No Hunting signs.

Tom Elder didn't like any part of this new nonsense; he lusted for the time of year when the others packed their station wagons and went home, and it had something to do with his sudden conviction that in these terrible times the talented who could retreat to snow and silence were perhaps morally compelled to do so.

He took great breaths of the squeaking clean air.

Striped pine siskins rattled the cones of a nearby tree; their wings and tails flashed yellow. A jay screamed and flew like sky against the snow. And there motionless on a cedar stump was a saw-whet owl. Saw-whets are singularly unafraid; perhaps they know that people like them. Who wouldn't like a little owl not six inches high? Tom stepped toward it; the wings that it raised once and lowered were barred and the big yellow eyes inquisitive: you could believe them friendly, if you chose.

How many can stand in a companionable silence with a saw-whet owl?

Precious few.

Below him the sea simpered. Gentle as June, it patted the boulders at the foot of the forty feet of plummeting broken rock, nestled upon the sand and waved at him only the most frivolous scarf of foam.

He stepped briskly down the bank and stopped, astounded.

Underneath his house, athwart the knickknacks and the gew-gaws, a thirty-foot log lay like a battering ram. It had missed one piling by three inches; the other end, a good three feet in diameter, had missed another by even less. If it had hit, it would have taken out the house.

Incredulous, Tom looked at the deceptive water.

It beamed back.

3

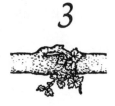

THE PILGRIMS didn't even get to Plymouth until 1617, for cat's sake. And then in that bad second winter, they got help from Maine. It was Monhegan fishermen who loaded the Pilgrims' holds with mackerel and halibut and hake and sent them back to their women.

In sober fact, the first permanent settlement in North America was Fort Popham, on the banks of the mighty Kennebec. Well, fairly permanent. The *Gift of God*, with one hundred and twenty colonists, anchored in August of 1607. Before freeze-up they had built a storehouse, fifty domiciles and a church, but in December all but forty-five of them went home and most of the forty-five lost interest by spring. It was too cold, there wasn't any gold, fishing was hard work, the Indians were unfriendly and didn't have many furs. So they all sailed away on the

Virginia. Nevertheless, it had been a settlement, and meant that the English had dibs on Maine.

These facts should be more readily available than they are, and Jessie Thorne was probably the one to see to it.

"Lipperty, lipperty," thought the new ungenerous Jessie. "Here come Br'er Rabbit."

This was not fair of her nor even accurate, since there was nothing about the new man in town that remotely resembled a rabbit, except that he did move in lopes and bounces. And he was ubiquitous; it was hard to avoid meeting him everywhere: at the supermarket, at the liquor store, at the post office, a youngish man with an extraordinary capacity for wanting, if not for making, friends. Everyone knew who he was, of course: he told you. What no one could figure out was what he was doing on Crow Point.

Or properly speaking, almost on Crow Point, because the house which he either rented or had been lent overlooked the cove, just where the Point road turns from the highway. Angus (everyone, he said, was to call him Angus) was probably borrowing the house, since it is only people who need money who have to pay, and it was plain that whatever Angus needed, it was not money. Look at the car he drove.

Most people found him attractive, but Jessie didn't.

"Hey there!" he called to her now. "Wait up!"

There was very little way that she could not wait up, since her car was parked on the short steep driveway and he had stopped his so that he cut her off. Having decided that since no one else was making available the facts about Jacataqua and its illustrious environs she, like the Little Red Hen, would do so herself. Jessie was caught at the old library, her arms filled with precious musty volumes and her sneakers slipping on the thick, pungent carpet of pine needles. The old library used to be the old schoolhouse, before the new schoolhouse was built of haphazardly mortared stone and then abandoned for the Jacataqua Central.

There was no new library. Anyone wishing the heady stimulus of fairly current reading had to go up to New Bristol. Anyone content with the treasures within the wee one-room building had to wait, because it was open only one day of the week and six months of the year. Mrs. Charley was in charge.

Jessie looked at the new man critically. He was tall, he was robust, and he was young enough. But he was groomed in a way that did not please her. His gleaming hair was full in a way that betokened an expensive cut, and he was not dressed properly for the island: he wore a modish turtleneck and espadrilles. She should have been more tolerant since she herself, when off her native grounds, was liable to error, as Howard had pointed out. She had once met Howard at an important cocktail party in something appropriately misty and floating but in walking pumps, because she couldn't drive unless her feet were supported.

"Other women solve this problem," Howard had said. "Couldn't you have changed in the car?"

It hadn't occurred to her and didn't occur to her now and anyway, this character wore a beard that she found offensive. She shifted the burden in her arms and looked down on him coldly.

"Yes?" she said.

"I'm Angus Allister!"

She believed him.

"I've wanted to meet you."

She said, "Why?"

"I've been told you know everything about the island."

"Then you've been misinformed," she said.

"No one can tell me, why Jacataqua?"

Jacataqua was an Indian woman. Call her a princess, if you will. Jessie had had to ferret it out for herself and saw no reason to share it with a stranger. A phrase of Charley's seemed appropriate.

"I don't know," she said. "I'm sure."

She looked at him levelly. People with those fair skins flush easily. The sun struck down through the branches of the pines;

in the full cove the water lisped and lapped. He had a kind of awkward dignity and too much pride to play the fool.

"I see," he said pleasantly. Then he accelerated admirably; not fast enough to indicate a state of rout nor slowly enough to show a lack of purpose.

Since they were headed in the same direction, Jessie waited a minute in the sun to let him get ahead of her, so that she would not seem to be in pursuit. Even so, when she rounded the cove slowly (because it is a damn-fool driver who does not slow on the Crow Point road) the back door at his borrowed house was just closing. As she fled slowly by, she wondered at the depth of her hostility.

Was it because, like Howard, he wore a beard?

Howard's beard was dark, short, and well-trimmed. Each morning of his life he leaned lovingly to the bathroom mirror and with a nail-scissors sternly disciplined each hair that was out of line. The stranger's sunny beard was shaggy.

If a beard was enough to curdle her courtesy, she was in a bad way. Much of the damage we do to one another results from confusing the proper objects of our hostility. Bitter she might be, but she was not stupid and should not claim the exemptions of stupidity. Perhaps she was a bad person, since she was punished with two such heavy losses, but even if one were wicked, there is no reason to be rude. Very well, then. She would not search him out, but the next time she met the fellow she would apologize, and that would be that.

Thus absolving herself (nobody else can do it), she pulled sharply aside, having seen in the rearview mirror that Lydia Pullen was behind and coming up fast. Lydia was too polite to honk and fey enough to pass, which cannot be done on the Crow Point road. Jessie didn't want Lydia fretting behind her when they reached the marsh; it was better to let her by now and to receive a grateful wave. At the marsh she herself purposed to stop and to contemplate the easy ways of nature, where all things prey upon one another but not upon themselves.

Here it was, open to the afternoon and stretching on either

31

side the road (that was like a little dike) to the distant woods, for all the world like meadowland except for the water glinting through the golden, blowing grass. Here the last waters of the cove gave up, saw they were not going to reach the bay and made do with the company of frogs and the tall blue heron. There was silence here. The wind in the trees sighed far away, and the rote of the sea. Among the stands of cattails red-winged blackbirds flashed, noiseless and bright as sparklers.

Only at one time of the year the marsh shook with sound, on April evenings when the air was pierced by the loud, madding chorus of the frogs. The air cold then, the sky paling, and the peepers piping like the pipes of Pan.

Next spring, she thought, I will hear the peepers cry.

For Jessie's love of Maine she had her parents to thank: they were such awful people.

Her father was an ugly drunk who used to tell her that he had been molesting children in Franklin Park and that the police were after him.

"They'll be along anytime now," he would say.

About the third time that the police didn't come Jessie decided that there wasn't a word of truth in what he said, but long before she knew the meaning of the word *fantasy* she found it an unpleasant and unsettling fantasy. He died early of some ordinary cause and in the odor of sanctity.

Her mother was a cold blonde who upon the demise of her first spouse married again and removed herself to the Argentine, where her new partner had a cattle ranch. Neither suggested that Jessie come along or even that she visit. Her mother said the Argentine was no place for a child. As a consequence Jessie was sent off to school earlier than most and continued to summer with her grandparents. Many a child has been pulled through by the grandparents.

Her grandmother taught her many interesting things. She took the child in the early mornings into the salt meadows while the crystal spiderwebs still dangled from the grass and showed

32

her how to tell the architecture of the one from that of the other. She kept her up at night to see the constellations shifting in the sky and in August, to watch for falling stars and northern lights. Once every summer they drove down east and, cold and sleepy, watched the sun come up over the farthermost eastern point of these United States. She took her to Damariscotta to see the middens where the archeologists had found human bones that had been cracked to extract the marrow. Perhaps those early people had been hedonistic cannibals and perhaps only frugal.

Also she taught Jessie how to make Indian pudding, build a clambake, split a lobster with one stroke — the heart beats for a bit. She knew where to find the high-bush blueberries and the wild strawberries and the lady slippers, which you must not pick, and the wild columbine, which you do.

Jessie's grandmother was an optimist and did not feel that there was much of which to be afraid, but what there was, she mentioned. Avoid strangers and rabid animals and, in a thunderstorm, trees. That loose sand in the tidal river is not quicksand but pretend it is; it keeps Canadians from crossing over from the Park. There are no venomous snakes in Maine; it was not really necessary for the congresswoman to urge that bill that forbade snakes to pass the state line because the one she had in mind had escaped from a carnival; perhaps it seemed harsh to forbid carnivals to cross the line.

The white rocks are safe but the black ones slippery.

Above all, avoid undertows and riptides and the mouth of the Kennebec. Don't swim alone: never trust the sea.

But since she had been a happy woman and unafraid, Jessie grew up happy and fearless and no doubt would have remained so had her grandmother not erred by dying and if she had not erred herself by marrying Howard. In her own defense she could claim that he had seemed to be a happy man who required to complete his felicity only the opportunity of taking care of her. Only that once when he struck her had she recognized in him a touch of the cold madness of her parents.

33

As she drove home she pondered on these things.

Cravenly, Angus Allister would not unload his loot until the sound of her car had faded down the road. He was inordinately attracted by the young woman's great gray eyes and inordinately hurt that their gaze had been inimical. It was only lately that he had become used to being among people, and those he had been among had proved friendly; Jessie Thorne's rebuff made him want to scuttle like a crab for a cranny, but if he did so that would be the old Angus, and he had no intention of ever being the old Angus again. Living in the world but not of it had already cost him enough.

He stood now in the summer kitchen with his arms filled with gin, mail and groceries, including five pounds of mussels about to burst through their damp paper sack. Leaning far to the right, he tried to ease them down upon the pumpkin pine table and just made it: out they spilled, blue-black jewels on the weathered orange wood. He hadn't the slightest idea what to do with them, but his hostess probably had a book somewhere. The man at the fish market had vowed that they were not dangerous; there was at the moment no Red Tide. Had the water been invaded by that poisonous algae he would have been permitted to buy lobster but not molluscs; coming from inland, he had not the slightest notion why.

Outside the screens, the leaves stirred on the apple tree and inside, light and shade danced through the open room. He liked the idea of the summer kitchen, where a woman could keep cool even while she kept the range up for the Saturday baking. From the cramped front hall where the steep stairs slanted up, the tall clock spoke. In there the windows of the tiny rooms had tiny panes, there was a great deal of bric-a-brac and on the small chairs with ribbon backs and slick seats upholstered with horsehair, one slid. It was all alien; why was he here? Why wasn't he in Montana, where he belonged?

It was his own doing.

A year ago no one, except for his ex-wife and his aunts, had known or cared what his name was. For years he had made a modest living writing television scripts, mostly for daytime drama, a profession that sounded more exotic than it was. When June had said that she would marry him, she thought he was going to do it in New York. But he went right on doing it in Helena.

It is true that from time to time he did go to New York for conferences, where for brief periods of intense strain he met with the three other writers responsible for *Hidden Lives*, and with the man who directed the whole like an orchestra. At these meetings future episodes were blocked out and distributed to him who was best equipped to cope. Once in a while there were unscheduled panics when the death or desertion of an actor forced abrupt changes in the plot.

At these times Angus saw little of New York but hurried home to push on; those scripts had to exist well in advance of need. So on the rare occasions when June went with him she saw nothing but the inadequate hotel room and the bad lobby. Even in the elevator she was afraid of being mugged, and when room service brought a sandwich, she had him leave the tray outside the door.

Back home in Helena, Angus would disappear into his study, which was the only place that he felt safe. He felt a deep respect for men who had to go forth every day and hold their own against others, and he admired their courage. He himself had, from the time he was a boy, labored to learn his trade just so that he could shut the door and survive in solitude. As long as his fingers rapped the typewriter keys he was oblivious to pressure and to threat.

"Anyway, you like those dumb characters," June said.

Yes, he did. He had grown fond of him and of her and of the grandfather and the lawyer and the twins. When he wasn't writing about them, he watched them.

"You never even get the credit," June complained.

That wasn't true. Once in a while, when the program ran a

few moments short, his name, along with all the others, was rolled rapidly by. If you happened to be looking closely you saw it: here he came. "And Angus Allister." There he went.

Then because of one of those internecine warfares that begin with ratings and end with the rolling of heads, the show was canceled.

"Good," said June. "We can go somewhere."

But Angus, who was not comfortable except when he was working, had begun a novel. June didn't stay around long enough to know that it was good. The characters that prowled its pages were real men and women, the complications that beset them believable — indeed, true. He knew the setting; Bannack in the old days when Montana was still a Territory. He knew his protagonist, a subtle and educated sociopath. He knew the agonized girl who was no silhouette but a strong woman with an honest choice to make. His prose, cut back ruthlessly to the stem, blossomed like a plant.

It was a great help to him that he had never read anything because he was not afraid of being imitative and was deeply moved by his own book. He wanted to call it *Forever Amberley*, but the first house to which he sent it retitled it and rushed it into publication.

It sold one hundred thousand copies.

One of the first things he did was to send a whopping check to his ex-wife because he liked her. June had not left him because she was grasping but because she was lively and could not adapt herself to the interminable hours while he tapped at the typewriter nor the ensuing silences while he thought about what he would next tap.

Besides, it did not seem fair. They had once known a man whose wife divorced him because he would never take her out for a steak. The next year, he married an airline stewardess and went all around the world, half-price. In a way that is what June had brought upon herself, because with the arrival of the first mammoth royalties, Angus had lumbered forth like a bear blinking in the light and had discovered a whole world out there

36

filled with pleasures and excitements: admirers and first-class tickets and talk-shows and the best hotels with the best accommodations, while June had gone back to her old job and was working nine to five in Denver.

No — he could in no way fault June, except for not recognizing that he was addicted. Not only in these terrible times but in all terrible times the poor human creature, a little higher than the ape but less than angels, has sought escape in liquor, foreign substances or sexual collisions; all of them more a distraction than an anodyne. But those among them whose illusions are just as real are less destructive: they retreat into the life of the imagination where, poor forkéd fools, they win an hour's respite. June didn't know that she could no more distract Angus than you can distract a wolf struggling in a trap.

Neither did he. This is what makes success so dangerous; it separates the addict from the dose.

At first, like a child with its hands on real money, Angus bought everything in sight. He turned the old Chevvy in for a Mercedes. He paid off the mortgage and put in a patio that looked up to the blue jagged peaks. He bought shoes of kangaroo and two gold chains and an earring, which he returned. He sent his aunts sweaters of zephyr-weight wool and tickets to Montego Bay. He bought a tangerine-colored typewriter, which anyone could have told him was a mistake, because on his new typewriter he wrote nothing but letters to new friends.

After a while his agent grew restive. His agent pointed out that twelve months had gone by and that with production taking as long as it did, even when the new manuscript was ready it was not going to be in print overnight and that people forget very quickly. His agent reminded him that the only safety for a writer lies in writing and reminded him of the young man who had such a success with *Raintree County* that he gassed himself in the garage. His agent suggested that he absent himself from felicity awhile.

Hence Maine.

Agents are useful. They do not represent geniuses nor artistic amateurs: for those they can do nothing. But the mere talented need a lot of help. Angus's agent happened to know these people who were going abroad and whose enthusiasm for the arts overcame their prudent fear of artists.

It might be, his agent suggested, that having discovered the rich lode of American history, he should mine it again. His agent said there was a lot of old lore lying around Maine.

It was that old lore he pursued in wishing to know Jessie Thorne, even before he knew she was long-legged and grave-eyed. One thing that many do not understand is that a writer in search of material is hard to peel away as tar.

So he would try again.

Meantime, he must do something about the mussels. Those who should know had assured him while they are alive, clams squirt and lobsters wave their fronds. How do you tell about a mussel?

Maybe he would boil them. Boiling sounded safe.

4

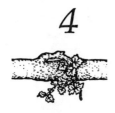

THE PEDERSENS were the only people on the Point who had, so far, built to winter. It was a great consolation to Edgar Pedersen when he retired from a profession that he had loved with an icy passion. People usually love the things that they do well: Edgar Pedersen had been teaching for three years before he discovered that he was a gifted teacher.

It had come about it this wise.

One morning with the clock crawling to eleven and faced with forty drowsy, doughy pupils in whom the light of intelligence flared but feebly, he was trying to explain Gresham's law — granted that there is little about it that was blood-tingling, except to himself. *Bad money drives out good.* Then he remembered what a good teacher had bugled at him in his young days and he swung upon them and demanded,

And shall Trelawny die?
And shall Trelawny die?

Literature was not even his discipline. But eighty eyes looked up, startled. Forty brows scowled in dissent.

Here's twenty thousand Cornish men
Will know the reason why!

They breathed to the bottoms of their lungs, their hands tightened at their sides, their dull eyes were shot with lightning.

At the close of class the youngster for whom he had most hope lingered to ask, "Who's Trelawny?"

"I don't know," Ed said. "Let's go look it up."

Sir Jonathan Trelawny, it appeared, was imprisoned in the Tower of London in 1688 along with six other prelates who had their fill of James II.

"Now," said the youngster, "who is Gresham?"

"*I* know," Ed Pedersen said. "You look it up."

When he got home he found his wife up to her elbows in diaper suds. And so he bugled at her, too.

And shall Trelawny die?
And shall *Trelawny* die?

Her little pink face deepened to rose and she raised a sudsy fist.

"Certainly not!" she said. And then, "Who's Trelawny?"

He swung her until her apron strings flew and then he kissed the damp nape of her neck.

Later she said thoughtfully, "That's dangerous. Look at Hitler."

He said, "I'm no Hitler."

She said, "But that's because you're good."

He would do anything for that woman.

40

By the first of July everyone was there and as soon as everyone was there, the trouble started.

Crow Pointers were neither indigenous nor homogeneous, so that what pleased the one did not necessarily assuage the other. Furthermore, they were divided into natural groups which, although they inhabited the same terrain were either indifferent to each other or downright hostile. The smallest and most predatory phylum was composed of the first families and the larger, of the lemmings who had migrated in the last twenty years, building their nests and lairs where for so long there had only been open shore and unviolated woods. The first families resented the loss of their kingdom and the newcomers resented that they were resented.

Of course in each species there were subspecies and sports.

But on the whole — and the new people found this hard to understand — it was among the first families that you found your heavy drinking and your nude bathing: Lydia Pullen had been heard to mutter about why France fell. Even now, when there were little children on the beach! True, very few had actually seen the nude bathing, but they knew that it went on under the cover of darkness or of dawn, and it is hard to relax when you are convinced that just beyond those rocks little John-Joe may come across old Mr. Rafferty with his parts dangling or Mrs. Rafferty playing bridge attired only in her diamonds.

It was embarrassing to bring this up at the Association meetings and useless, too, since the first families never attended those meetings and it was a brave soul who, in person, agreed to bell the big cats.

With certain ukases the old families conformed if they seemed sensible. They no longer threw their swill overboard, though this was less in consideration of the others than because it was a town ordinance, and the old families had old and close associations with the town. Besides, now that there were fifty dwellings on the point where there had once been four, even the aristocracy could see that the easy days were gone: they gave nary a thought to the tumbrils; they didn't want cornhusks washing up on them.

41

Because of a basic disparity in aims and wishes and also because some people like hard feelings and enjoy that rush of adrenalin that accompanies offense, small feuds erupted every summer that resulted in odd and temporary alliances: the Armstrongs had those tall and unpleasant dogs and Mr. Baker, who very much liked to walk, did not like the way the dogs looked at him.

Neither did Lydia Pullen, who had small nieces and nephews whom she did not wish to be frightened; her sister would hold her responsible for it. Neither did Mr. Fisher, who, when he wanted to visit friends, pretended he was headed for the Raffertys' tennis court and casually swung a racket, with which he meant, if it proved necessary, to lob the dogs upon the nose. There was some talk of invoking the fairly new leash law or of calling directly to the game warden, and in fact the game warden did show up. The Armstrongs' feelings were very much hurt: their dogs were dear to them.

Just an example.

Rosemary Ross, the dearest dumpling of an academic widow, turned truculent and circulated a petition to prevent the portrait painter from putting his studio where it commanded the north light. It was not that she objected to his using the north light, but the studio honestly was an eyesore. And then guess what! One of the teenagers who was helping to circulate the petition asked the portrait painter's wife to sign. The bad blood that ensued was only aerated the next year when they all closed ranks against Lydia Pullen. With all her talk about natural beauties, it was Lydia who painted footprints on the rocks. She claimed it was to guide her nieces and nephews safely over the rocks: there had to be a better way than splayed and comic toes and heels, and it was not the sort of thing you dash right out and do; Lydia could only have done it with malice, foresight, and defiance of the common weal.

So it went. But these were personal battles. No year went by without a hue and cry in which everyone was involved. Year before last it centered around trees.

The town had widened a section of the road and in doing so had cut down several dead spruce and two old giants who were merely dying; also, they had cut back the brush. One faction accused those selfish people who were willing to sacrifice natural growth to their own convenience. Since there were three new houses going up that year it was indeed easier for the construction trucks to get down, and pretty plain to all who the selfish people were. Nonsense, said the opposition. Those trees were a fire hazard anyway and the way that some people drove it was too bad that more brush was not cleared: that way, at least, you had a fighting chance. As it was you had to honk all the way, and how do you suppose that sounds to your wildlife?

As a matter of fact the town had not consulted anyone but had just done it, as the town often did; but the general theme having been sounded, it was curious how often the issue of greenery came up that year. One family which wintered in Florida was missing an extremely attractive spruce. The jagged stump yawned like the root of a broken tooth; it seemed plain that somebody who lived closer had taken it for Christmas. Perhaps they should all look about more closely. It was all too possible that one of them was cutting trees to sell.

The bad dogs did not bite anyone but with their urine scalded the Scotch pines by some so lovingly planted. And one unfortunate, having asked permission of his neighbor to take down the two tall pines that blocked his view of the water, took down the wrong trees.

Last year the dissension centered over the hiring of a constable. This constable was to sit at the mouth of the tidal river all day long in her truck and prevent. It seemed a lot of money to pay someone just to sit in a truck when everyone knew that the violators came after dusk with their cans and their condoms and their smoldering logs.

This year the annual malevolence was shaping up over those who wished to winter.

"Five selfish people," said Lydia Pullen, who seemed to be in a sort of verbal rut. "Willing to change the whole character of the Point for their own considerations. Telephones will come next."

Little Mrs. Jones looked up with interest. She had to call her aged mother thrice a week and had to go way out to the post office to do it; many a night she lay awake and worried, picturing the phone out there ringing frantically in its glass closet, with no one to answer.

The tension was not eased by the fact that of the five, three belonged to that impervious first group that didn't give a fig for the others: it was not *they* who had changed the character of the Point. There was nothing legal about the Association except for those who must contract for their summer water and who, were they in arrears, could not frequent the beaches. The early-ons would like to see anyone keep them off the beaches, particularly after Labor Day.

Edgar and Irma Pedersen were left with a status as undefined as it was uneasy.

They stood that July morning on their porch, smelling the smell of new wood and looking through the dim-dazzle of new screens. Since one was fretting, the other fretted, too. The Pedersens did everything together.

"Then what did she say?" asked Edgar.

"It wasn't so much what she said as the way she said it. I told her we'd been planning all along, else why the full foundation? All she said was she said, 'Oh?'"

He was disturbed because last summer Lydia Pullen had been Irma's friend.

"Petty," he said, "you're not to think of it."

Irma was not strong and had never been strong: he had always taken care of her and was glad to do it. Edgar had spent his whole life doing what he thought ought to be done.

Once he had discovered his powers, Edgar had moved right up the scale. Perhaps he was a little rigid, accustomed to instant obedience from his staff if not from the students — students have no decorum anymore, but it would be a brave student who dared to face Edgar Pedersen's controlled hysteria (unfortunately this does not work out as well with sons); sharp with his subordinates and haughty with his peers: he had never had much money because principals are not monied men, but his position was impeccable and he was troubled to find himself in the wrong camp.

Nor was it fair to Irma, who had not really wanted to move down here in the first place. She wanted to be closer to their son, who, upon his graduation from the University of Maine, had moved just as far away from them as he could get.

But Edgar, once he had seen Crow Point, knew that was where he would retire. He had bought the land years ago before it had gone galloping up in price, and had mortgaged the house in China Falls in order to do so. They couldn't build the new house until they could sell the old, so for a long time they had been Sunday owners, driving over for the day to picnic on their own cliff overhanging their own ocean, and walking the road to meet their new neighbors, who were friendly and courteous and remote, because nobody wanted anybody new.

But it was hard to resist Irma, who was so much like a nice child, and when there was enough of the house up to camp in, they had found friends, and Irma had happily trotted off with several of the ladies to examine, according to their interests, the antique shops in Hallowell, the handsome old houses in Wiscasset or the paintings at Bowdoin College; then they had lunch. She had explained to them that she herself no longer drove, because of her eyes; they didn't mind a bit. Actually, they felt safer at the wheels of their own cars, although about this, they were mistaken. And then there were couples who met more or less regularly for bridge, and this the Pedersens found pleasant because they both were excellent players.

So when his son wrote wanting to know if Edgar had given any thought to Mother; after all, these were her retirement years, too, Edgar had answered smugly and honestly that Irma had just as much social life as her fragile health permitted her to enjoy.

So far this summer there had been little talk of bridge.

45

Of course the season was not yet in full swing. Many who rented in order to keep up with the taxes preferred to rent in June when it is cold and rainy, and besides, school keeps well through the month. Officially, the season proper begins on the Fourth of July. This was only the eighth.

As a mark of his emancipation Edgar had grown a gingery mustache. He plucked it now, absently.

"I'll tell you what," he said. "You write a little note and I'll drop it off at the Humphreys'. We'll invite them first."

He did not notice the slight anxiety that fluttered across Irma's face, because his attention was deflected by the welcome arrival of the carpenter.

When the Pedersens said that their house was finished they of course meant fairly finished. That was because they had hired Parker Redlon and his crew. Parker's work was good and his ways pleasant; he was well known and well liked all over the island. But he did not keep his promises. Smiling, he accepted all jobs offered him and smiling, he got each started. After that, he dealt out what he considered your fair share of his time by the day or half-day. Look at it this way. He can't build in the winter so in all fairness to his crew he must take every job that he can get in the summertime. Parker will probably get around to you in time.

People react to this in differing ways, according to their temperaments. Many lose their tempers and a few men shout, but it is less exhausting all around if you just wait. You could of course have hired some builder from away who would stay on the job till it was done, but that would be foolhardy, because after that builder went back to wherever, you are going to have emergencies and need repairs: then Parker either will come or he will not.

The Pedersens' house was pretty well completed, or would have been if Edgar Pedersen had not reached a new conclusion. It is true that Parker had never sent anyone down to fill in around the dishwasher or to hang that cupboard in the bathroom, but the dishwasher worked just as well and the cupboard wasn't in

46

the way all that much: Edgar kept magazines and an ashtray on top of it. Both of those jobs together weren't going to take Parker more than an hour or so, and he was going to be down the next rainy day.

However, Edgar decided that he wanted a sun-deck.

On Crow Point there were two schools of thought. Some felt you wanted a screened porch because it was nice to eat out without the damned mosquitoes. Others said that the screens cut your view and that a porch was cold all summer long. Whereas with a deck you could sit in the sun and look out over the leagues of blue bright water and if the deck is on the sea side there is too much breeze for mosquitoes anyway. Of course you can't sit out there at night; who wants to sit out at night?

Irma wanted the porch and had it; she said when it was muddy, you didn't step right onto the new carpeting, which was true, and she said (wisely) that in wintertime they could leave their boots out there and stack firewood. But he still saw himself leaning against a rail, his face lifted to the wind, a lean, strong man of a certain age facing the sea as from the bow of a ship.

"And here's where I want it, Parker," he said. "Right here above the cliff."

"Oh, I can *do* it," Parker said. "Wouldn't be much room between the deck and the drop."

Fortunately the house was L-shaped there and the deck would fit nicely into the L.

"I want it heavy," Edgar said. "Not one of those little afterthoughts. And bonded just as tight to the house as you can do it. Sink the posts in concrete."

"Well," Parker said, "I can *do* it. Around here most folks think it's best to keep a deck loose and light."

"Why?" And Edgar gave him a long level look meant to remind Parker that he, Edgar, was not born yesterday. Here on the coast things weathered quickly and an exposed deck, if flimsy, was going to need repairs right along, which would be profitable to someone if not to the owner.

Parker gave him his look right back. "Easier on the house," he said, "were a blow or high water to get to her."

Edgar Pedersen nudged a rock over the side of the cliff and watched contemptuously as it danced and bounced down, down the steep granite slope to where, far below, the restless water moved in and out of the broken boulders.

"I guess we won't worry about that, Parker," he said. "Just do it my way."

Parker tucked his pencil behind his ear, eased his belly over his belt and smiled his wide warm smile. No sense in telling people anything.

"So then," he said. "We'll be down toward the end of next week, probably."

Edgar went back to Irma feeling pretty fine. If you were both knowledgeable and firm, you could handle anyone. His son had suggested that at their age they ought to take a nice apartment; give up responsibilities and not take them on.

So much for his son.

The house was still so new to them and so grand that at least once a day, hand in hand, they walked throughout it marveling. They had never lived in a new house before nor in one so spacious. Their own bedroom had room for a four-poster, an armchair for him and a chaise longue for her because sometimes she rested. There were two smaller bedrooms, too: one was for their son and his wife and one for the grandchildren; this, until there were grandchildren, Edgar used for his books and pipes and papers. Irma loved her kitchen, which was big and bright and filled with every appliance she had ever wished for or that he could discover, but she was intimidated by the living room, which had two walls of glass; she had difficulty remembering which panels were windows and which doors. What seemed to her like acres of carpeting covered all the floors.

Their son said it was too much house for where they had chosen to build it. He said such houses were a fine investment, but not where no one wanted to live. He said it would be hard to turn it over. What he meant, his father thought resentfully, was that he would find it hard to turn it over, which meant that he did not expect his parents to live as long as Edgar Pedersen intended that they live. Was that any way to think about your parents?

He put his arm protectively around his wife.

"You're going to like a deck," he told her. "We'll get some redwood chairs." For a moment he stood entranced, looking out where his deck was going to be. The Atlantic was very blue today and as far as the eye reached, flecked with white under a light wind. Far out beyond the black rocks sailboats skimmed like butterflies.

"And now," he said, "about the Humphreys."

The Pedersens never had words; that didn't mean that once in a while one of them didn't find the other inattentive.

"Edgar," she said, "I *told* you. Her sister's here from Elizabeth, New Jersey."

"Good," he said. "We can have two tables."

"The Johnsons are having a little party for her," Irma said. "For the sister."

The Pedersens had not been included.

Edgar in truth was a thin man, not a lean one, and perhaps not quite so tall as Irma made him feel, but he was resilient and resourceful.

"Who cares," he said. "What say we skip over to Boothbay for a shore dinner?"

"Ooh, *fun!*" she said.

He felt a savage satisfaction to think that the Johnsons and the Humphreys and the Pullens must go back to where they came from, while he and Irma, in their real house, were the only ones who belonged.

5

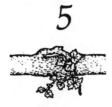

"YOU KNOW WHAT YOU'RE DOING?" asked Jessie's new friend. "You're cracking up."

"I am not," she said, but without conviction.

"Most people I know take it as a sign of grace."

Well, not most people that she knew. Howard, for instance, thought cracking up was weak, and much as she hated to agree with him about anything, about this she did. For a long time they had agreed about so much; it had been both comfortable and companionable to nod together over the behavior of their friends.

Her eyes brimmed and flowed over.

"See?" Angus said.

There was so much solicitude in his voice that, for the moment, it seemed natural to confide in him: that she had trouble sleeping, no longer liked to eat, resented everyone. He had proved more attractive than she thought, especially since he had caught on to what you do not wear on the coast of Maine; Mrs. Charley said the local girls called him sexy. That did not interest Jessie much, but she was influenced by other factors. Angus was observing — and ought to be, considering what he considered his profession. He had the pleasant, unpretentious good manners that she had noticed in other westerners, and it might be rather fun to show him around.

She had certainly not intended to become his friend. But Jessie thought a great deal about what was right and wrong — always had — and so did Howard, who said it was part of their inheritance. Don't laugh: the greatest thinkers about right and wrong have not, in themselves, always been faultless. Her conscience nagged her: it is wrong to be rude to a man you don't even know. And when he turned his cheek and came to call, he had destroyed the muffler of the Mercedes on that big rock that she had never had removed from her driveway. Most people knew it was there. What's more, trying to bind the muffler up with baling wire (which Jessie did supply) he tore his shirt and came near putting out an eye.

She pretty much had to ask him in for a drink.

He turned out not to be as loathsome as some men. Perhaps artists don't have to defend themselves as much. No, she took that back. Tom Elder defended himself like a terrier. But perhaps she was being harsh: she had never liked Tom since, when she was six and he old enough to know better, he had pulled down her pants and then complained to his mother because she kicked him in the gut.

And then, Angus was not an artist. Howard was a snob: he read not only *A la Recherche du Temps Perdu* but also *Jean Santeuil*. Jessie's taste was fiercely eclectic, but the fact that a book had sold a hundred thousand copies did not in itself impress her. She came by her snobbery naturally. Her grandmother used to stand at the window of the town house on Easter Sundays and watch the brand new bonnets and bags go by.

"There go the cooks," she would say.

But Jessie would not permit her critical acumen to prevent her pleasure in showing off her house. Houses. The little one was a one-room cabin that had been built by Captain Joshua Drake with his own ax and for himself alone; before the land belonged to anyone he had squatted there to get away from people. Even before she had espoused misandry, Jessie had admired his judgment; who, who was able, would not wish to live on Crow Point alone? Whether or not he was a veritable captain no one knew, but one did know that he was able, because he had left behind a kind of journal in which he had recorded his ability: he had fished and crabbed and like a clean animal, covered his waste. For those few things he could not wrest from nature, he rowed across the bay.

Not even Charley Pratt knew what became of him; one hopes the town did not take him away.

Jessie's grandparents had meant to take the cabin down, but they saw at once that it wouldn't do. With a new floor and the stone chimney repointed, it was a perfect playhouse for a child or a retreat for a kindly man who was tired of children, and Howard had thought to have a study there. Ha! But because it stood on a high point of rock and was all too visible, they planted a windscreen of spruce around it. Spruce grows fast.

Because they could not build the big house with an ax and because there was still no road beyond Gin Beach, every board, shingle and nail had to be brought by barge, a fact in which Jessie had always taken a singular satisfaction. In those days, people didn't expect things to be easy.

"You're wandering," Angus said.

"Is that a symptom?"

"Seems to be." He patted at his beard as if he were surprised to find it there as, in fact, he still was.

"You don't think," Jessie asked, "that for a mere acquaintance you're a bit outspoken?"

Angus was bending down to peer up the chimney of the fireplace, for what purpose she could not imagine. He straightened up and said, "Perhaps. But I've been through it."

Then people did get through.

Jessie said, "You've cracked up?"

"No. But I've been divorced."

It seemed incredible to her that he could speak so cheerfully of what was, after all, an amputation.

"Toward the end," he confided, "she said I was a third-rate writer."

Jessie cringed as if he had read her thoughts.

"It has advantages," he said. "Mostly it's first-raters who crack up."

Well, if that was the price first-raters had to pay. Perhaps it was through the capacity for pain that one became first-rate, although she could not see that all this hurt had brought out any hidden powers in her. Third-rate or not, she looked at Angus with a new respect. Writing was hard work. Not only do you have to get it all down, but you have to know in advance what you are going to get down. For all her efforts she had only three beginnings, none of which pleased:

The history of Maine is more interesting than the reader may suspect.

The pursuit of the history of Maine is more rewarding than you may suspect.

How interesting and rewarding is the history of Maine!

She sighed. Angus looked at his watch. It was well past noon. "Are you eating enough?" he asked.

If that was an invitation to be invited, he could forget it. After he left she would down a glass of milk. One way to get him out of the house was to show him the outside of it.

She said, "Don't look back," and then she led him around

53

from the back door and down the long lawn past the captain's house to the beach.

"Now!" she said.

He was speechless, as many a one had been who saw it from the sea. For the house was schizoid. All within was *gemütlich*: the living room was flanked by two long halls, each lined with spartan bedrooms through which the sweet cold sea air flowed. These rooms were as bare as the living room was comfortably cluttered with wicker work, braided rugs, oil lamps; with pouncing china dogs and plaster lobsters and bookshelves topped with snapshots in ornate and gilded frames. The interior was redolent of tennis rackets, hot porridge and cold baths.

The exterior was that of a Greek temple across whose open atrium marched four tall Doric columns — calm, white, and gloriously inappropriate.

"They brought them all the way from Boston," Jessie said, and proudly, "They belonged to Samuel Gridley Howe."

His ignorance was profound.

"You do too know. His wife was Julia Ward Howe."

Well, if she said so. He himself got Julia Ward Howe mixed up with Harriet Beecher Stowe.

Jessie was unbelieving. Mix up the authoress of the "Battle Hymn of the Republic" with that of *Uncle Tom's Cabin*? How could one do that?

"I forgot you're from away," she said. "Harriet Beecher Stowe lived in Brunswick, and Laura E. Richards lived right here on Jacataqua."

"Ah," he said.

She couldn't imagine an American child who hadn't read *Captain January*.

"They were all wonderful women," she told him. "There were more wonderful women then."

Surely she joked?

No, she didn't. They were intelligent and self-educated and they had strong opinions but were contented in their homes, where they shaped the characters of their husbands and their children by the sheer force of their example: they were brave and self-sufficient and probably on the whole, more chaste.

"They were like hell."

Which was a good thing, he said, for his particular line of work.

Jessie thought it was nice to laugh again. What's more, unless you despise him, there is something soothing about the personal interest of a personable man, and Angus Allister was not despicable. She kicked her way through the deep sand of her own beach, or what was good as her own beach since though no one could own below the turf line, there was no way to get here without trespassing across her land. Since when her grand-parents bought the land was cheap, only their shocking lack of foresight confined Jessie to the ten acres that had been left to her. She might well have owned more, in which case she could sell it and be a wealthy woman. Only she wouldn't. If Jessie owned it all she would cherish every foot and when she died, she would give it to the Audubons.

Not that she cared for his interest. Or she guessed she didn't. But when an ego has been bruised by one man, the attention of another is therapeutic. Except that with relationships as fleeting as they are, one knows pretty well what an estranged woman can expect, and if the new admirer proves either rapacious or conde-scending (most of them will so prove), that ego may be further frayed.

Unless the woman herself turns condescending or rapacious. Maybe both?

This time of the summer the adolescent gulls were big as adults but still brown; you could tell them apart anyway because of their behavior. The social behavior of gulls is both interesting and illuminating. Jessie had once beached a dory on the Black Rocks with Howard; there several colonies of gulls lived in un-easy truce. Each colony defended its own boundaries, which seemed reasonable, but Jessie was appalled to find that, even as it is with us, the adult gulls savagely attacked any young that did not belong, and that the young in turn, even as it is with us, ganged up beak-to-beak and back-to-back, in order to defend their own.

Of course it is easier to be patient with one's own. Ahead of her now a baffled and beleaguered mother attempted to defend the limpet or the crust or whatever it was that she had wrested from a harsh environment for her own; her child followed, crowding and shrieking.

"Scat!" Jessie cried, her sympathy all with the rattled mother. But of course both squawked and in the moment while they wheeled away a tern shot down and got the morsel. Terns do that. Jessie, like all philanthropists, sighed and moved on.

She was headed for her favorite place of all, although Jessie had many favorite places. Usually every year she raced to visit each of them but this year, because this year was different, she had saved and savored the thought of the little cave.

It wasn't a real cave but a formation in the process of becoming one; a roof of rock under which and over centuries, the abrading tides had chipped and rubbed and washed away the infinitesimal detritus until now it was deeply undercut. When you sat beside it, walled in your little room of granite, you looked up at the gray eave where in pockets of thin soil the bayberry grew. Below the sea swirled in and a kaleidoscope of light danced on the overhang and mirrored the dance of the watery light below.

The sound of the advancing and retreating waves, their sigh and grumble, the slight slough of the wind and the slow fireworks of reflected light were pleasantly hypnotic. More: here your solitude was safe. Here, inaccessible to invasion of any sort, was a secure hiding place where, highly as you may hold your grandmother, the sure sneakers will not follow nor the voice that quizzes about what you have learned. And in the height of the sun, the low of the moon, Jessie had learned much here: it was the place where she had first made full love with Howard.

She stopped now with her hands pulling on a boulder ahead and her feet pushing at one below. It had been a mistake to share that place with anyone and she would not make that mistake again. Jubilant, she scaled the crown of outcrop and looked down to where the deep dazzle of the water should have been sheltered by the great gray roof of rock.

It was gone.

6

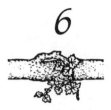

THE CROW POINT ASSOCIATION met at Gin Beach on the tenth of August and on the eleventh, Tom Elder committed his first lawless act.

The meeting was no more annoying than usual and perhaps less so, because the tide was high and the members had to huddle on the narrow sands. One might think this would make things worse because it was easier to spot hostile groups by their huddle; on the other hand, you couldn't hear the speakers over the crash of the water, so you were not offended by what they said. Their faces reddened and their gesticulations were fine. Meantime the water banged.

Eventually the bang, the long suck and the little rattle of pebbles in between caused part of the audience to become comatose and part restless. Tom Elder was one who became restless and he tried to shoulder closer to the speakers without seeming to shoulder, since he prized his vote highly and when it came to a show of hands he wanted to know if he wanted to show his hand.

This year there were some strange alignments. The woman who hotly said that if she wanted to winter, before she would ask for the road to be widened she would bring her groceries in on snowshoes was unexpectedly supported by a person who had never been her friend. This was because they both bitterly opposed the mother of adolescents who hoped to clear the whole top of the hill and build a center with slot machines to keep the young people's minds off sex.

She in her turn was challenged by the couple who wanted a by-law to prevent exotic animals upon the beach, which the mother of adolescents took as a direct blow at her eldest, who went to the Rhode Island School of Design and was known to be interested in peacocks. There followed a certain amount of discussion about the derivation and meaning of the word *exotic* which was highly irritating to the Callahans; they felt there were too many academicians settling on the Point and jested sourly that, if anything, professors should be excluded from the beach. Mrs. Callahan admitted freely that she didn't know why she was so offended by the man from the very good private school except that he smoked a pipe and rode a bicycle in what she took to be a superior way. It was not that she was opposed to education per se; if anyone cared to check they would find that she herself had been graduated from Bates College, class of '37, with admirable marks in Physical Education.

But since the subject of adolescents had come up: the growers of rhododendrons had discovered that someone (they were not going to mention names) had planted marijuana amongst the rhododendrons. Lydia Pullen had not meant to mention, but had reconsidered: Did we not wish to keep everything native? It was her belief that rhododendrons were not native. The owners of the two black bad digging dogs agreed.

Meantime all those who could not hear concerned themselves with matters of more general interest. Take your clam chowder.

Is it permissible to substitute bacon for salt pork? One would be well advised not to; bacon has nitrites. Yes, but salt pork has salt.

Had anyone seen anything of Jessie Thorne? Anything at all?

No, but then, Jessie had never been very friendly; she never dropped in to pass the time of day and there were those among them who had never seen the inside of that extraordinary house. There were even those who had never seen the husband. They certainly hoped what they heard wasn't so but goodness, everyone got divorced these days, even those who had not bothered to get married.

Someone said thoughtfully, "Her land is very valuable."

It had been his experience that matters could turn ugly if property was concerned.

There happened to be a brisk wind that day. The boughs of the spruce trees whipped like the arms of the speakers. At the conclusion of the meeting many were surprised to find they had voted for the new by-law: there should be no exotic animals on the beach. Then, gathering their sweaters and their children and by twos and threes, they drifted home.

Tom Elder was surprised to find that it was his own mood that was turning ugly. Who were these who intruded upon his personal paradise, imposing their opinions, their regulations and their presences upon him?

When his own camp had been built there had been just two other houses on Crow Point: the Thornes', which had been there forever, and that one place on the bay side. Except for courteous speech at the post office they never communicated and would walk miles to avoid the sight of one another. There was room for three.

Now signs blistered the trees everywhere; not only rustic or vaguely nautical clues to the directions in which all these people might be found but horrid printed placards in electric colors: NO HUNTING, PRIVATE ROAD, STAY OFF THE DUNES.

Doubtless, next year, a new one: NO EXOTIC ANIMALS. What kind of animals did they fear? Aardvarks? If Tom could think of an exotic animal, he would acquire one.

By the time he regained his home and sat with the first dark brown drink of the day, he admitted that, so far, it was not turning out as he had hoped. To begin with, during the pleasant years of his marriage he had become more uxorious than he had realized and he missed his wife's cool and cheerful manners more than he had intended to; also, her tranquil presence in his bed. In other summers this had been perfectly all right. During the week while she was occupied at her office he had enjoyed being alone and made do heating up little messes in the skillet, and then every weekend she arrived and restored him. This year Brigid was acting oddly. For two weekends in a row she had not come at all and her calm and affectionate explanations did not compensate for her company.

She said she found it necessary to see her dentist but he thought the truth was that she was not so enthusiastic about his company as she had once been. Once or twice, had he had a telephone, he would have called her, but the prospect of driving to the post office at night deterred him. She might not be home. Then he would have to drive all the way back.

All right. He was lonely. As the long blue light failed it even crossed his mind that he might drop in on Jessie to renew — what? Old irritations? For it was Jessie who had pushed him off the pier. He had risen choking and sputtering from down there where the piles were painted with slime to see her with her brown bare feet planted firmly and a look of malicious triumph on her (at that time) small face. She hadn't even bothered to deny it.

Of course there must be elation in an egregious act, one that you get away with. Not anything that would damage anyone, just some refusal to follow the pack. He thought of something that would separate him from his neighbors, which would be irritating to them and satisfying to him.

He would dig clams. And not content with exceeding his legal limit when he had a legal limit, he would dig where no one was allowed to dig. Why, he felt better already.

Nature conspired with him. Brigid had given him a tide-clock with which he was not much pleased. Tide-clocks have to be adjusted according to where you are and then only tell you whether you're headed toward high or low. As a boy he had judged by custom and by eye: midtide flowed north or south around the Dragon Rock that lifted above water even when the tide was at full. At dead low, that rock was big as half a house. His parents had preferred the *Old Farmer's Almanac* for accuracy, and he turned now to the Old Farmer. Low tide half an hour before sunrise.

Nothing could be better.

Because satisfactory though it might be to act in defiance of authority, it would be less satisfactory to be spotted. At that hour it would be quite light enough for his purpose and he could not believe that any official would be at the clam flats before dawn.

He slept and rose and, leaving behind his usual equipment, started forth. The hod and hoe would give the show away, digging by hand you do not break the shells, and he honestly thought that he had tucked a plastic bag into his pocket in which to carry home his loot.

Everyone should get up earlier. The air was sweet as Eden, dim in the wooded aisles but bright on the horizon. It was so quiet you thought to hear the dew drip from the grass. Mosquitoes snarled and zoomed; you cannot have everything. In order to attain the flats you have to skinny around that chain that keeps the cars from the salt meadows, and there Tom paused to read the notice. One phrase sprang forth that slightly shocked him.

$500 Penalty

Did that mean him? He had been thinking in terms of twenty-five. Surely it was directed at commercial diggers? He read it again. No, it meant Tom Elder, too.

62

But he pushed on. First you cross the meadows to where at the very head of the inlet the true marsh begins. There through the last sand the last little braids of water still trickled toward the sea and he saw, dimpling the low mounds in between, the myriad breathing holes of the clams. The salt smell was strong. Toward Portugal the foam was pink and the sand salmon and where the sun would presently come up, a sky of robin's egg was ribboned low with tangerine and gold. An artist sees the universe as freshly as if it had just spilled from the hand of God. In all that brightening space, Tom saw no man and nothing that man had made. Exultant, he bent to his work.

His reward was immediate and pleasing. The clams were immense — big three-inch beauties with thick rubbery necks where you used to find those thin-shelled little ones that shrink when you steam them. These cried to be chopped, stuffed, and baked with curls of bacon. But for whom? There was no one on the Point before whom he wanted to cast his clams.

Meantime his natural reluctance to thrust into those holes where his naked hand might encounter not a clam but a sea-worm continued to give way to cupidity. It was not easy because his back began to ache and the sun was suddenly hot on his bare shoulders; the plastic bag was not in his pocket and he had had to sacrifice his shirt, in which he was going to have to wrap and carry his slippery and uncohesive burden.

When he made his momentous discovery he was still on his knees, which was not unfitting. A painter such as he planned to prove must cast a unique glance at substance, so that the viewer perceives what he has not perceived before. Up until now, Tom Elder's glance had not been unique. Naturally, his canvases leaned rather heavily on Maine. Among them there were those from which in streaks of rose and blue and smudges of pale gray and magically, sea and sail materialized. But he did not want to be a Marin.

And those in which the clouds were bruised and beautiful and outlined with brown heavy lines. But he did not want to be Marsden Hartley.

There was one with a sun shining through a mist to touch a dory and a wharf as if God's finger had touched working men. But he did not want to be Claude Montgomery.

He wanted to be Tom Elder.

And crouched there on the sand he saw that he could crowd a canvas with a clam. For the clam, unexciting when incidental to the shore, is quite another thing taken in itself. Closely observed, it is pure shape and subtle banded color. And with form subdued, a miracle of shade and texture can be wrung from a periwinkle, a crab's claw, a yard of sand.

Excited, he straightened up with his wet, grainy hands on the small of his back. And someone was observing him, although fortunately not with binoculars. Even art bows to exigency; rapidly, Tom assessed his position. The figure was motionless and male and silhouetted against the shrinking sun, which had risen big and scarlet and now streaked, paling, up the sky. He couldn't tell if the man was uniformed, but he did know that from that direction he himself was more visible, even perhaps identifiable.

Certainly what he was doing was identifiable. No one who watched him bend and rise was going to think he was doing calisthenics on the clam flats. Casually, he tied the corners of his shirt together; it dripped salt water and was cumbersome, but though it obviously contained something, perhaps the observer would take it for a beach ball? What he should do was to sling it easily across his shoulder, since that so often is what you do with shirts, but he might spill the evidence. You can drop fish back into water, but there is no way to return a clam to its hole. So with both hands Tom clutched the sodden bundle to his stomach and with such insouciance as he could convey, strolled quickly toward the safety of Crow Point.

But conscience doth make cowards. Pressed between the footfalls of a pursuer who did not pursue and the approaching patter of a jogger who indubitably was there, Tom knew he must reach the bend in the lane and get up and around it before the two converged. But his sodden sneakers slipped on the last grassy incline and instead of inching around the iron chain he slid

64

beneath it; as if winged, the clams flew everywhere. He rested with the wet shirt bunched about his chin. Then he looked up and the jogger was looking down. Fit, breathing easily and bright of tooth and eye, it was Jessie Thorne who was witness to his woe.

He assumed that she smiled with malice, but he was wrong. Nothing so ameliorates malice as the opportunity to add the soubriquet "poor" to the given name.

"Poor Tom," Jessie said. "Let me help you."

He lay for another moment, more at ease. She had nice legs, brown, slim and shapely. As an accessory after the fact, she could not rat on him.

"If you help," he said, "I'll split with you."

For the first time they were not old foes but new conspirators.

Jessie said, "We could have lunch. I've got a bottle of wine."

7

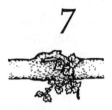

FAR ACROSS INNER RIVER the mysterious figure moved and was no mystery at all, except insofar as all of us are mysteries, but only Edgar Pedersen.

He had come early out because he could not sleep, was deeply troubled, and didn't want Irma to spot it. She was quick to spot. Naturally he had seen Tom Elder clamming, but his interest was of the mildest and lay only in the fleeting thought that the young man's methods were inefficient and his scrambled retreat inexplicable. He glanced around, and seeing nothing of which he himself should take prudent notice, he shrugged and, with his pants rolled up, began to wade back across the river.

It was that time of tide when about your ankles cold little tongues of new water converse with warm little tongues of old, and when around the haunches of the Dragon Rock a shallow puddle lingers. Edgar's tennies (he was one of the few left who called them tennies) were tied together by their laces and hung about his neck; before he put them on he would dabble his long toes to get the sand off and dry them in the new sun. He sighed. The day before, he had received a blow, a severe blow that might have consequences. It might prove that his son was right and that he himself was wrong, which was intolerable. Somewhere along the line the child whom he had lived to shelter and who, although he had not always minded, had never questioned that he ought to mind, had turned critical and wished to reverse their roles. It was now, in the opinion of the son, the father who must be prevented from such egregious acts as might threaten his own security and that of those he loved.

It was now necessary for Edgar Pedersen to question his own judgment, which it had never before occurred to him to do. If he had erred in such a way as to in any fashion inconvenience himself, it was of no moment. But if he had endangered Irma!

Yesterday he had driven her back to China Falls to see her doctor.

Irma was fragile. Throughout their happy years together (they had been very happy) Edgar had fought for her with strength and cunning and with courage. They had not been six months married when she had appendicitis and, before it ended, peritonitis. Two late-in-term miscarriages had followed and one long tearing birth. A tubal pregnancy had assured that there would be only the one child. Later her thyroid was removed and her gallbladder and then there was the hysterectomy: thank God, that was caught early. From how many hospital beds had she looked trustfully up at him, her pink little face alive with hope!

> O Lyric Love, half angel and half bird,
> And all a wonder and a wild desire.

He always had liked Browning.

Her troubles now were chronic and controllable: a mild arthritis, cataracts that had terminated her use of the car, a lazy heart. But she didn't have to drive, she didn't have to lift anything or do heavy housework or even light. He was there.

He himself had never required the services of a physician because he had been of robust — you might say rude — health. So his acquaintance with her doctor only nodded. After he dropped her off for her checkups, there were always demands on his time. The new principal wanted advice, or the old teachers, and then he had many friends in China Falls whom he wished to see.

Their pleasure in seeing him again was honest and was limited. His clout was gone. Of all things they would like to chat with him, but there always seemed to be a faculty meeting or else he with the temporary stop had just been told by his dentist that the new crown was ready. Edgar urged them to visit on the shore and they always said that there was nothing they would like better; if not this weekend, then the next.

So while she was reassuring him by seeing her doctor (she and her doctor were old friends: she called him Bill) he drove around by the old house. Some things the new owners had done were well done and some were not. The leaking gutter had been replaced and they had put a hard-top on the driveway. But they had also cut down the birch. Birches are short-lived, but it did seem to Edgar that the puny maple, no thicker than his wrist and no taller than his shoulder, was a poor substitute. When they tore down the garage and put in a breezeway, he had known he didn't own it anymore.

There were some things you could say for the old house. The wood had softened up so that when you repainted, the new paint either vanished or it flaked. Every April Irma relined the pantry shelves but she knew and he knew that the mouse was still getting in. They had made some mistakes, like varnishing. There were naked pipes everywhere but there was room for everything.

One of the hardest things about leaving was getting rid of things. When he was little their son had drawn astonishing pictures with which Irma did not want to part. As an educator, Edgar recognized that it is a dull child whose drawings are not,

68

in the true sense of the word, remarkable: it just happened to be a fact that the drawings of their son were witty and Edgar felt worth keeping, though he was content to have Irma be the one who insist upon the keeping. He himself wanted to retain the electric train although it had been a disappointment because the boy's interest in it, after the first delirium of delight, had lapsed with the absorbing task of putting it together. One thing which could not be destroyed was a report card signed by a Miss Snodgrass; it suggested that their son's sensitivity was as great as his ability and that perhaps the fact should be kept in mind at home. So that had to be kept.

But there is little sense in hanging on to a damaged saucepan because in it Irma warmed their son's first applesauce. The pan was now dimpled with years of use and its rounded bottom rocked a little on the burner. Edgar bought for Irma a whole new set of enameled pans that gleamed white and were colored with baked-in carrots and with parsley. Irma said it chipped.

Well, you could go from room to room finding things with which it was hard to part, but the nice thing was that you could go from room to room.

Shaking the sand out of his tennies, Edgar looked up at his new handsome house, as simple and as useful as a box.

Irma had said to him once, "Do you miss doors?"

In the old house there were lots of doors and you could close them. When Irma got sore (and of course sometimes Irma got sore) she sewed in the sewing room. When Edgar got miffed (of course he got miffed) he studied in his study. When their son sulked he had a place to sulk and if Edgar didn't like his records, they could both close doors. Though as far as the records were concerned, when he attacked, she defended. She really liked Elvis Presley.

"Mama!" her son had said.

"Well, I do."

No, there is something to be said for cumbersome old houses with bad roofs and many rooms. Up at the new house the sun gleamed on the glass and then one panel vanished. Irma stepped out upon the new deck, so small a figure at this distance that he saw only the bell of her skirts (she was one of the last women to wear skirts) and the white handkerchief she waved at him. She was the one of the last to have handkerchiefs; Kleenex does not wave properly.

Breakfast was ready.

The doctors' office had not changed much over the years. Way back when Dr. Weller took the new partner in, there had been a flurry of new carpeting and an outbreak of new prints upon the old walls and because everyone was on the bandwagon now, a measling of small offensive signs that thanked you in advance for not having smoked.

Edgar snorted. He was thinking of the last time he had his glasses changed. The same signs were in the optometrist's office, and that man also had canned music, played so softly that it distracted without interesting. A young woman of impeccable poise was smoking and because there were no ashtrays, flicked ashes on the floor. Perhaps, the receptionist suggested, she had not seen the signs?

"I wouldn't be here," said this secure young woman, "if I could see the signs."

Dr. Weller appeared in the fairly Moorish archway. He was a handsome, melancholy man who would, he confided, have preferred to be a concert singer. He was fond of Irma.

"Edgar," he said. "May I have a moment?"

Ah, we all know that moment. While you sit more or less at ease and wait for a routine reassurance, some dark direction has been turned: between one instant and the next, there goes the meaning of your life.

Dr. Weller, to offend no one, affected an empty pipe. Before Edgar was well seated he whipped his black bundle around Edgar's upper arm and pumped away.

"Ha!" he said. "Thought so."

Edgar felt that his frontiers were violated. What right had the man to think of him? He was not the patient.

The doctor snapped his fingers. He said, "You could go like *that*."

And that changed everything.

What would she do in the dead of wintertime, snow on the road, the plow not yet down, no telephone, no neighbors and no friends and she not able to lift him nor to drive the car nor to reach help?

If he went like *that*?

8

JUST BEFORE LABOR DAY one of the nicest couples on Crow Point
had a bad idea. The Bakers proposed a cocktail party in order, as
she said, to wind the season up.

It did.

What they had had in mind was to draw together in amity all
those who otherwise might withdraw to their winter homes with
all their summer discontents, but because the hostess was too
gentle for her own good and the host unobserving, the guest list
was disastrous. She felt (her name was Joan) that everyone
should be included. He felt (his name was Hank) that their
machinations would be less obvious if they included other
islanders and even a few from New Bristol.

Joan said that would prove expensive, and who knew anyone
from New Bristol.

He, for one. He had met some nice men while golfing.

But if they invited those from New Bristol, they were going to be invited back. Was he sure they wanted to be known in New Bristol? And think of the liquor bill alone.

He felt he could afford it.

Joan said that in that case she would like to have the party catered.

Hank wondered why. If he helped and since she had insisted on the freezer, they could manage a cookout by themselves.

Joan said she was sick of managing and that a cookout was not what she had had in mind.

But at a cookout, beer would suffice.

That didn't work out well. Hadn't he noticed that at the wine-and-cheese parties that were popular of late, there was always a full bar in the kitchen? And besides, next time he came up he could stop in Portsmouth for the liquor where it was so much cheaper, and they could take home all that was left over.

Left over!

Marriages have dissolved over less than this.

And had she noticed that since the last time the price of vermouth went up, everyone who made do at home with vodka on the rocks became choosy at parties and drank scotch?

They both laughed.

Marriages are sustained by less than this.

The motives of those who accepted were obscure. So were the motives of those who declined. Had you been a mouse in the wall or a carpenter ant, you would have heard: she had already packed the one dress she had brought. He didn't like to drive on the holiday. She had never found much to say to Joan. He had a lot that he would like to say to Hank, who always parked so that no one could pass. If they accepted, they would have to retaliate.

On the other hand, if they did not attend, who knows what might be said? At the very least, that they had not been invited.

The history of parties on Crow Point is not good; sensible folk avoid them. Serious drinkers do not entertain wine people, who are inclined to be critical and have total recall. Wine people are nervous about serious drinkers, who have been known to have a few before for fear of what they will be offered: the results are uncertain. Unlikely alliances are formed and wars erupt. The wandering road is annually scarred where people have gone off the road.

It is best for congenial friends to meet alone: three couples is enough. With any luck, if you go off the road, Harry Higgins will come right out with his truck and although in the morning everyone will conjecture, no one can be sure. And then, if you drink with your friends you do not have to dress.

On Crow Point nobody knows what to wear. Your host may wear a T-shirt or a cummerbund. Pant suits used to be safe; not now. Those smoky frocks necessitate real shoes. The heels of the real shoes dig up the lawn and if the evening is fair, you can forget your lawn. If the evening is wet, your lawn is safe but your house isn't.

On the night of the Bakers' cocktail party, it rained.

Irma said, "Where do you think we ought to park?"

She was wearing her strapped slippers.

"As far back as possible," Edgar said.

Irma had never been what you would call a dresser. She had one long skirt and two tops and when he had been made principal he had taken her to Boston and gone straight to Delman's and had paid fifty dollars for the sandals in which she did not wish to maneuver.

He was good that way. He put the key back in the ignition and the wiper snapped again.

"On the other hand," he said, "it's better to be facing in the right direction in case you want to leave quickly. So I'll drive you to the door and then turn around."

The Pedersens were always punctual, but as Irma hovered on the back porch, not wanting to go in without Edgar, already others were arriving. Most of the women who were more accustomed than Irma was to social life on Crow Point were carrying paper bags with their shoes in them and wearing sneakers. Irma felt for Joan Baker, who in the morning would not only have to

74

deal with the ashtrays and plastic glasses but with the leftover shoes, and would have to inquire all over before she matched them with their owners.

The big living room with its stone fireplace filled rapidly; so did the long screened porch where the bar was positioned.

"Munchies!" the hostess cried out gaily.

She was no fool; having observed at other parties the cold cheese slide from the crackers while the hot hors d'oeuvres charred in the oven, she had hired an island girl to pass the hot crab and the stuffed mushrooms right now, while they would still be noticed. The island girl was some connection of the very young man who was the bartender and kept a careful eye upon him; he had been known to take advantage of his office.

Those plastic glasses are confusing and since none of them is stemmed, an innocent mistake was made. Irma received from her host what looked like sherry but proved to be bourbon. Never one to call attention to an innocent mistake she drank it down, and then she had a sherry. The bourbon was not as palatable as the wine, but its effect was pleasing. It seemed to her that none of these people was as formidable as she had thought; particularly she had felt ill at ease before the New Bristol bunch, who clustered together in what had seemed to her exclusiveness but what she now saw was simple shyness. Irma began to draw them out.

In the meantime Edgar engaged seriously with the bishop.

The old Raffertys had for years made their tiny guest-house available at a pittance to the bishop and his pretty wife, because curates cannot afford vacations. As he advanced rapidly up the ecclesiastical ladder, it became obvious that he could now afford it, but it was too late to bring the matter up and the young Raffertys could only hope that he contributed a good round sum to charity; no doubt he did. Although the bishop was High Church and the Pedersens Low, the two men found a lot in common: both were grievously disappointed in the President and were as one in decrying the new liturgy and the construction of seawalls.

So far, so good.

During the second hour the disintegration was gradual. There was a steady progress to the porch, perhaps in search of fresh air, since the living room grew hot and fuggy. The island girl had given up passing trays and leaned in a corner with her arms folded. Jessie Thorne arrived late with a nice-looking man who had lately removed his beard; you could tell because he now seemed to wear across his upper face a darker mask, like a raccoon. Jessie had conceded to the party only a white shirt and a bright scarf, below her jeans (clean ones) her brown ankles were bare and her sneakers speckled with wet grass.

Irma was pleased to find the young man was Angus Allister. "*The* Angus Allister?" she asked. Why, she had read his book!

He too was pleased. "Let me fill your glass," he said. "What are you drinking?"

"Bourbon," said Irma, brightly.

Oh, there were signs. One of the golfers broke away from those discussing birdies, bogeys and Sudden Death to shake his finger at the glass in the bishop's hand.

"I've heard about you Episcopalians," he said. "Where four are gathered you will find a fifth!"

The bishop's laugh was testy. He had encountered the facetious gentleman before on an occasion when he had publicly attacked a frightened young clergyman with a sick wife.

He now saw fit to remind him of it. "That was a disgusting performance you put on the other night," said the bishop. "Nobody ever heard of you outside of Maine; you aren't even congressman anymore, and all your money is inherited."

Among the *Comus's* crew from New Bristol there was a stately and raven-haired Californian who seemed to be a sort of guest of a guest.

She said now to her present hostess, "How do you do? I have to pee."

And since she seemed about to do so, Joan helped her to the bathroom and balanced her upon the seat. It was not easy because she was about to remarry, and listing to the left and right, became emotional.

"I am not going to hurt his children!" she cried, giving the game away. Of course she meant to hurt his children: otherwise why would it be on her mind?

"Of course not!" said Joan, trying to direct her flow.

And when she returned, Lydia Pullen's voice was lifted above the rest. "Five selfish people are behind it all."

Since this was not to the purpose of the party, Joan cried nervously, "Lydia! Did I show you the snaps of the little boys?"

"No," Lydia said. "But perhaps it can wait."

The bartender had romped through the Chivas Regal and the Beefeater and had now brought aboveboard the Poland Springs. Had the Bakers thought that would not be noticed? Amused glances were exchanged and some that were not so amused.

A landscape painter, a handsome man just this side of elderly, began to pinch the ladies. Some were offended, and some were not.

The wise began to slip away.

The bishop watched his wife carefully, not because she was not flawless but because from time to time other men noticed that she was without flaw. There had been a sudden last surge of late arrivals of whom he could not approve. Ragtag and bobtail. Even the host did not seem to know who they were. They must have spoken to someone on their way in. Perhaps the waitress?

A tall young woman from New Bristol with a petulant, disappointed face watched them sternly, and then as if she held Lydia Pullen accountable, swung to her and said, "I understand your grandchildren are a public menace."

Her friend said, "Helena is so direct."

On the porch bawdy song erupted. That sort of thing cannot be tolerated unless you are the one who is singing and the hour is late. On either side the fire two women who had attended the same college looked at one another. Then their pure voices soared.

O Colby, Alma Mater dear . . .

"Foss Hall?" asked one.

"No," said the other modestly. "Mower House."

The academician had lately been elevated and was now a dean. One cannot imagine why he felt it necessary, but he glanced about as if to challenge anyone who questioned his command of languages. Then he too, sang.

Vita nobis brevis est. . . .

Lydia Pullen said, "I hate this sort of thing."

Gaudeamus igitur!

The bishop subsided on the sofa.

Now the attractive old landscapist pinched Irma on her behind (she was flustered and flattered) and then with his surly mate in close attendance moved on to the bishop's lady and managed to brush her upper parts.

"Pretty titty," he said.

The bishop was at a disadvantage. The sofa was deep, the cushions soft and the adversary standing. But, trained neither to give nor to take offense, his wife spoke not to the aging satyr but to his consort.

"Such joie de vivre!" she said.

"He's a dirty old lech," said the wife.

Then rose the bishop in his wrath. Had he been stoled he could not more have suggested authority; perhaps he may have touched his collar.

He said, "Come, Martha. This is bestial."

Later some people thought it was at this point that the hostess burst into tears. But in point of fact, she did not notice the clerical departure.

"Can't someone say," she sobbed, "what I should do to be happy?"

And as the Pedersens departed by the kitchen door, the waitress and the bartender quarreled.

"Mama said I was to drive," she said.

Irma never failed to astonish Edgar. She trotted happily beside him in her stocking feet.

"What a good idea!" she said.

Before them the headlights of the departing sliced through the treetops. The skirts of the fog hung low.

She swung her sandals by her side. "Stockings are cheap," she said. "Wasn't it wonderful?"

He grasped her by the elbow.

Oh, she skipped along!

Somewhere the dean was caroling. *"Freude! Freude!"* The dean had a strong voice. *"Tochter aus Elysium!"*

There was a crashing in the underbrush.

Edgar was confused. Somebody certainly said, "Somebody certainly should look after Madge."

"And don't you think," Irma asked as he got her into the car, "that we should have a party?"

9

ON A BLUE bright September morning Jessie Thorne was climbing carefully on the rocks. You have to be careful on the rocks. Every summer there are casualties even among the abstemious, and people limp around or wear slings or openly display bruises, contusions and lacerations. The bishop had been cut quite badly sending off fire balloons from the beach. The trouble was that the salt air, the shining sand below, the beckoning water bring on a euphoria that make the most sensible attempt to bound like goats.

Jessie was too much the old Crow Pointer to err upon this issue: she would scorn to be damaged on the rocks. But she was going to swim, whether or not it was wise to swim alone. Anyway, this time of year you could hardly call it swimming. Already the temperature of the water was dropping rapidly from its midseason high, which, to tell the truth, is never very high, no matter how dazzling the air or hot the sand.

If you sat first on the sand and grew comfortable, you were lost and would remain where you subsided, so what you did was to drop your towel and keep going up to the water and into it, not pausing at the cold that slashed your ankles and your knees. Then you fell forward. And then as you flailed about it didn't seem so bad, though this might be because you were numb.

She got out right away. The bright sun threw a shawl around her and she dropped down to where, supine, she lay below the razor's edge of breeze that stropped itself on her wet skin. She sighed with pleasure. In spite of every effort she had made to cling to a just resentment of the way that a pernicious life had battered her, Jessie was getting better. She had been four months alone on Crow Point, and nothing the nervous nellies had predicted had occurred: she wasn't lonely, she wasn't drinking too much, and she had not been frightened.

"You ought to get yourself a dog," Charley Pratt had said.

No. She wasn't ready to spill forth affection.

"Whyever?"

"Because it's not the way it used to be."

"Meaning?"

But she knew very well what Charley meant. In the good days nobody locked a door from season's start to season's end; it wouldn't have been friendly. What if somebody wanted to borrow something? And it was a common joke that after Labor Day the sheriff checked the houses and left a card to say that he had done so and to alert thieves that he had come and gone and would not be back. Nothing was ever taken. You could leave that bottle of Jim Beam out in plain sight.

Now a rough local crowd broke in after anything electrical that could be detached and you were wise to detach it first yourself. You were advised to keep a list of serial numbers and with a special pen the sheriff would supply to scratch your name into your property, but great-grandmother's desk had no serial number and should not be initialed.

"But Charley, they all know I'm here."

"And they all know you're alone. You ought to get a dog."

She loathed those brutes big enough to tackle people and did not want to be responsible for anyone a big brute tackled. Chows and Dobermans and shepherds and like that.

"You ought to get a beagle."

Ho! That gentlest of animals?

". . . would let you know someone was coming. Your grandma had some right nice things down there."

What's more, last year the Coast Guard moved in on drug smugglers close as Arrowsic and on another in Boothbay.

"You ever think a cutter could anchor off your beach?"

"Oh, come on, Charley!"

And then, these days there were more of your natural nuts.

Jessie was thinking that they always told you noisy dogs were a deterrent, but they didn't tell you that dogs will wake you from your sleep with your heart crashing when all in the world they hear is a skunk. Then, ready for fight or frolic, they yap at the door for you to open it. And what if there should be somebody standing, silent, on the other side?

Thanks ever so much. No.

She had a gun and she could handle it; anyone who thought she couldn't had another think coming.

"That goes for you too, Charley."

He said, "I know a fellow's got a beagle."

Jessie rolled over in the sun. In Maine, September is a lovesome month. Mornings are clear as crystal and as cold as ice, but at high noon from the blue bowl of the sky the sun pours a heat like midsummer over the clean and empty beaches, and you can stroll in silence beside the splendor of the empty sea. Bright buoys bob out there, but the lobstermen have long reset their traps and gone; the sailboats are put up and the noisy pleasure craft,

82

silenced now and sullen behind the station wagons, have gone down the Maine Turnpike.

Jessie pillowed her head on her hand and sighed as a traitorous sense of well-being overtook her. Those habits instilled early are hard to break and in the face of facts, the child habituated to love and to contentment will, as an adult, succumb to happiness.

No, she could not deny it: every day in every way she was getting better and better.

She was even losing her animus toward men because really, she liked men: always had. Once in a while she even missed Howard — not the one who had so reduced her, but the one she trustingly had married.

Be honest: she missed him in her bed.

Not only for the customary purposes but for other amenities. No electric blanket warms like a naked body. And when, at three in the morning, you awake with that primordial panic, nothing else comforts nor gives you the generous joy of comforting. And then, in what she had thought their special marriage, another thing had been nice. When the sky paled, they had their first coffee and their best talks. Howard would hump up on his pillow, balance an ashtray on his knees and tell her of his dreams.

Like, "All night I was cataloguing the mythical compositions of Ralph Vaughan Williams."

Or, "It was my mother all right, but it was also Rimbaud. In some ways they were not dissimilar."

And though he was troubled by her shoes, he was also proud of her and said so. He said she had a bright, interesting little mind, if not well trained. She felt that while she could not refute him, many a dolt walks around with a bachelor's degree. They took turns getting the coffee.

Of how much had he bereft her!

The warm sand cupped her breasts and mounded under her like a warm belly. The wind lifted her brief hair and behind her, the water played its slow game. *Ping . . . pong . . .* A drop slid down her grainy cheek and by God was not a tear but real salt water. Her thighs pimpled with cold; she hadn't toweled well enough.

Or was it that someone was watching her?

Jessie lay sprawled, bare and defenseless, with that feeling everyone has had: eyes are upon me. All the advantage goes to him who is erect and clothed. Had she done this by lingering upon the thought of Howard?

> I can call spirits from the vasty deep.
> But will they come when you do call for them?

Yes. Yes indeedy. If it is Howard, Jessie thought, I will kill him. She opened her eyes, swung her head, and looked into the eyes of a raccoon.

You do not see raccoons upon the beach. Raccoons eat fresh-water fish and everything you put out in the trash. Crow Point is loaded with raccoons. You can put rocks on the garbage cans, lock the garage doors and pile firewood in front of the locked doors; they will still get your trash. Everyone knows they wash their clean fish with their small prehensile paws and everyone thinks that an attractive trait. Then there are their nice little masks. Because of all this someone always tries to raise a raccoon kitten as a house pet, which is a mistake. They will ride on your shoulder. They will also get into your flour. Jessie remembered one pet who liked to upend beer cans in his clever little paws. The trouble was that when he got drunk he got ugly.

Raccoons do not belong upon the beach.

This one smiled at Jessie. Along its muzzle hung a line of froth.

Rabid. *Any wild animal whose behavior is uncharacteristic should be avoided.* Like the plague.

True and furious rabies, an acute disease which can be communicated by inoculation to all warm-blooded animals, even birds, and causes them to act offensively. The desire to do injury is irrepressible. Do you suppose we are all rabid?

84

Once (this was years ago) one of those little red foxes that surprise you because they are so little had chased her to the back door. She wouldn't have hurt him, but he should have thought she would.

When therefore an animal, contrary to its habits and natural inclination, becomes aggressive, one should take precautions.

Her grandmother opened the door and Jessie slammed inside and the door banged behind her but the red fox stayed, smiling and snarling on the other side. And once she had seen, smack in the middle of the highway, a fox doing battle with a dog. The fox looked sick: under its patchy fur its sides caved in.

Expect paroxysms and paralysis.

This raccoon did not look sick. Perhaps a little puffed about the head, and swollen. But it was out of place and as she scrambled to her feet it ambled toward her, badly balanced.

In human beings the premonitory stage is characterized by great mental depression and disquietude, together with restlessness and indefinite fear. There is an unusual tendency to talk. After two or three days of suffering of the most terrible description, the patient succumbs.

Of course there is treatment, but the treatment is long and painful though almost certainly sure. If, of course, it is started in time.

Jessie raced for the rocks and fled up them, careless as any neophyte. When she attained the turf she stood shuddering because of what had not happened and because of what must now happen.

She was a good shot and had dropped many a beer can, but she had never taken life. She was not offended by hunters of pheasant or quail or even deer, any more than she would be offended that a bass be hooked or a flounder speared; since such fills the larder it would be sentimental to object. She just didn't care to do these things herself.

But the raccoon could not be allowed to slouch off again. Heaven knew at what place in what deadly chain the creature took its place, and the fox or the mate that had nipped it surely was panting or rotting in the woods. About that she could do nothing, but she could crack the link before the raccoon, who no longer recognized its natural enemy, encountered something . . . someone . . . who did not recognize his natural enemy. Perhaps, even at this time of year, a curious child.

Jessie had always claimed she could handle anything that came up, even if she had not expected it. That is the essence, isn't it, of things that come up: that you do not expect them. As soon as the rifle was in her hands she was steady as a ledge. She broke the gun, loaded it, made sure the safety clicked and, carrying it muzzle to the ground, paced rapidly and naked down the long lawn. She hoped the raccoon would not have moved or not much, because where it had been she had a safe shot at it; if she missed (she wouldn't miss) the bullet would not ricochet from the rocks but would spend itself harmlessly in the sand or water.

Jessie stepped to the belt of boulders and looked down.

The raccoon wasn't there.

Her thoughts swirled like a whirlpool. Relief that she didn't have to be the one to translate that pelt into a bloody sponge. Disappointment, because she could have done it. Fear. Because if the raccoon was not on the beach, where was it?

If she had a beagle she would know where the raccoon was. And if she had a telephone she could reach the game warden and with no more ado turn the problem over to him and let him earn his keep. As it was, she was going to have to drive into town. There went her morning. But she was not about to go ranging through the woods after that animal nor did she wish to spend the next days peering around her doors and rather more than not expecting its jaws to close around her ankle.

Well, the whole point in being able to cope is coping. If you can't, everyone else is right and you should not winter by yourself on Crow Point. So Jessie dressed, dashed for the garage, hesitated at its dark corners with their moist earthen smell and their attractive trash and then leaped for the front seat of the car. The car groaned and whimpered and cried aloud.

86

But it would not start.

That was the beginning of the *Drang nach Telephon*. No matter what Lydia Pullen thought, it was not a conspiracy but a simple decision by those who for their sundry reasons had reconsidered. Jessie had decided that a telephone would make her more independent and not less so. She would, of course, have a privately listed number and would give it to no one except to Charley and Mrs. Charley.

Tom Elder was lonely. Perhaps he had counted too much upon the company of his hi-fi and the pleasure of playing it at what a tactful friend had once called concert strength, which because of the neighbors made Brigid critical and uncomfortable. Here where there were no neighbors the joy of shaking the windows with Mahler's sixth and Bruckner's ninth first contented and then abruptly palled.

Then in the face of Brigid's inexplicable refusal to join him on weekends, he had begun to drive of nights into New Bristol, where in a variety of public places he encountered a variety of young females who were quick to see in him an amusing companion. While it could be maintained that these close, sudden friendships were quite innocent, he did not particularly want to explain them to his wife. If by means of a telephone he could establish that Brigid was in Boston, he could more comfortably fare forth. Brigid would never call him back again to check. She was too careful with her pennies.

Naturally he did not go into this with the others. To them he only said that if he could persuade Brigid to take a winter holiday, she would still want to be in almost daily contact with her office.

Jessie Thorne raised her brows.

Of course when he drove in and out through town, the Pratts might notice, and Jessie and the Pratts were thick as thieves. But they had no way of knowing that he did not, as he had casually suggested, spend evenings at the library and indeed, one of the girls was a librarian. Besides, his feeling about Jessie had ameliorated. He still disliked her brutal honesty but was now convinced that she did not insist on it for others. As long as she herself was the only one concerned he did not give a fig and could watch her headlong assault upon a reasonable mendacity with interest and a certain sympathy. She had not ratted on him about the clams.

Edgar Pedersen's public reasoning was not equivocal. It would be nice for Irma to reach her son at will. Also, back home in China Falls she had spoken daily on the telephone to her friends and could still do this, within reason, since a toll call to China Falls was a small one, as toll calls go. Therefore the Pedersens would go along.

Privately, relief reduced him. If they had a telephone Irma could call a doctor, a hospital, an ambulance. She could call the road commissioner, who would send the snowplow down. Or the sheriff, who had been known to dispatch snowmobiles in such emergencies. And while she waited, she could call on either of these young people; whatever their private vices were they were not the kind, he was sure, to grudge a neighbor help.

But that they were now a determined nucleus did not guarantee that they would get their phones. Far from it. The cost of running lines down through Crow Point was astronomical and New England Telephone was not about to do it without a given number of subscribers; quite a given number, too. Edgar Pedersen had a directory of Interested Owners. They went over it.

"What the hell," Jessie said. "We can try."

Jessie and Tom had portable typewriters and the Pedersens only an old massive upright, so it was more sensible and more fun to meet at the Pedersens' where, while the others wrote the letters, Irma licked envelopes and served popcorn, brownies, and beer. They had intended to proceed alphabetically, but Tom Elder had an excellent idea.

"Let's leave the Pullens to the last. That way Lydia can't call the others up and frighten them off."

"Oh, good idea!" said Irma.

Then with the natural cunning of the shy, she had a suggestion of her own. The names of all subscribers should be kept in confidence except, of course, from New England Telephone. Once the telephone was a *fait accompli*, even Lydia's closest friends couldn't be blamed for gracefully giving in, and Lydia couldn't know who had not waited to give in with grace.

Edgar Pedersen, tacitly recognized as the most reliable, was entrusted with mailing the letters from New Bristol, since the town postmistress was totally reliable but had no gift for deceit. Back on the shoulder of the road Jessie and Tom paused to breathe deep of the autumn dusk: salt, mist and leaf-mold. From the Pedersens' you looked down on Tom's roof.

To his surprise he said, "Come have a drink."

"No," she said, not at all unpleasantly. "I'm expecting a guest."

That's what he meant. Had it been he, he would have covered up a little and said "guests." On Jacataqua Island word gets about as if by osmosis; unless you are very careful you may sprain your ankle in the morning or go to Portland and by noon, the town will know. This does not mean the town will criticize or even care but only that the town will know; if Jessie had said "guests" she could conceivably have meant the Pratts.

By "guest" she meant Angus Allister.

Tom shifted his typewriter case from hand to hand. "Well, back to the old drawing board," he said.

Jessie had been much interested in his plans and had even offered to help him search for subjects. "How's it going?" she asked.

So far there was only the one painting, but it was almost done. "Great. Just great. Couldn't be better."

The moon, trailing skirts of mist, sailed up beyond the firs. An owl hooted.

10

DURING THE FIRST WEEK in October when the woods shouted with color, Charley Pratt backed the old blue Packard out of the garage and drove around.

Oh, yes he could. According to the pestiferous law if you were over seventy-five you had to go to New Bristol every two years and prove to the State of Maine that you were just as good as the whippersnappers. Which he was.

So Charley still had his license. He resented the whole thing very much. They hand out licenses free-for-all to the young, who have no experience and no judgment and no common sense. But Charley Pratt every other April had to go to the new Registry (you used to have to go up to Augusta) and demonstrate again that his eyes were sharp as needles and that he never forgot to come to a dead stop before he crossed the tracks where the trains no longer ran.

Much of the year he didn't care to drive any more than he had to, which meant just up to the schoolhouse and once a week into New Bristol so Mrs. Charley could stock up. He wasn't frightened by the traffic but he didn't like it; it was no pleasure, on the highway, to have to look at and consider streams of strangers and go at the speed they chose, which was too fast to look around you and too slow to get anywhere and back without wasting time.

But in the fall when the skies were high and blue and the ground carpeted with scarlet and with gold and it was brisk enough for his old coat-sweater and all the summer people had gone home, he liked to mosey around and see what they had been up to this time. On these occasions, Mrs. Charley did not care to accompany him. It embarrassed her. It was all very well to say the summer people had gone home, but what if somebody came back? With Charley peeking in their windows? Because he did peek into any window that wasn't shuttered, and if they were shuttered he would still poke around the yards and garages. He wasn't supposed to be on Crow Point at all, since it was now all private property and so posted.

"I don't pay any attention to that," Charley said.

"That's what I mean," said Mrs. Charley.

So she was not with them when they started out that morning, Charley and his friend, though she had stood at the door of the garage as she always did, ready to shout out if he got too close to either side and was in any danger of scratching the paint. The paint was flawless.

"I've never put a mark on it," said Charley.

"That's because I always shout out," said Mrs. Charley.

The Packard was a deep source of pride to them both. Charley had bought it brand-new back in nineteen-fifty and they had coddled and cared for it ever since: it had been constantly waxed, shined and polished, inspected and repaired and repainted. The nap of the upholstery, in spite of constant vacuuming and mothballs, was short in places and had faded and the rust was gently nibbling at the Packard's skirts but not — like other old cars — until they looked like lace. Salt on the winter roads will do it

91

and salt in the sea air. Everything rusts by the sea. But one admits no flaw in the beloved.

"Why don't they get a new one?" the town said. "They can afford that and some."

They didn't get a new car because new cars were ugly and the blue Packard beautiful: more than one fellow had come around from the Veteran Motor Car Clubs of America and tried to buy it. They claimed that in Boston on the Larz Anderson estate there was a museum for classic and antique cars where the old Packard could be protected and admired. No-sirree-sir.

Mrs. Charley's hands folded under her apron. "I notice you don't go down there in the summertime," she said.

That wasn't because he was afraid of being asked to leave. There wasn't a soul on Crow Point would ask Charley Pratt to leave. It was because he didn't like any of them well enough to talk to them. And he tired of their reverent courtesies, as if he were an ambulatory monument.

"Don't go and fall down anywhere," she said.

She was a nice person but like everyone, annoying. Now Charley made a nice adjustment to the rearview mirror and slid his hands lovingly over the real wood wheel.

"Best buy we ever made," he said.

"Yes," Mrs. Charley said.

And then she smiled and waved.

The Crow Point road is all ups and downs and mean quick little turns and though the town cuts the brush back in the spring, the bushes move right back into the road so you can't see much ahead, which is another reason Charley Pratt avoided Crow Point in the summer; nobody sensible wants to meet a summer person on the Crow Point Road. Even after the summer people leave, you can't trust them, because one of them may have asked a workman to go down: workmen are always in a hurry, especially if they have forgotten something and have to go to New Bristol for it, and they have always forgotten something for which they have to go to New Bristol. When they get back it is lunchtime.

So Charley was driving so slowly that without even stopping

he could pass the time of day with the writer fellow, who was raking up a scattering of bright dry leaves. It seemed to Charley that he had kept the yard up nice.

"He's not the worst of them," he said to his companion, who expressed no opinion.

Beyond the trailer (where he waved at the lobsterman's pretty wife) he saw no one and could stop now and then and in the sunny silence hear grasshoppers crackling in the grass. This part of the long road had not changed, not enough to speak. The blueberry bushes burned with a motionless flame, the flames of the burning maples stirred in the blue wind. Way across the marsh he could see the blue glitter of the bay. Many a time with a horse and buggy he had come here courting.

But the hooded old eyes were not looking for evidence of the past but of the present. You heard all about the summer accidents, but it amused him to see the veritable places where they had occurred. Briar Hill had a sharp drop-off on one side and down there the birches were broken where the VW went over. One thing about those light little cars; the VW had just hung there and no one had been hurt. This season's skid-marks and rutted shoulders were still visible where numerous drivers in similar haste but with varying degrees of skill had left the road in order to avoid a head-on. Sometimes the marks went both to right and left. Into the single tree at the fork of the road disfigured by directive signs, the Emerson boy had crashed like an ax and the signs had flown like chips. He said his friend was driving. Most of the possessors of the signs had gathered them up but had not yet replaced them. That was pleasing.

Through the marsh Charley had noticed, on both sides of the causeway, a few new pieces of big driftwood that had traveled quite a way from the bay. They lay dark and spiky among the old salt-whitened ones. So when he reached the Bombing Gate Charley stopped the Packard and got out and stepped down to where the beach began. Since this time last year the channel of Inner River had swung violently back and forth, digging sand here and pushing it up there. Well, Inner River did that every year. But this year the turf was undercut. The Raffertys had lost a foot of lawn and the big tide that took it had tumbled upon its side a raftlike rock where everybody used to like to sit. "Hmmmn," thought Charley Pratt.

Brigid had at last been on Crow Point for almost twenty-four hours and it seemed to Tom Elder that whereas on Friday afternoon she had proved a pleasant guest, she had spent much of Saturday morning teasing him in an unfriendly manner.

If he had come right out and asked, she could have told him why, although whether or not she would have is another question. Again, he had not lived up to her expectations, although as an intelligent woman who read and looked around she knew that the holiday of being away from one another was not necessarily going to change dross to gold. It is no wonder that for centuries sex was a forbidden topic: it was more fun that way. Now that it was casual as a cigarette it was just about as exciting, and all his joking references to pussies and to cocks was not provocative.

That was what made Howard dangerous. He understood that foreplay does not occur in bed, but begins when someone looks directly into your eyes and does not smile. This indicates that something momentous is abroad. If you had met earlier, kingdoms might have toppled. They may yet. So did Troilus look at Cressida and Tristan at Iseult, and what came of it could not be laughed away. All the cosiness of marriage cannot compare with that delicious thrill of mortal fear.

She was sensible enough to see that you cannot go around in a state of mortal fear, especially of someone whose toothpaste you purchase and whose socks you put away. She did think that even yet, Tom should once in a while look into her eyes, a thing he never did unless he happened to be angry.

Last night had been wretched. By the time they were in bed she knew exactly what not to expect, which was any recognition of her: Brigid. And so it had turned out; the old pattern. If he didn't feel like it he would pat her hand. If he felt like it he

94

would pat her elsewhere. Then having identified his intent, he would for two minutes rub her briskly in the wrong places. This was not all his fault. She herself had made the initial and old, old mistake. She had moaned once in simulated ecstasy, after which, in his generosity, he had thought, ah — that's what she likes. Often it was perfectly all right for her and she knew it was usually all right for him, because you can tell. But something is missing if you lie linked only in certain parts.

Why didn't her husband kiss her on the mouth? Why did he laugh at the act of love, which leads so often to mayhem and to murder? What's to laugh? Though we all know now that no penalty accompanies the occasional attraction, Howard's dark gaze was still a threat and his firm hand about her wrist, a demand.

"It isn't enough fun," Brigid said now, "to drive all this way just to watch you batten down for winter."

She was stretched on a log mother-naked but with a towel handy just in case. The last sun of the season. It coarsens your skin and blisters you with wee cancers, but who cares?

He noticed that she looked slippery as a seal. She was a brown girl — skin, eyes, and glossy hair, and she looked warm as an agate. But that she was bare-assed annoyed him, because he himself was dressed in high-laced boots against the briars, buttoned from wrist to neck because of the flies — oh yes, there still were flies — and he had one of her bandannas around his neck to arrest the sweat from rolling down into the shirt.

What he was going to do was to widen the path up to the road. The summer guests he had were limber and did not mind climbing over the puckerbrush, but when the winter guest was snow, Tom was going to have to shovel, and although if the path were wider it would take more shoveling, it would be easier to get supplies down on a sled. Until he had to think of supplies he had not thought of sleds. Do they still make Flexible Flyers?

She looked warm and cool and brown and inviting. Last night had been glorious. She had arrived with Boston scrod — many think Boston scrod is any baby white fish; not at all — and with

95

a better wine than he could find in New Bristol. For some reason the State Liquor Store cannot sell wine or beer; in the supermarkets the supply is plentiful but dull. Also she had brought a running Brie. Also she had done the dishes.

He hoped very much that she would not hear about any of his young women. But why should she? People do not repeat hurtful things unless they are hurtful people.

Brigid sighed. She said, "Can't you stop? It isn't going to snow tomorrow."

"Sit up," Tom said suddenly. "Cover yourself. Here's the old man."

Brigid was old-fashioned. She always blushed in any room where there were more than three men she had slept with. Naturally she covered herself because that is courteous, but only because of that. One thing she knew was that Charley Pratt was not prurient; Charley Pratt was amused but not particularly interested.

From his vantage point above them Charley said now, "You've got a nice spot here. Your mother liked it."

Below the fall of rock the sea curled and caressed. From up here the little house looked vulnerable, but it was Tom's belief that it was only because you could see through under it.

Charley Pratt said, "That's some big old log."

The eyes of all three rested upon the big old log. In June wild iris had perked up about it. Then the wild raspberry took over and the blue gentian and the nightshade.

Charley said, "If I was you, I'd move her up and back." He didn't mean the log.

Tom Elder saw his little house swinging through the air, the shingles scaling off and the partitions parting.

He said, "That would cost a fortune."

Charley said, "Cost a fortune to lose her, too."

Tom didn't like to be told anything. Nobody does. It wasn't so much what he said as the coldness in his voice.

"It's been safe a long time right there, Charley."

Suddenly they antlered like two bucks in a clearing.

"Sure has," Charley said.

When the old Packard bumped away the Elders were left troubled.

Tom said, "I wonder what moving it would cost?"

Brigid said, "How's the work going?"

When you have been married for a while, you know the difference between a tactless remark and a malicious one. What she meant was that to think of moving the house was a pipe dream, since he had scamped his job and was eating up his capital. What she meant was that she expected no more from his painting than she would expect from the absorbed activity of a child.

The day lost some part of its charm. Above the towel Brigid's shoulders puckered as thin soiled clouds raced overhead and then hung, hostile.

Very well. Then he would not share his new excitement with her. She was probably incapable of sharing that excitement anyway, since she measured everything with the calipers of stocks and bonds and any interest she had ever shown in his art was (he decided) bogus. He tossed his saw aside. Where he had thought to garner a little kindling the rotted wood crumbled and the things that lived under it crawled out.

He said, "It's not the easiest thing to work when you're here."

She could have taken this as an allusion to her powers to bewitch and distract, but she did not.

She said, "I don't come up that much."

"Yes," he said. "I've noticed."

Charley Pratt went on down the road, rather more pleased than not. It did no harm to shake folks up a little. Down the line he stopped to examine two new houses that had gone up this season. They looked to Charley like two great big old chicken coops, though he knew for a fact that they had cost a pile because the town assessors told him so. He prowled around one of them and because the owners had made the mistake of relying upon draperies, he peered in. They had also made the mistake of carpeting; that sent the taxes flying. The other house was on the bayside flats and the bugs were going to be fierce.

He stopped again where the whole half-circle of Gin Beach was clean and empty and where, many years ago, he and his love had loved while upon the shore the sea sighed in and out.

> Ah, love, let us be true
> To one another! for the world, which seems
> To lie before us like a land of dreams,
> So various, so beautiful, so new . . .

Would that surprise you? Shouldn't. He had been a fiercely thoughtful child.

> Hath really neither joy, nor love, nor light,
> Nor certitude, nor peace, nor help from pain . . .

Very few things got under Charley Pratt's hide but one thing that got under it was the summer assumption that the towns-people read nothing but the *Coastal Journal*.

> And we are here as on a darkling plain
> Swept with confused alarms of struggle and flight

Nothing changes much, does it.

> Where ignorant armies clash by night.

The trouble with the young ones was probably not that they had not read Matthew Arnold but that they had not thought upon it. Someone must stand beside you in the last retreat. To have a battle-mate you have to choose first and then you have to stick.

He stood beside the old Packard with the changing wind in his face. The clouds lowered and skidded overhead. The sunlight left the woods. The bayberries trembled and tried to catch the light and the last shadows sifted across the sand. The tide was going out. The weather changes with the changing of the tide.

Charley had not got much from *Empedocles on Etna*, but any man who has lived beside the sea understands "Dover Beach." Way down there at the graying margin of the water, the pebbles and coarse sand sucked out ceaselessly. There went his parents and his cousins and his friends, the kid who sat beside him in the third grade and his severe and rosy teacher and the Reverend Pritchett and the basketball coach and everyone, and left Charley (except for Mrs. Charley) alone upon the naked shingles of the world.

Ah, love, let us be true.

Charley had been true to his love and she to him.

His friend whimpered. Charley turned back to his automobile. After all, that was what he had come for, wasn't it?

To introduce Jessie to her beagle.

11

IN NOVEMBER, which is a dull month, flocks of starlings shake in the quaking-aspen trees.

In November, Irma's son called and said, "Are you alone?"

It just so happened that she was.

He said, "She's pregnant again."

Oh, it had been so hard for them, the disappointments. Irma said, "When?"

"It's supposed to be March," her son said. "I don't want you discussing this with him."

Irma felt that was unfair but on the other hand, pregnancy is private, and Edgar had got too excited before. She vowed that she would not discuss it.

In November, Jessie was scared to death that Howard would telephone and scared to death he wouldn't. The operator, under penalty of being boiled in oil, should not give out an unlisted number, but it might make a difference when you knew the operator. She found the instrument unnerving in a way she had not anticipated; it was as if the beagle barked when there was nothing there. And it had rung twice, bringing her to her feet with adrenalin pumping through every vein. The first time, the operator wanted to know if her phone had rung. The second was a wrong number.

Each time, the beagle wailed.

The beagle was a year old and totally engaging, but timid; Jessie found it necessary to have him constantly by her side. Fortunately, his soft dappled coat smelled of sun and, oddly enough, of juniper.

"Down, sir," Jessie would tell him sternly.

He would look at her, incredulous and hurt.

Their scheme had succeeded with singular ease; apparently Crow Point was populated by husbands who would stay longer if they could reach the office, wives who were nervous without their husbands, and parents whose children were on student tours in Europe or simply batting around the country with their friends. Even the Pullens had succumbed, though Lydia wrote indignantly to say that while she would not cut off her nose to spite her face, she considered the telephones the beginning of the end.

Jessie had hers installed on the wall beside her bed. It was not convenient in the daytime, but if she should need help at night it was the logical place and if it rang at night she didn't want to go pitching and scrambling through the dark to answer it while the beagle bayed in terror. It is impossible not to answer a telephone that rings: it might be a warning. Of what? Perhaps a madman, loose and wandering. More reasonably, fire. The island was heavily wooded and from snowfall to snowfall, fire was a dire possibility. You would not want to be anywhere on the island in a major fire, but particularly, you would not want to be cut off on Crow Point.

So if you were going to have a telephone at all it was wise to have it by your bed and besides, she had a small mean hope that one night Howard would call, and she would have Angus answer it.

Though that would just be a lucky accident because Angus wasn't there all that often, not through the night. Since they began to go to bed their relationship, she supposed, had been of mutual comfort, but he was too conservative for her taste. That is, he would not spend the night. What she missed almost most was company in the dark and conversation in the morning; Angus was too conventional to see any reason why two unattached people should not go to bed but stubbornly refused to let her, as he put it, risk her name.

"Name of God," Jessie had protested. "Who's to know?"

He'd like to remind her that there was only the one road off Crow Point, and while it was all right in the morning to be seen driving in, it was not all right to be seen driving out.

"But there's no one to see!"

Not true. "There's Elder and there are the Pedersens."

The Pedersens were not malicious. "And Tom would only be amused."

He would not expose her to amusement.

"Rubbish," she said. "Who cares?"

Angus did. He cared very much. He would not consider, either, permitting her to stay with him. In her case, it was all right in the morning to be seen driving out but not in, and anyway, he didn't think it would be considerate of his hostess.

Exasperated, Jessie said, "Antediluvian! You're not living in the time of your poky old book."

"That's what my wife called it," he said wistfully.

She hadn't meant to remind him of his wife. "Sorry," she said. "But all that old stuff about who sleeps with who. Nobody's all that interested anymore."

If she thought that, she pulled the wool over her own eyes. "People are always interested in adultery."

"Fornication," she reminded him.

Whatever. Let him remind her that she was separated but not yet divorced.

"And anyway, have you read my book?"

No. And it was unfair to have spoken like that when she hadn't read it. She would look it up at the New Bristol Free and Public Library.

Perhaps because New Bristol was ringed at reasonable distances by small good colleges with big good libraries, the Free and Public had been allowed to drowse along in a sunny somnolence, an impression reinforced by the yellow brick of which the small Gothic building was constructed and by the lazy little park in which it stood. What changes had occurred had occurred out there in the park. The last time the Dutch elm disease went around, six tall wineglass elms went down and the park looked surprised and bald. The parking space kept encroaching on the lawn. This year trash cans were placed about in which the young did not trouble to throw their beer cans and wine bottles, not with the wading pool available. People were getting used to the handsome if inexplicable statue donated by a local sculptor of international acclaim, if not to the fact that all through the winter it was covered by a wooden hut not unlike the smelting shacks that at that same time of the year brightened the ice floes on the river: should not a statue designed for the out-of-doors be able to withstand weather? Yet in the summer tourists with wallets were drawn into town to stand before it in puzzled awe.

Within, the Free and Public was poorly administered by little old ladies, a personnel which must have changed from time to time but did not seem to. Their dress was impeccable and their grasp of Library Science tenuous. Regularly they cleared from the stacks all interesting and possibly valuable materials in order to make room for Taylor Caldwell and, one may be sure, for Angus Allister. Jessie had once, in search of the book section of the *New York Times*, inquired for it.

"We don't take the *Sunday Times*," she had been told. "On Sundays, we're not open."

So Jessie would read Angus and in the meantime, she was tempted to do something nice for him to make up. She had taken him around to public places, and they had seen Fort

Popham and followed the Kennebec up to Augusta in the wake of Benedict Arnold, lunched at the Stowe house (ruined by a gift shop and an adjoining hotel) and had visited the Longfellow house in Portland, where Angus, as westerners will, grew glassy-eyed to find that Longfellow had existed.

Then they had lunched at Boone's.

Happily, the beagle seemed to feel fairly safe in the car. Jessie was getting used to driving with his paws on her shoulders and his sweet breath in her ear. And fortunately he didn't mind sleeping in the car, indeed, insisted on sleeping in the car, because twice they were gone overnight. Once she had taken Angus up Cadillac Mountain and once they had stayed at Moosehead Lake (neither of them knew anyone at Moosehead, so that was all right); and on the advice of the innkeeper they had gone to the dump to watch for bears and had seen nothing but others waiting to watch bears.

That morning she had wakened happy; the lake light shook through the rented room and she lay snug, thinking about the ways in which men felt and of how lucky she had been never to have waked with a puny one. He slept soundly. Finally she resorted to subterfuge. Later she clasped her hands around her knees.

"What do you think about Stendhal?" she asked.

"Excuse me," he said, and got up to make a note.

But she had not shared with him one private place. Anyone can write about Benedict Arnold and many have. Since she had given up her own ambition to preserve in print the best of Jacataqua Island, he might as well do it. He had told her sternly that he was not to be interrupted before noon, but pooh. He had also admitted that his manuscript was not progressing. Besides, it is one thing to drive into a body's driveway honking and requiring entrance and quite another thing to spin a dial. The other person always can hang up.

Jessie spun the dial.

"Want to see my sphagnum bog?" she said.

He certainly did.

Angus wanted to do anything these days that would keep him from his desk. He was not used to being rich, he was not used to being idle, he was not used to being alone. Every day he picked his way through the small rooms heavily occupied by small fat chairs and fragile tables; sat, sighed, waited. Nothing came. Few things are so frightening to a writer. Panic. *Othello's occupation's gone.*

Therefore he had no right to be roaming around with Jessie Thorne; it was too pleasant and too unproductive. She was of no use at all to him as a type. She was too nervous, too blunt, too restless: too modern. She was both distracted and distracting and what he should do was to tell her that he couldn't see her today and probably not tomorrow.

"Well?" Jessie said.

"I'll be right down," he answered.

Perhaps something would emerge from the sphagnum bog.

Many people who summered on Crow Point had not seen the sphagnum bog nor even heard of it. For the most part they followed the beaten paths from house to house and beach to beach, and there was no true path into the bog nor out of it. Those who had heard had also heard that it was wet in there — not damp, but wet.

"Not that it ought to matter," Jessie said. "Everyone's got an old pair of sneakers."

It happened that his sneakers were fairly new. "How about rubber boots?" he asked.

She said scornfully, "If you like."

He thought he did like the idea of boots and big thick socks inside them, too. Now in November, though the rains had not yet come, the cold had, and the days were either dim and chill and wreathed with mist or else they clanged: the earth iron, the bare metallic branches scraping, the harsh wind impertinent and the sky pale.

"What's that for?" he asked suspiciously as she folded a plastic sheet into her knapsack.

"To sit on," she said cheerfully. "From now on, we can't

afford to lose a picnic." And she added a thermos of hot coffee, one of bloody marys and two thick sandwiches. "I would have brought hot dogs," she said, "but nothing in there's dry enough to burn."

As they trudged down the road she told him what he could have expected of the bog in August had she, in August, been ready to trust him with the bog.

The bog might be a thousand miles from the road and a million years, and there are plants in there that you have never seen and perhaps ought not to see, because they are upsetting. Here where the fickle firs and spruce spring up so quickly and give way so quickly to maple, oak and ash, this land that within the memory of man (Charley Pratt has faded snapshots) has been cropped nude and has gone back again to woods, here where unless Lydia Pullen has her way the woods may again retreat before the asphalt and the bulldozers, the bog has lasted for a long, long time.

How did she know? Sphagnum is a peat-building moss. Each year it decays and binds. "Wait till you see how thick it is," she said.

Uneasily he asked, "About those plants?"

"In the spring," Jessie said, "the moss is covered with what looks like flowers but isn't; like tiny red heads of pins."

Then came the true flowers. Two of them. One was the sundew. Something about the way her eyes lighted, telling of it, made him uncomfortable. It had, she said, a tall stalk from the base of which rosettes of round leaves lifted, covered with reddish hairs on each of which a drop of sweetened liquid hung to entice insects. Because the sundew was an insect-eater. So was the other.

"Pitcher plant," Jessie said. "*Sarracenia purpurea.*"

This had a high stalk, too, on which a heavy petalled round flower nodded: the horror lay below. There in a cup of swollen veinous leaves, striped bright and gaudy as a gourd, water stood and flies floated. The thick lips of the cup were lined with

106

downward-pointing hairs so that the struggling flies slid down to drown.

Angus was not attached to insects; he found them lacking in appeal. Nevertheless, carnivorous plants offended him. What next? Perhaps next they would walk.

Jessie said, "Nature, red in tooth and claw."

But surely Tennyson had meant animals, and not plants.

"Come on," she said.

The bog was an irregular circle around which conventional growth flourished; within, dense draperies of spruce and cedar and bayberry clutched at the thinning soil and bunchberry and cinquefoil, so pretty with its little yellow stars. Next came a spreading, waist-high conifer, unlike anything with which Angus was familiar. The needle was long, the stem rough; as in all gymnosperms, the true cone depended from the branch but ended in a kind of penis. It looked like something that would have been laid down in rock and fossilized a million years ago, or that would take over a million years from now.

In there, it was deadly silent. No bird sang.

Beyond this point you stepped upon a thick, saturated sponge that worried the beagle. Getting his dander up, he tried to follow and then waited on his haunches, wagging his tail and whining. The thing was that the deep moss trembled and in some places broke and let you down ankle-deep into cold mud, with a thin glass of ice inside your sneakers. When this happened Jessie frowned, but only because the sneakers left the spoor of man. From the cold mist that clung in the conifers and blew in tall sheets, Angus would not have been surprised — not really — to see a stegosaurus lumber or a pterodactyl rise on great kite-like wings.

She seemed suddenly subdued. November is subduing.

Of the troublesome flowers nothing was left but scarified and desiccated stalks.

Jessie said, as if seeking comfort, "Howard says the bog's not big enough to attract. I mean, commercially."

What for? Well, the moss was absorbent and florists made a lot of use of it. And it used to be used for surgical dressings and sanitary napkins. "But I don't know about that anymore."

It is not always easy to know what is going to comfort women. Because her attachment to the bog was obviously very great (although in his opinion, morbid) and because she seemed to fear that human greed or human footfall might whittle it away, Angus suggested that it might all take another turn. Who knows? All of Crow Point might one day be a sphagnum bog. And since it was she herself who had brought up Tennyson with his amazing gift of thinking in eons, Angus reminded Jessie of something else that that strange poet had perceived.

> There rolls the deep where grew the tree.
> O earth, what changes hast thou seen!
> There where the long street roars, hath been
> The stillness of the central sea.

"Ho!" she said. And uneasily, "Not in our time."

"Don't be too sure," he said.

You could no longer confuse the cold mist with the steam of a primeval swamp. A sudden snappy wind straight down from Canada scissored the fog and flaunted it in high rags; far overhead there was enough blue to make a Dutchman's britches. On the beach now the sand would fly in needles. They would have to take the bloody marys back to the house.

Then Jessie did an unfair thing. As uncontrolled as a child, she wept. Big tears coursed down her cheeks, the gilt hairs curled around her brow, she wailed like the beagle. What was he to do? From the first moment when we leave the womb, we hunger for the nurse's arms; he put his arms about her and was surprised to find, since she was a tall girl and since they had never measured lengths while standing up, that her damp blond head fitted beneath his chin.

"There," he said. "There. What is it?"

She shook convulsively against him. He could no more have

108

turned her loose than he could have kicked the beagle, who hovered with great kohl-painted eyes bright with distress.

"I don't want anything to change!" she cried. "I don't want anything to *have* changed!"

Perhaps all women share this maddening trait: that they impose their will upon reality. Angus had not much missed his wife, whose cold demands that things be other than they are had made him feel so impotent — though, as things turned out, only her own impatience had prevented her from entering Eden. And seeing no reason why he could not enjoy without possessing or, worse, without being possessed, he had not meant ever again to put his neck in the noose of caring.

"I want my grandmother!" Jessie stormed. "I want my child!"

And he was almost saved by irritation.

But then she quieted and hiccoughed in his arms. No man can turn his back on suffering he has eased. Besides, a fearful thing had happened while he wasn't noticing, a thing he wasn't ready for and hadn't meant ever to be ready for and couldn't handle and couldn't not try to handle.

It was too late. He loved her.

12

DECEMBER IS DISAGREEABLE. Even on Jacataqua Island the chains clank and the tires spin cold mud. The ice skims and then thickens on the cove. Wet winds slip bony fingers down your back and the dogs shake and shiver. At night the lone streetlamp by the post office sways and sends long shadows convulsing on the frozen dirt. Those who are about to die, do so.

On Crow Point everyone had been busy for a month, squirreling up for winter. Jessie had kept two bedrooms open; she had an electric blanket in one and kept her stores in the other, where, presumably, it would not get cold enough to burst cans. The road commissioner cut and sold wood on the side; his heavy truck rattled and rang on the iron road down to them all. During the early days of November some small and provident animal beat

Tom Elder to the punch and, trying too hard for security (there may be a lesson here), got trapped between the walls and died.

This meant that as the days grew nippy, Tom had to leave the windows open, paint in his outdoor clothing and stop to warm his hands over the stove; in spite of this and of Odors-Off, the sweet vomitous smell of dissolution permeated the camp. As a consequence, for weeks Tom spent more time in New Bristol and less time in urging Brigid to keep him company. He had quickly forgiven her aspersions upon his art because she was a businesswoman and as such, one could say that it was almost one of her functions to misunderstand his art. But in the meantime he understood it.

And one of these days he planned to miss her very much. But he was justified: he flourished. All those long hours of lying in the sun paid off, and whereas before he had been bored with dories, he found that he was not bored now by a barnacle. Canvas after canvas he eased lovingly from his easel, and each exquisite tracery of line and light seemed to him so fortunate and original in both concept and execution that the walls of the big room were soon lined with the evidence of his genius. After he finished work and before he went to town he spent a good deal of time walking about and observing the pictures in the exhibition, and he looked upon his labor and saw that it was good. Had Brigid been present with her comings and goings and her incessant dusting, he would have had to isolate his beauties against the flying smut of a clean house.

But because his conscience troubled him — and in the first flush of the novelty of the telephone — for a while he called her twice a day, once to ask what was going on and once to hear if it had.

But it grows tiresome to receive reports when the reporter has done nothing but — granted with skill and finesse — manipulated other people's money. It was with a kind of comfort that he accepted the moment when their mutual interest tipped on the fulcrum and Brigid's accounts of herself changed to excuses.

After her dentistry, which had apparently been extensive, her Toyota was in the garage, and Tom felt very guilty to feel glad to hear it.

"Is it the carburetor?" he asked.

"Oh, I don't know," she said. "One of those things."

Finally she merely said that she was busy.

Eventually the stench disappeared, or else he had got used to it. When he found that he was too much picturing the small shrinking carcass and wondering whether the matted fur was still wet or had dried in spikes and if the color of the fur had faded with the liquids of the eyes, he recognized that he needed an old comfort and stimulus that the librarian had not been able to supply. Tom Elder stood sniffing and sniffed nothing; there had been one sharp freeze and then another, the days were drawing in, the nights black, he had left *Così Fan Tutte* too close to the stove and the record buckled; he was sick to death of pollock and of the chowder that you make with that soft flesh.

Tom put down his brush. And the day had come, and he missed Brigid very much.

She had put his need for solitude before her need for him. But how was he now to persuade her from her consideration of his needs?

He could see only one way to do it.

So he sat down and wrote to his wife about all the young women whom he saw in New Bristol. The next morning he drove out and mailed the letter from Falmouth Foreside, which he could count on to confuse her.

He signed it, "A well-wisher."

Naturally, she told Howard all about it. They were lying on his bed, too fatigued at the end of the day in their separate offices to be interested in more than talk. She had her shoes off, but just so as not to spoil the spread; Howard was partial to his spread and, in fact, quite canny about many things. Brigid, although she understood the impulse very well and had always been the one who, unostentatiously, had lifted glasses and slipped coasters under them, did not find it an attractive trait in a male. It annoyed her that Howard was careful and it was, she felt, unmanly.

He had already disappointed her in several ways and she was beginning to think that she should have stayed clear of the whole thing. Had he brought the walls toppling? He had not. After she had given in to the tempest of his desire and she lay ruined and brave enough to face the consequences — he slapped her on the fanny.

They are all alike.

"It's so childish," she complained. "Even if he used another typewriter, doesn't he know that I know that he can't spell *occur?*"

Was there to be no blood and no disaster? Apparently not.

"Let me get you an ashtray," Howard said.

When tall Troy was afire, did Priam offer Helen an ashtray? She saw that he was going to talk about his wife again. "Speaking of children," Howard said, "have I told you that Jessie is defenseless as a child?"

"Upon innumerable occasions."

Silently, they sipped at their wine. Howard said, "One nice thing about white wine is that it doesn't stain."

With wrath, she regarded the bedspread upon which she had only once been ravished and thereafter, merely romped. A small frown crossed the crop-curled brow that she had honestly thought looked like Pan.

"Perhaps I was unfair to her," he said.

Who cares?

Although if he were going to insist upon his guilt, she thought it self-indulgent. And then because she was schooled in profit and in loss, she saw that he was suffering from loss and that his wife was somehow mixed up in it. Brigid felt that his initial investment had been unsound, but he seemed to think that he himself had damaged it. It did not seem to occur to him that

113

she, Brigid, had been damaged — but she saw now that what he really felt was that a loose woman is beyond damage. It is the enchantress who gets short shrift.

Howard had been an error. But there was no reason why she should not avail herself of his nice little legal mind. If he would not play Iago, perhaps he could prove Polonius?

"Advise me," she said. "What am I to do now?"

"About what?"

That was the heart of the matter, was it not? That while she lay (although dressed) upon an alien bed, he could ask, and with interest, upon what she wished to be advised?

She said, "I was thinking about my husband."

"What about your husband?"

This took some thinking about. It implied that her husband was of no moment. This in turn implied that her marriage was of no moment and that implied that she, Brigid, had used bad judgment when she elected to get into that particular arrangement and was, in fact, a fool, as she perceived now that she was; but not for choosing Tom. Because she was, on the whole, a good-natured young woman and perhaps because she had been a business major and not into the fine arts, she had never found it helpful to become emotional. And in fact heretofore she had observed in the behavior of others that unleashed emotion is detrimental to whatever project you happen to have in mind.

Now Howard looked admiringly at his toes. They were long, straight, and clean.

"What do you think I ought to do?" she asked.

"It depends, doesn't it, on what you want?"

Certainly. But what did she want? For one thing, that Tom cease going through his money like Sherman to the sea. She doubted very much that among his female friends one would appear who was a serious threat, but entertaining female friends comes high. She wasn't quite ready to have him back in Boston because she was still enjoying having the apartment to herself; if she indulged her indiscretions elsewhere it was not so much to avoid the interest of the neighbors as to avoid disarrayal of her towels. But neither did she feel happy about leaving Tom unattended in Maine. She did not think he was a very good painter, by which she honestly admitted that she meant he had not made any money at it, but living there alone with no natural corrective, he might very well decide that he was a good painter, which in the long run could only be disappointing to him and, in the short run, to her.

"I suppose," she said, "I want him to be having a hard time."

"Then why don't you go and give him a hard time?"

The effect of their remarks was pretty much to terminate their affair, if what they had been up to could be dignified by such a designation, since she had indicated a continuing interest in her husband and he, that he was glad to hear it.

"Because," she said, "I want him to change plans, not wives."

It had begun to rain, one of those mean city rains that oil down dirty windows. The heavy draperies were musty, being rented. In the hired light his very own crystal wineglasses glinted, but the corners of the room were dim with other people's disappointments.

She said, "This place is very dark."

Most of Brigid's affairs had taken place before she married Tom, and so they didn't count because they had nothing to do with him. But she began to think that this one counted, if only because it seemed to her that Howard was callous about Tom.

She knew him to be proud of this apartment on the Hill, of the twisted stairs and the cupboard doors that didn't close and of the cobblestones below that he — among many — had quarreled and paraded to defend from the city, and probably even of the sirens that nightly shrieked down on Cambridge Street, so she said, "Very dark indeed. It can't hold a candle to the one you had with Jessie." Then she stretched to her full length, which was not very long, and reached for the ashtray.

"Careful of that," Howard said. "It's Meissen."

Her fingers tightened on the tray. She said, "You know, when I first met you I didn't like you very much."

"You didn't?" Howard asked, surprised.

No. And she didn't like him any better now. There is this to say about seducers (although one does not speak of seducers nowadays): their long look indicates that they alone see the essential you; then it turns out that they are only interested in the essential them. Brigid's mother had said that every young girl should read *Anna Karenina*, so that she recognize the ephemeral quality of philandering and the permanent and malevolent power of society. Brigid thought perhaps she was right, although the malevolence seemed to belong to the philanderer.

Moreover, his pleasure taken, the seducer is amused, which is insulting. At this moment, Howard poked at her nipple as if he rang a bell.

"Poor old Tom," he said.

She rose with the ashtray in her hand, considered for a moment and then flung it at him. It caught him right underneath the chin, where it left a cut that could be accounted for by careless shaving and did not hurt him very much.

But it made her feel a lot better.

Thus it was that on an afternoon of steel-colored rain, damp, chilled, and perplexed by her peculiar problem, Brigid followed the weather up the coast and arrived at Crow Point with three suitcases. Before she headed down the hill she sat in the closed car and smoked a last cigarette, still considering what she had considered all the way from Boston, over the bridge that hung in mist at Portsmouth, past the vast board figure of the fisherman at the state line — the rain dripped from its hard yellow slicker — and the one of the Indian at the store where you buy hard moccasins with iron laces that hurt your feet. Was the false letter to be mentioned?

If she did not mention it he would think his ruse had succeeded and that she had come flying to protect her property; which, in a way, of course she had. But if she mentioned it she would have to add that she knew it to be a fake. In that there would be a certain satisfaction, but it would bring up the whole ambience of infidelity, and Brigid was not sure she was ready to do that, particularly since she had retained the ability, if ability it is, to flush until her dark skin reddened like a peony. Tom was not going to think she blushed for his indiscretions.

A pretty problem.

The sea was rolling in great gray sullen combers under the whips of the rain. The wind sent the gutter water smoking toward the earth. She stubbed her cigarette in the metal tray that over-flowed and stank and stepped out into the clean smell of salt, woodsmoke, kelp. And into a brutal cacophony. The waves boomed and between and above them *Also sprach Zarathustra* masked the sound of her horn and the sound of her shriek. What was the sense of battling three suitcases when you had a husband?

Then she saw that he had, after all, been thoughtful; the red sled waited for her, its runners poked into a snowbank. It is impossible to tell precisely when you will arrive from Boston unless you call from Kittery and possibly from Brunswick and again from New Bristol to report your progress, and it was reason-able for him to play his record at concert strength, since he knew full well that once she had arrived she was not going to like his doing that again. She could send him back for the suitcases, but perhaps that would be small. So she loaded the luggage and the groceries and the half-gallon of good gin on the sled — there was a rope handle to drag it by — and then stood wondering what her best bet would be. Apparently Tom had not shoveled since the last snowfall; the steep inadequate path was bumped with snow and glazed where the cold rain was freezing. If she let the sled out ahead of her and tried to ease it down, it might get away. If she attempted to pull it behind her, it would nip her heels. She tried both ways and it did both, and the big bottle slid off and shattered.

So Brigid was not in the best of moods when she stamped her boots and entered to find Tom warm, dry and at his easel, to which she suspected he had leaped when — she withdrew the benefit of the doubt — he had heard her car. Nor was she partic-ularly pleased with the quality of the greeting she received from the man for whom she had given up a passionate if perfidious lover.

"Look out, you're wringing wet!" he cried.

The canvas he was working on was nearly finished, and one of a dozen he had completed since she had last been here. Brigid looked at them all thoughtfully. She found them profoundly pleasing, which troubled her. She knew that about such matters he thought her taste was poor, but surely if she liked his pictures, others would too. He had more talent than she had guessed and perhaps more drive, and she might have to change her plans to include a gifted husband. In that case she had better do it gracefully, since gifted husbands have a way of taking off.

"They're very good," she began.

"Aren't they," Tom said.

It is one thing to praise an artist and quite another to have him anticipate your praise. Because of this and because she was wet, cold, and had broken the Beefeater, Brigid again felt hostile to him. And memory deceives: she knew very well that the camp was not going to be comfortable, but while she could not have imagined the cartons of dried leaves, grasses, weeds, burrs and branches that choked and blocked each corner she should have remembered that, setting aside the subject, the ordinary impedimenta of the painter are not neat nor, in themselves, attractive.

"Where am I to put my bags?" she asked.

"Why, in the bedroom." Where else?

But the bedroom was hardly big enough for the bed and the closet was filled with the television upon which Brigid insisted and to which Tom had an aversion only slightly mollified by the fact that when it was not in use one could close the door upon it. Unless the bags went under the bed she was not going to be able to open the closet door; he could call it soap opera all he liked but she called it daytime drama and since she almost never had a chance to watch it, meant now to take advantage of the daytime.

118

Then when he had struggled in with the bags he compounded his offense by asking, "Did you have to bring all this stuff?"

And back in the living room he said, "It was at Milton Academy that I first knew I was talented. At Milton Academy we all had to take art. At Milton Academy . . ."

Brigid said, "Shit on Milton Academy!"

As soon as Brigid was old enough to understand her name, she had been furious with her mother for naming her for a neighbor just because that neighbor was good and kind and had a gentle voice. People would think her Irish, and people did. It was not that she had anything against the Irish but that all too often the others lump them as angry naifs who harbor all their lives the sense that they are underestimated.

"God save Ireland, say the heroes . . ."

How come they identify with heroes? What's so heroic about bars and ballgames? So the others thought.

Brigid grew up in Waltham, which is no-man's-land, neither South Boston nor Beacon Hill; but as she ventured abroad in the pursuance of her education she increasingly encountered the others and found them bloodless, supercilious and given to bland assumptions which were all the more infuriating because they were baseless.

When she was a graduate student at the Harvard Business School, they said to her at parties around the Square, "Ah. You must know all about Honey Fitz."

Not unless they thought she was ninety.

She would like to remind those cold blond young men that she was no more from Southie than she was from Louisburg Square and that they were no more at home in the Athenaeum than she was and that there are a whole lot of people in Massachusetts who are neither this nor that.

She didn't hate Milton Academy. She just hated the cold blond boys who went there.

But Tom refused the gauntlet.

"I understand," he said.

And she believed he did. Which might prove difficult, because it is hard to hold your own with someone who is willing to understand. If his new confidence mellowed him like this, Brigid might well end up without a leg to stand on.

13

EDGAR PEDERSEN did an ugly thing. He snapped at Irma.

"What are those pills you're taking?" she had asked.

He felt the blood flood through his head and had again that near-to-bursting feeling.

So he said, "Since we married, I have had no privacy."

Naturally she was mad as hops. But then she stroked his hair. "I saw a grosbeak today," she said. "A Canadian Pine!"

To tell the truth, Irma was getting bored. While the hills were still the color of tanagers and haze powdered the blue of the wide skies, it had been pleasant to walk through the woods, over the ruined gold of the leaves, by the shore. But it was no fun now that the days had soured and saddened. She had never been much of a one to read, which was just as well now that she found reading hard, and she had frankly never liked the daytime shows because they were too much like life. Naturally, she did not say this to Brigid, who had become her unlikely friend. And even Brigid found that the interest of the shows diminished with their availability; they did not really rivet when all you had to do to see them was to glance up.

Therefore the ladies thought that they would lunch, and once or twice they did, at one or the other of the two places in New Bristol that are available to ladies. It had been Irma's thought that they would each have one cocktail, eat, shop and return home through the quickening dusk. However, she found a curious and somewhat disturbing thing. Brigid, usually so amenable, wished to have two drinks and to linger over them so long that on both occasions when they came to order, the specialty of the day was gone. While she prolonged what should have been a pleasant little outing, Brigid gazed in a penetrating and critical way at every young woman in the place: guests, hostess, harried waitresses, and they excusably gazed back. Brigid commented coldly upon these women and though her remarks were undecipherable her manner left no doubt that she was not pleased with the service, the menu, nor the company. Irma felt that their reappearance would be greeted with no real warmth.

"Do you suppose he steps out on her?" Edgar asked.

"Not with them all," Irma said. "He couldn't!"

And so the luncheons lapsed.

Neither of them was much with her hands. Every year Irma still knitted one toy animal — with heavier yarn and on larger needles, which she then wrapped in Saran Wrap against the time when there were grandchildren. Every day Brigid called her office. Something about the toys made Edgar very sad and the telephone, when he was not using it himself, drove Tom wild. Finally the husbands conferred and bought binoculars and Field Guides and for days, the wives watched birds. This they could do because the men put up bird feeders. The bird feeders also attracted squirrels, both the little rat-tailed red ones with eyes like watermelon seeds and the big gray plush ones. Squirrels are fun.

The men didn't think the squirrels were so much fun. They

do damage and if they get inside the house play havoc with the wires: you could burn up. But the wives were adamant that the squirrels were neither to be shot nor trapped, not even with the Tender-Traps that everyone uses now. The wives suspected that any creature behind which that small door slammed would be taken into the woods and not released. There should be none of that.

And then the twenty-second of December dawned like a miracle with a pale summerish sky banded with lemon and pumpkin and grape. The sun came sparkling on clean snow and dark green armies of spruce marched toward glistening fields. Below the Pedersens' deck the water swung lazily. The waves lifted traceries of foam as if for their approval and then dropped them gently down. It was the very sort of day, Edgar saw, to make Irma restless. Right now she was on the telephone with Brigid.

He heard her say, ". . . a Canadian Pine grosbeak. Oh, but I think so! Rosy breast? And just the size of a robin but with white bands on the wings." There was a moment's silence in which Brigid obviously challenged Irma's claim. "Well," Irma triumphed, "this *is* a cold spruce forest and Peterson says 'winters erratically throughout United States.' This bird acted erratic."

When she hung up she said, "For a young woman, Brigid is not very flexible."

Beyond the big doors to the deck icicles glittered, as bright and uniform as if they were for sale. Irma said, "I haven't done anything about Christmas yet."

Edgar himself had planned to spend the day thinking about death. Like any reasonable man he had spent a lot of time in contemplating last things, but they had concerned horrors that happened to others, not to himself. Everyone has felt this: since we have not died before, it is unlikely that we will do so. But friends die; so do the darlings of one's friends. After their son was born, terror stalked constantly. Infants suffocate in their cribs; sometimes it is months before you know they are not normal. Perhaps he might never walk. And then when he did, he might totter off and be lost or drown in a shallow brook.

Smile if you will, these things do happen. Later pneumonia might develop. His bicycle might swerve into a truck, football is hazardous, everyone knows what happens when they start to drive. And hovering over too many of those years had been the fear that infantile paralysis might still those perfect limbs, in which case, Edgar had always thought, all but the most selfish parents had better pray for the black angel.

Irma had never laughed at him about any of this, because he had never told her. Now he did not have to worry in this way since his son had grown to be a strong, self-sufficient and hostile man. But in the end, a man has to consider his own death and try to evaluate the chances of those he loves to survive whatever it is he has done wrong.

At his shoulder Irma said wistfully, "What a super day for shopping."

Shopping for what?

Usually her assault upon Christmas began well before Thanksgiving. She made fruitcakes and cranberry chutney as small, affectionate gifts for their friends, who could no more afford real shopping than she could, and long before it was reasonable she went through all the old, beloved ornaments and reluctantly replaced those which had had their day. And then there were the Christmas cards, all but the locals requiring personal notes, so that during November she made few calls on Edgar's time.

But this year the new kitchen had not tempted her to more than cursory cooking and — like many others — they had decided against Christmas cards, in order to punish the post office. The box for their son and his wife had long since gone. As far as he could see, that left only him. Good. She could shop with Brigid. It was a wonderful day for the girls to go to town. The road was plowed, until today there had not been sun enough to melt the snow so that it froze at night in skiddy sheets, and along the cove the piled banks were frozen hard so that the ladies, who were always afraid of hurtling into deep water at high tide or rocks at low, could glide against that barrier at will and in safety.

That meant he could get on with his contemplation.

On that black day he had said to Dr. Weller, "Nonsense! Not at all! Never felt better!"

The doctor's dark melancholy eyes were sympathetic. "You've got to watch out," he said. "She's a killer."

What he meant was that you could very well feel that you felt good, and then — boom. "Could be heart," he said. "Could be a cerebral accident."

Edgar said flatly, "You mean a stroke."

The doctor shrugged. Laymen's terminology. If you're dead, you're dead.

Anyone wants to go easily as possible, with no pain, no fear, and if possible, no notice in advance. From that point of view the doctor's news could almost be considered good; however, you must consider those you leave behind. She who he, in that event, would leave behind tugged at his elbow now.

"Want to drive me to town?"

The sun lay in cold gold plates upon the deck. Edgar said, "If you're after my present, surely I shouldn't be along?"

One thing he missed about the old house. The old house was decently dark and when a beam of yellow light sliced through you saw motes dance. The new house was so clean that the slopes of sunlight held no motes.

Irma was saying, "But you never go right into stores with me."

No, he didn't. Nor into Mr. Jacque's Salon de Beauty, which is where he had left Irma on that day when he consulted the New Bristol Free and Public Library. The medical dictionary which he found there was bound in new, cardinal-colored limp leather, and not one page was yet creased except the one that dealt with hemorrhoids. *F. Hémorroïdes, fr. L. Haemorrhoidae.* In short, piles.

What he was after was some information with which Dr. Weller would not part. "What type of hypertension?" Edgar asked.

"We don't know yet. Now, if you want to go into the hospital . . ."

No, he had not wanted to go into the hospital. Going into the library was bad enough. The reading room was sunny and silent and the chairs a little too small and too straight. Did he have intracranial hypertension, a syndrome of increased intracranial pressure and papilledema? With no neurological signs to warn in advance when the thin pinkish walls were going to buckle and the colorless cells to flood?

And anyway, what was papilledema?

On his brow a light sweat broke out. Putting his glasses on the medical dictionary so that no one should think that he was through with it, he detoured to your regular dictionary. Papilla: nipple, epidermic cell. *Medical*: choked disk. Papillitis: inflammation of the intraocular end of the optic nerve. One morning Irma had said, innocently enough, "Your eyes are bloodshot."

He said he was hung over. He was not, although it was true that he was drinking a bit more than usual. Thinking about it on this later day he felt his irritation bubble to a boil, which he understood was worse than moderate drinking. Anyway, he didn't smoke — never had. So that, he felt, more than balanced out the moderate drinking. But it was Irma he was trying to protect: why couldn't she just let him do it? Without personal comments and suggestions and plans with which he wished to have nothing to do and the consequent gathering of precisely what he should avoid? Humors: choler, bile, melancholy, spleen.

"Get Brigid to drive you," Edgar said. "You can take our car."

"I don't like to shop with women," Irma said. "They rattle me."

He was remembering the library and the innocent, deadly dictionary. It might be malignant hypertension that he had: accelerated severe hypertension with poor prognosis. This was the one he feared. Suppose that in spite of the pills and of the careful diet and of keeping his temper as well as he did, he was stricken out of the blue when the doctor wasn't even looking? Perhaps she had better get used to shopping with women.

The sun had shifted and Irma for some reason had become very quiet. In fact, she wasn't there. So she had probably taken his advice and was calling Brigid. Then suddenly he realized that his advice had been ill considered. Although he hadn't noticed it, for the last minute the radio had been speaking to him. Now the radio said, ". . . and changing to sleet by late afternoon."

Incredulous, Edgar looked at the dazzling water and the flawless sky. A jay flew by, bright as an exclamation point against the shining snow. Surely they jested?

Irma had little confidence in the Weather Bureau. He knew what Irma would say. She would say, "Pooh."

But Edgar believed from the evidence of his whole life that qualified people do their jobs with quality and if the Bureau said it was going to sleet, sleet it would. In which case he was not going to have Brigid Elder driving his wife. Or, for that matter, his car. He had always prided himself upon his ability to go on almost indefinitely without comfort stops, but at this moment he was sharply attacked by a real need for comfort. Edgar trotted across the living room, coursed through the bedroom and flung open the bathroom door.

Irma turned, startled. She was just stepping into the shower.

When you are growing older it is a shocking thing to see the one you love stripped. Now that he thought of it, for a long time she had worn those posy-colored night-things with long frilly sleeves. She never wore bathing suits because she didn't swim and saw no reason to sit around in one as if she suddenly might swim. Edgar had always found her reticence sexy. He still did. Everything he had touched and fondled had slipped and softened, what had glowed and was taut was not, and the firm little silky muscles had loosened everywhere. It didn't matter. There was no reason for her eyes to round with fear.

"Privacy," she said bitterly.

He fled, distressed and delighted as a boy, and relieved himself from the deck, which is a thing any man likes to do.

Why, he had moved like quicksilver. Perhaps, after all, what he was suffering from was neuromuscular hypertension, a condition of hyperexcitability and hyperirritability; also called an anxiety tension state.

That is the one he chose.

14

ON THAT SAME MORNING Angus said, "What shall we do for Christmas?"

Jessie raised her brows slightly. We?

She asked, "Are you accustomed to cavorting?"

"No," he said, she thought a little wistfully. "We always meant to. Once we got a tree as far as the porch, but that was as far as it went."

For some reason Jessie thought of people who lived in the West as poor: and it was true, wasn't it, that his comforts had come lately? She saw a shabby bungalow with a scrappy porch where a lean tree was propped, its branches whipped by mountain winds while the needles dropped on the bad boards and inside, the two held bitter speech. And she felt sorry for him.

"What do you do that's Christmassy?" he asked.

"Oh — I haven't done anything Christmassy since my grand-mother died."

They looked at each other and laughed. She didn't mean, of course, that she thought her grandmother's death was Chirstmassy.

"Maybe we ought to do something," Angus said. "This year." Well, why not?

The ornaments were all in the big house in Belmont, or had been when the house was sold: the gilt angels and the veritable crystal icicles and the faded red ropes and yellowed silver ones and the glass balls from Germany with painted figures of little girls in muffs and ice-skates.

"We never had a Christmas here. I wish we had."

Why, because then it would be traditional to have a tree here now.

He said, his eyes either shining or aglint, however you looked at it, "Maybe it's time to start some new traditions."

There was no doubt about it, Jessie was being wooed for the first time in her life; her opinions were solicited, her comfort connived at; before she rose from their daytime bed, he brought her glasses of cold milk. He was more adamant than ever about not staying over; perhaps westerners were not only poor but prudes. This had all made her very wary, and she was not made less so by this talk of tradition: what is the point of a new tradition unless it is to become an old one? And yet, in spite of his careless height and almost too adult behavior, there was something about his face (younger and gentler than it had been with the beard) that made her think of the hundred neediest cases.

So she said, "I know where there's a corker."

Of course Angus would not allow her to cut the corker, which did happen to be in Lydia Pullen's yard. Must a man in love be bossy, as if he and only he can protect you from bodily harm, future challenge and possible criticism? Apparently so.

But deep in the woods they found a nice little tree that had somehow escaped the elbowing of its brothers and that spread to the winter sun a perfect parasol of branches. Jessie would have preferred pine because of the cones; you can gild them, but Angus wanted spruce. Well, he was the needy one.

In Angus's car — it was part of his new protectiveness that she should not touch a wheel unless the roads were dry — the two of them drove to New Bristol after folderol for the tree. The winter solstice had just passed and the sun hung low but with surprising strength; at noon the road was deep in puddles, and on the highway the cars splashed and sent the water shining from their wheels. There was a good deal of waving and of calling back and forth.

Yet even an hour later, when they all ran into one another in front of the drugstore, the low sun had dipped, a gray haze was creeping up the sky and the temperature had dropped enough so that Brigid stamped her feet in their little high-heeled boots. The Elders had come up for liquor and the Pedersens for a poinsettia. A strange thing happens to Crow Pointers who encounter one another off Crow Point. There is a feeling of both covert camaraderie and displacement like the reaction of fellow travelers who meet, but not by appointment, after the cruise is over. And then, they all were cross, though not with one another. The Elders had been cruelly embarrassed at the liquor store by the deprecatory gaze of the bonneted woman with her bell who accosted them when their arms were so filled with Four Roses that they could not reach their pockets although (she made it silently clear) they had reached their pockets easily enough before.

And Irma had found only a pink poinsettia. "Pink!" she said. "What is the good in that?"

None of them was much pleased with the street decorations, perhaps because the wreaths and ropes had been up since well before Thanksgiving, were old and tired and had lost their original zip; the plastic ivy climbed but languidly about the light poles and the MERRY CHRISTMAS that swung over Front Street had lost two r's. They were all somewhat critical of one another. When Brigid beat her mittened hands together and said you could not, *could not* shop in New Bristol, Irma, who had been

131

thinking the same thing, felt that it was not very loyal. And Edgar refused Tom's suggestion that they all stop for a drink with a testy alacrity that suggested that it was far too early and that those dependent upon alcohol endangered those who were not.

Irma felt this was rude, but in no way indicated to Edgar what she felt. Nor did she have to. There is a way of not glancing at one's spouse that makes all perfectly clear but does not open one to recriminations later.

"Well, it's beginning to sleet," Edgar said. "The driving will be bad."

This, although she felt already the cold moisture on her face, made Brigid angry and Jessie uneasy.

So when the Pedersens departed and Tom shrugged and said, "How about you?" Jessie surprised herself by saying, "No — I think we should get home."

Which, any way you wanted to look at it, was the wrong thing to say. It both rejected the Elders and admitted that she thought of Angus and herself as "we" and of where they were going as "home."

So she felt doubly guilty as they watched the Elders cross to the Emerson House and while they themselves, their arms filled with their bright junk, slid into the delicatessen and downstairs to the nifty little bar not everyone knew about yet. A fire burned in the low dim room and the hot air swung the paper bells. The waitresses wore holly at their throats and glowed with seasonal warmth. So did the bloody marys. Jessie had two and Angus three, though that was not the reason why what happened later happened.

It was three o'clock when they emerged and already growing dark; the colored lights looked better in the dusk and a true sleet was falling. It froze on the sidewalks as it fell and many a merry voice was raised in warning. On the big bridge the cars slid toward the guardrails; there were no merry voices lifted, and the road out of New Bristol was sheer hell. While Angus edged the car along he bent to the windshield, which was already icing up. The wipers whined and struggled.

Because of the weather, that shift had been let out early and everyone from the shipyard was trying for home: nervous, alert, and afraid to slow for fear the car behind should not be able to do so. And yet the windshields must be scraped. Here and there a driver more timid than the others, or perhaps more foolhardy, nudged off the road and hunched, shivering, scraping and swearing. After three miles Angus found — perforce — a widening into which he could slide. He had no scraper but Jessie had a pocket comb: the back was rounded, but what can you do?

She refrained from saying that in her own car she carried a scraper at all seasons and also a spray to soften ice. But she was much relieved to cross, without incident, the metal bridge that threw your car badly even when it was dry, and the narrow one at the foot of the steep hill by the post office. Angus signaled wildly with both his directional and his hand and made it safely onto the Crow Point road; they were, at that point, the only ones to try to leave the caterpillar of home-going cars. He skidded badly but made a quick recovery and anyway, that was well before the cove.

Once past the cove you are not likely to be killed. Even Jessie, who was fearless (but that was in the summertime), did not trust the frozen banks. They would probably hold. But if they did not, she could not remember how far you were to let the car settle before the pressure equalized and you could try to open the door. It would be awfully cold.

At Angus's house the lights glowed with welcome. He always left them on because they didn't show in the daytime, and it was no one's affair at night.

"I could stay here with you," Jessie suggested.

"No, you can't," he said.

And, to be sure, after that the road was somewhat better, although his weak headlights, because of the sharp swings and the short abrupt hills, were thrown into the black and massy woods and not upon the road where they were needed. In the vast and tumbled recesses of those low hills there could be anything: trolls.

Jessie, who was herself not nervous anymore, said, "You seem nervous. Haven't you driven on bad roads before?"

"In my part of the West," he said, "you can see a long way before you."

She thought of suggesting that he return to his part of the West.

"At any rate," he said, "there isn't anyone behind us now."

Nor was there. But now Angus gunned the car (cautiously) to turn a corner and make the steep rise up the hill where the Volkswagen went off, and there was someone in front of them. Edgar Pedersen had almost reached the top before he slipped back and, in slipping, veered. Now the front of his car was buried in the bank and the rear end hung above the drop. Worse: the reason Angus didn't hit the Pedersens broadside was that there was a car behind them and it was that car that Angus hit. He slid straight into it. There was a sickening crunch of metal and then, a foul smell of fumes.

It had been a new car. In the driver's yelp Jessie recognized the agony of Howard Thorne. Her heart jumped in a way that she resented. Why should it jump? He was not worth her thought and indeed, she had lately given him very little thought. Separation from someone you have loved is surgery, and however necessary the end may be, the process is not pleasant. Jessie had tried to anesthetize herself with anger, but at the sight of the lost member the pain flooded back.

Howard was looking very well. He had a new belted coat with a deep beaver collar. While she had no way of knowing whether or not he had really needed the new car, she doubted that the old coat had broken down, and she suspected both were for the purpose of impressing somebody — somebody small, dark and female. Because of this she was glad to see that however unreasonable it might be, he was not pleased to find her in the

134

company of a man. She knew this from the way he raised his dark and eloquent eyebrows and then rubbed ruefully, first at his black mop of curls and then at his neat beard.

"All of Maine," he said, "and we have to run into one another."

Angus said, "Let's have a look."

It is not much help to the injured party when the injurer suggests that they have a look. The car had been a sprightly little one and of an Oriental cast. The Mercedes had clipped it smartly and the trunk was deeply dented.

"Don't worry," Angus told him. "I'm insured."

Jessie knew that Howard would take this to imply that he was more interested in expense than in perfection — particularly because although he acknowledged no familiarity with Angus's name, she knew he knew it. Howard had been one of the first to read that book and then to deprecate it.

"The material's good," he had said. "Any hack could have written it."

Maybe so. But then Howard was one of those who, loving letters, always had believed that if he had the time he could write a book if he could just run across some material. Right now he clapped his fur-lined gloves together.

"Do you have any idea," he said, "how long I've been sitting here?"

The sleet hissed on the oak leaves.

Jessie said, "How long have they been sitting here?"

The Pedersens were very cold. You can't keep the heater on unless you open the windows so wide that it doesn't matter that you have the heater on. Edgar had wrapped Irma in the car robe, from which she peeped out like a mouse. He himself was indignant. Jessie recognized that indignation is proportionate to distress. No, they could not have walked home. It was too far and too icy and too black. If Irma fell, how could he carry her? And then, how could they have trudged off into that inky sleet and left the car behind? If he left on the lights, the battery would run down. If he left the car straddled as it was, the next person along would have clobbered it. Some people have only the one car. She looked with satisfaction on the Subaru, because it was much better that it was the car that was clobbered.

However, he needn't have taken it out on Jessie.

Edgar crawled from his car like an animal from its lair. "Considering the taxes they extort from us," he said, "you'd think the town would sand."

Jessie said, "They will, when they get around to it."

"And what are we supposed to do while they get around to it?"

Jessie certainly hadn't meant to get cross with Edgar Pedersen, but this is what she had always expected from new people.

"We're supposed to wait," she told him, "while they make sure the ambulance can get through. And the school bus. And the people who have to get to jobs. And the fire engine."

"And what if we should have a fire?"

With his wool cap covering his pate and his ears pushing out underneath, Edgar really did look like a New Person.

"If we should have a fire," Jessie said, "tough titty. Nobody passed a law that said we have to winter."

A welcome heat was rising from her wrists to the nape of her neck. She glared at Mr. Pedersen. He growled at her.

Small Mrs. Pedersen said, "It isn't Jessie's fault!"

"I don't consider that it is," he said, making it plain that he considered that it was. Was she not hand in glove with the town moderater?

The two younger men were suddenly at her shoulders, which made her remember with whom it was that she was angry.

Angus was too cheerful to please anyone. Since no one could proceed until the Pedersens' car was straightened out, he said to Howard, "If you and I both pushed on the one side . . ."

"And if we both got hernias," Howard said.

Edgar said, "And if, in the process, my car went over the grade?"

Angus put his hand on Jessie's shoulder as if he claimed her, which she found pleasing and comfortable.

"Well, then, somebody's got to go for help." There was a fighting chance that the Mercedes could back up, and maybe even find a place to turn around.

So guess who?

Jessie's teeth suddenly chattered. She said, "You'd better take the Pedersens along."

Edgar thought it a sterling idea that Irma should go back with Angus and wait where it was warm, but while he meant no offense to anyone, he did not propose to leave his car with the keys in it. Jessie's two men looked at one another in momentary accord. Was the man mad?

"You understand," said Howard, "that I'll be here?"

Edgar was silent.

Jessie whooped; she couldn't help it. Edgar, too, thought Howard untrustworthy. Howard's whole professional career depended upon the fact that corporate officers took one look into those level, steel-blue eyes and entrusted him with all their maneuvering — but Edgar Pedersen saw deep. No, Howard would not steal a car. But had Jessie not been besotted at the time, she would have known him for a thief: who else would take off with her love, her trust, and eight years of her youth?

"Well, if I have no takers," Angus said.

He vowed to be as prompt as possible, waved, and began to ease the Mercedes down the hill while Jessie watched with interest. One has heard that westerners are more resourceful than your average man; it seems reasonable. Look what they deal with: blizzards, cows, droughts, Chicanos. Wolves. The headlights of the Mercedes blanked her eyes and she marveled, knowing that hill as she did, at how he backed at all, with the drop on one side, the ledge on the other, and only the little blurred red circles of the taillights to back by. Now his headlights veered to the right, precisely as they should, and as the Mercedes' bottom dropped, its yellow eyes caught the ragged top of the tall trees and the tattered moss that flew sideways in the wind.

Then the lights raked the sky and tipped and dipped steeply.

"What's he doing that for?" Howard asked.

Edgar Pedersen said to Irma, "You see? You see?"

Irma was not surprised. She said, "Well, dear. If *you* couldn't do it."

Then the taillights rose slowly, like two cigarette butts in the dark.

Jessie said, "Oh, my God."

She had started to run when Howard grabbed her wrist in a way that she remembered well: it was one of his best tricks. But if anyone is so inconsiderate as to grab your wrist when you are trying to run on sheer ice, the effect is not sexual. When she had struggled to her feet she said nothing, because her attention was still down the hill where Angus clambered from his car that seesawed over the abyss.

With the rage that accompanies relief, she turned on her husband.

"What are you doing here?" she asked.

Angus was edging back up the hill.

"I'm visiting the Elders," Howard said.

Got him!

Remembering the Elders' retreat to the Emerson House, Jessie said, "I don't think they're expecting you."

Then she also remembered that Brigid was dark, ripe, and geographically available.

Surely not Brigid! The friend of a friend?

"No reason why they should," Howard said. "But if they're not there, I can stay with you."

Jessie said, "No, you can't."

"Why not?"

Why not? Because she was not culturally ready for it. Because she was not ready to be best friends with him whom she had never looked on as a friend. Because she had not given up on getting Angus to stay with her tonight.

She said, "Because I wouldn't prejudice your suit."

She turned the beam of the Pedersens' flashlight on Angus.

138

The wind had dropped. In the tunnel of light great single snow-drops like doilies were calmly coming down. They grouped and considered what to do. Half a mile back toward town there was a side road to a logging lot where a car could be turned around. Harry Higgins was going to have to drag them back there one by one and backwards, if need be.

It might take a block and tackle.

The trick was to get Harry Higgins.

And to do that, Angus was prepared to walk, but found himself reluctant to leave Jessie with her husband.

Howard said, ". . . and about the suit."

Jessie said, "We are not going to discuss our affairs before the neighbors."

Angus was hurt at being called a neighbor. He turned his collar up, pushed his hands into his pockets and began to walk. Behind him he heard Jessie say, "You can damn well go to the Emerson House."

Then she was at his side and slogging back toward town.

Once in a while the road was bare where it had been briefly open to the sun; where the trees loomed high the new freezing slush formed treacherous ridges. But it was warmer walking and he liked her deep and even breathing. Her mood was foul.

Angus said, "So that was Howard."

She said, "It still is."

He tried to take her hand. She refused it. Perhaps she was simply brooding about cars. If you cannot depend upon your car, upon what can you depend? Two things occurred to Angus. If she were frightened at the failure of cars, perhaps she would feel safer if he compromised his principles and started sleeping overnight, in which case there would always be two cars. Because if she gave up and went back to Boston, she would probably go back to Howard.

"You needn't worry," she said. "I'll stay with the Charleys."

He wondered what he was not to worry about. Was she

promising not to stay with him or not to stay with Howard? What went on in the capped head that he looked down on in the snow-light?

She slipped her hand into his pocket and her fingers interlaced with his.

15

THE NEXT DAY Jessie was wild that Howard had, after all, slept again in her bed.

Charley Pratt drove her home in the Packard after, following a word from him, Harry Higgins did get out and sand the road. At the sound of Charley's car, the beagle raised the roof. It hurt her feelings very much: the beagle was not supposed to bark at her. As soon as she stepped into the kitchen she saw how its affections had been suborned. Since when the beagle accompanied them it did not consent to leave the car, she had left it where it would be warm and she had, of course, provided it with food and water: good, well-balanced, nutritious and (for all she knew) delicious dry kibbles. Howard had wooed the dog with what was left of a perfectly good pound of hamburger and hadn't even bothered to remove it from its little cardboard boat, the ravaged bits of which now decorated the kitchen floor.

What's more, the beagle had been sleeping on her bed. The electric blanket was covered with hairs and there was a nice nest-like depression where it had turned around and around before it found itself comfortable. Why, she felt just like Baby Bear!

But worst of all, the sheets, the pillowslip smelled of Howard: utterly familiar, dear, and repulsive. She had no more expected this than she had thought to ask that he return his key. All right, it was just nostalgia. Nostalgia hurts. She threw herself upon the bed, his note crumpled in her hand.

"It was obviously not a good time," he had written, "to speak of money matters. See you soon."

What money matters? As far as she could see, they were about even Steven. He had his profession and she had her land.

Then Jessie wept.

Beside her the beagle wagged its tail, hoping as human beings always hope to be completely forgiven and totally loved again.

In the meantime, Christmas was at their throats.

By the twenty-fourth Brigid was bored to excruciation and saw to it that Tom was, too. She had never minded Christmas; it was nice to have champagne for breakfast, preferably in bed. But here on Crow Point you could breakfast every morning of your life in bed and the notion lost its zing. Besides, Tom was at his easel at seven o'clock. It was still black as the hinges but in the general direction of Spain, the sky was paling.

Presently the sun would come up like a hot copper penny.

"*Today?*" she protested mildly.

He said, "Ummmmn."

It was a pretty little thing that he was doing: the beach brightening through a filigree of bayberry twigs. So for a while Brigid was silent. But Tom went on painting for a long, long time. Hunched on the bed with a blanket about her shoulders — the small woodstove had its hands full warming the studio room — she watched while actors quarreled and, in the name of the season, were reconciled. Eventually they saw things more clearly.

Eventually Tom called, "Can you turn that thing down?"

Yes, but she wasn't going to. Her brown eyes narrowed.

Fortunately, she had not committed herself to more than a month and to that, only loosely. It was more and more obvious that this was an unintelligent and uncivilized way to live. Even the textbooks, the ones that tell you that you can spend twenty-five percent of your income for rent — what a laugh! — also said that in every decent domicile there is one room for every resident; Brigid did not consider this cupboard where she crouched a room, while the space that Tom commandeered was kitchen, dining area, workroom and living room, if you can call it living.

While in the commodious and gracious old remodeled brownstone on Arlington Street, the exorbitant rent rolled on and on.

What's more, were they in Boston on this day of all days when the city sparkles and from every corner and parking lot the carols clang, they could by now be drinking with their friends. As the hours inched along she sulked a little.

Married folk know when somebody is sulking, even if it is around corners or behind doors. Tom poked his head into her territory and said, "This was your idea."

This irritated her because it was true. He wasn't yelling but she said, "When you yell I can't hear," and then she reached into the closet and turned the volume up.

"Christ!" said Tom Elder.

In retaliation he played *Carmina Burana*. Those loud lascivious voices are just as bad in Latin.

Because people who majored in Fine Arts don't know anything he preferred that she didn't know anything, but as a matter of fact, she knew many things. She knew that the *Carmina Burana* were drinking songs. Now, to annoy him, she said innocently, "I've never understood, since it is Goliardic, why they sing Carl Orff in Latin."

This was the sort of thing he hated to have her know. But just because you are in business doesn't mean that you don't get around.

She said, "The Goliards were north European, and so was Orff."

143

She impinged on a territory that was his.

"If you remember," she said, making it plain that she thought he had little to remember.

Marriage is much like chess. Tom said, "Since you like it so much, shall I play it again?"

"I didn't say I liked it," Brigid said. "I don't like it."

They both saw that this was not going to do.

"If we were home in Boston," Brigid said winsomely, "we could be having rib roast at Locke-Ober's."

They both smiled, remembering how it turned out the last time they were at Locke-Ober's.

Tom said, "They have a pretty good rib roast at the Emerson House."

Was that where he met his women?

Tom said, "Why don't you take a little walk?" His brush jumped in his hand and he said, "Oh, shit."

Walk? Out there?

Because the day was dull and leaden, the air gray and gathering, the water motionless. A small sun hung angry in a heavy sky.

"I'll tell you what," Tom said. "If you'll be quiet for an hour, we'll have a drink."

Fair enough. Or fairly fair enough.

"Nice of you," she said. "You only offer because the light's so bad."

It was, too. Even the north light was bleached, and Tom squinted to his palette. However, a bargain is a bargain, and Brigid looked for something to use up an hour. If she were in Boston she would be wearing something pretty, probably the black lace. Clearly as she saw that Howard was selfish, opportunistic and impermanent, he was fun.

Brigid sighed. One could read.

But what? On Tom's meager shelves there were a few old favorites, mildewed and swollen by the winter damps: *The Last of the Mohicans, Ivanhoe, We Summer in Maine, The Sweet*

144

Singer of Michigan. Since the last was at least unfamiliar to her, she opened it at random and read.

> Oh, the view is quite compelling
> Down around Fort Snelling.

She returned the Sweet Singer to the shelf.

This week's *New Yorker* was late and when it came, would be skinny. Well, there was always the *Old Farmer's Almanac* or rather, the new *Old Farmer's Almanac*, still stiff and yellow and unexplored. Below wee pictures of the seasons and of Benjamin Franklin and Robert B. Thomas garlanded with fruits and flowers, it promised planting tables, zodiac secrets, recipes and weather forecasts; surely there should be something here to interest a restless wife. The table of contents advised that on page 34 she could read "Stars, Bright, How to Tell Time by," on 88 "Cow, Named for Neighbor's Wife" and on 156 "Hanged, Last Pregnant Woman." Since none of these appealed, she plunged into the body of the little book and was advised by the friendly editor that on the first of January she should don woolies. On the same page he philosophized.

> Sometimes I feel I am not looking up at our mountain but that it is looking down on me — almost sitting in my lap. It isn't, of course.

Of course not.

Brigid looked up to see that Tom had set aside his work and was pursuing an amusement of which he knew she disapproved.

"You know I can't work with anyone in the room," he said.

Did that mean that she was to spend the holidays upon her bed?

The bird-feeder was suspended from a pole, the idea being that the small ubiquitous red squirrels should not be able to climb the pole. They could, of course. Red squirrels can get anywhere. Observing this, Tom had devised a way to pass an idle hour. He ran a long string underneath the door and to the feeder so that while the little red beast clung to the plastic ball with its claws in the feed-holes and its tail twitching, he could swing it back and forth until the scrap of rusty fur went flying.

It offended Brigid very much.

"The birds won't come while the squirrel's there," he said.

Well. But what displeased her was his obvious pleasure in the animal's discomfort, which seemed to uncover layers of sadism of which she previously had been unaware. She said no more about it because she suspected that part of his pleasure in the mean deed lay in the fact that it distressed her.

"Got to discourage them," he would remind her cheerfully. "We could burn up."

Unwilling to give him the pleasure, she retired again to the *Old Farmer's Almanac*, where, to her glee, she discovered a thing that in turn, might give him a moment of distress.

"Tom, listen to this," she said. "On January ninth? There's an eleven-foot tide."

He raised his brows. So?

"And a new moon."

So?

"Suppose we have a northeaster, too?"

"Suppose we don't." But his brows drew together. "What does it say?"

"Clear and bright," she had to admit.

Well, there you were. "A full sea doesn't mean anything in itself," he said. "Not even if it's an abnormal height."

Still, he was troubled, just a little.

Brigid herself, being a city girl, had a comforting disrespect for the sea because it obviously couldn't do anything to you if you stayed off of it and out of it, but she had noticed that lately Tom had a tendency to stare at it thoughtfully. It was, she felt, the fault of the mischievous old man. Unreasonable it might be, but the thought of Charley Pratt made her feel anxious for her husband's comfort.

"Tom," she said, "you don't believe in this old book?"

But still he bit his thumb.

She still liked Tom and after all, it was Christmas Eve. "Why don't we get out of here for an hour or so?" she suggested.

His mood lightened. "You want to see the bright lights?"

"Yes," she said. "Both of them."

So they went up to New Bristol and to the Emerson House, where she was glad to see he didn't know anyone. The drinks were good, the rib roast excellent and the wine adequate: as a result they woke up on Christmas morning with hangovers.

But at least Christmas Eve had not been wasted.

During the night it snowed. All through the dark hours quietly, without wind, the leaden clouds let down their heavy burden. Angus awoke depressed. The living room was dark, the couch too short and his feet cold; he had had his way, but at a certain cost. Their attitudes had undergone a curious reversal, and Jessie had not wanted him to stay here at all, while he was the one who had been adamant.

"You never stayed before," she said.

Well, that was before.

"Before what, name of God?"

Before he decided he wanted her for keeps. But he wasn't ready to tell her that because she might laugh. Nor could he very well tell her it was to protect her from her husband, from whom he was not sure she wanted to be protected. Only the long shadow of Howard Thorne could have spoiled what would otherwise have been a first-rate evening.

"His note said see you soon," she had pointed out.

That didn't necessarily mean Christmas.

"It doesn't necessarily mean not."

Apart from that he would have been superbly happy with the big room so warmly shadowed and with the little tree that had turned out so well. At the last minute, discontented with the dime-store ornaments, Jessie had ransacked an old collection and now pale green sea urchins and white sand dollars and periwinkles gently swung and turned in the warm air. Under the tree there were packages: two of them. Jessie kept wanting to open these, which was silly because they looked nice there and anyway, they both knew what they were. What nibbled at the edge of his contentment was the thought that she wanted those presents put away and their wrappings burned, in case Howard showed up.

"He would have called by now," Angus said.

And by midnight, she forced him to the couch.

"How would it look?" she asked.

About as bad as could be. But what did she care? He thought she wanted the divorce?

Yes, but with dignity on her part and Howard totally in the wrong.

Because he was thinking about this in the cold blackness before dawn, he was surprised to go back to sleep again.

Jessie shook him awake. "Get up!" she said. "Come look what happened!"

The first light lay upon a flawless world: Howard had not been there and would not be; they were drifted in waist-high and the drifts were pink.

"Hurry up!" Jessie said.

The clean air stung their lungs. The beagle, baffled, blundered behind them. A rose sky brightened and a first lance of gold pointed the horizon. Snow light as feathers sprayed about them as they stumbled to the beach and when they reached it, the waters were still as Galilee and far away across the faultless blue, the light from Seguin shone as steady as a star.

Then the sun rose exulting and it was Christmas Day.

16

THE DAY AFTER Christmas was fine, too, and about eleven o'clock the Pedersens thought they heard the grumble of the snow plow. Edgar said he would take a look-see. He knew that when the road to town was choked with snow Irma felt choked, too, and the breath fluttered in her throat. Sometimes the mere fact that she knew he knew also made her feel that she was choking. Telepathy exists: ask any married couple. For this reason she concentrated heavily upon the kitchen cabinets — which she now wished had not been painted — until the back door slammed. Then she permitted herself to admit something.

Christmas had been hateful.

Where were the candy canes? Where were the children who should have smeared the furniture and ground the cooky crumbs into the carpet?

Edgar had given her a dress that looked almost like cashmere but would wash. She knew that Mary Lou Pepper had chosen it. Mary Lou always had liked pink. Irma gave Edgar a sweater which she herself had chosen and he said that he liked it very much but she saw him trying to pull the sleeves down to his wrists. She could have cried. In fact, she did.

Their son had sent binoculars and quantities of California fruits which had arrived not much frozen. But he had not called. Irma had not expected him to call and had not expected Edgar to expect it.

When his eyes kept shifting to the telephone she asked, "Don't you remember? They were going skiing."

"Oh," Edgar said. "Now I remember." Then he got up and made himself a drink.

Irma was appalled and exhilarated at how easily she lied. It was a gift that she had not known she had. However, having lied so easily, she ached all over.

Of course the chasm between the father and the son hurt the mother. It gaped as soon as the boy was tall enough to be a man. She also would have liked to have arrested the boy forever, but since she couldn't she had tried to make her peace with the gangling stranger. But Edgar said the boy was too big for his britches and the boy began to call his father The Old Man.

Sometimes she was wild with the son for reducing the father, and sometimes she was wild with the father because he minimized his son, and sometimes she was wild with both of them because she was in the middle.

It was so simple and so insoluble. Edgar questioned that his son loved him and had taught his son that it is unmanly to show love.

How do you straighten out that sort of thing?

With that in mind Irma admired the binoculars, which came in their own neat leather case.

Edgar said, "Very nice indeed." Then he replaced them in the box.

Irma looked out the kitchen window and worried because he was shoveling and all authorities are against shoveling. But he had never been what you would call a reckless man; his fluorescent cap was motionless and he seemed rather more to be observing the deep and gentle billows of the snow. Then she regarded her immaculate kitchen which was no fun anymore. No butter, no eggs, no sugar, no salt and no appreciation.

On an impulse she called Mary Lou Pepper, who was wild.

"It's all very well," Mary Lou complained, "to say nothing's right unless they spend the day with Mummy and Daddy, but much as I hate to say so those kids aren't well behaved. And who wakes up with the clean house? They do. Did the size suit?"

Irma thought of the turkey bones and the soapsuds gone to scum in the greasy roaster and all the glasses and of the way just one little boy messes up your rugs, and she didn't feel very sorry for Mary Lou. But she felt very sorry for Edgar, who was so afraid that he was going to let her down, when he had never let her down in his whole life.

Something exploded against the glass wall of the living room. A bird that thought it had clear sailing struck the glass with such force that Irma's hands flew to her throat. Now it lay iced on the deck and was a chickadee with a black cap and bib. Please, she hoped, only stunned. But as she looked at the angle of the little neck and at the claws that had abruptly frozen, she knew that it was dead.

Probably Edgar should not see it.

So she slid open the door, shuddering with cold and with revulsion, and gingerly picked up the too-light corpse. The black cap lolled against her hand. Irma stepped to the railing and flung it down the cliff and then, seeing that Edgar thought she was waving at him, she waved back.

Then in the bright barren beautiful room where nothing was like what she was used to, she thought to weep a little and then didn't, and when Edgar thumped across the porch she had fresh coffee on.

But she was more silent than usual. And when they had each settled to the empty afternoon, Edgar asked, "Do you wish that we hadn't moved here?"

"Certainly not!" she said. "What a thing!"

But after a decent minute she went into the spick-and-spandy bedroom where not one thing was comfortably out of place and scowled at herself in the sparkling mirror, and then she opened the closet door and kicked her shoes around.

But every day spent in feeling sorry is a day squandered, and none of us so rich that we can squander them. So Irma, who was not by nature a spendthrift, began to deliberately think of jollier things.

Because there was always New Year's Eve.

17

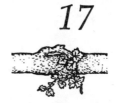

ON CROW POINT, there was some skepticism.

"What'll we talk about?" Angus asked.

Jessie said, "Something will turn up. What do we talk about at home?"

And nobody wanted to hurt Irma's feelings.

"I had to ask if I could bring you," Jessie said. "I thought that was kind of cute."

Everyone knows how capricious parties are; there is some safety within regulations, but not much. The most unpromising may prove saturnalias, but not often. To the best of her limited understanding, Irma had done well. There was enough food and liquor, as Edgar testily said, to sink a ship.

"You should have spoken up," Irma said with spirit.

Well: she had seemed so set on it.

Had she been in the mood to be insulted she would have been insulted. When a person says that a person is set on something he implies that the person, through a blind drive for satisfaction, ignores the comfort of the person who points this out.

"I didn't want to disappoint you," Edgar said.

He didn't want anybody else to disappoint her, either.

She seemed to him pathetically sanguine in her pink Christmas dress and the old Delman sandals.

"They're coming back," Irma said. "For so long shoes were so ugly."

He couldn't see how she could walk on them, held up as they were on little needles by a cobwebbing of straps. But she did have pretty legs.

He was afraid that she expected too much.

For instance, she expected them to dance. Because wall-to-wall carpeting does not roll up, she had installed the radio in the kitchen. And also the bar. On Crow Point everyone comes and goes by the back door, if the back door is what it is. You would think that because the front door fronts the ocean that it would be the front door, but that is not how it is. Since what should be the front door cannot be approached, you would think that someone would at least remove the garbage cans or get the dog's dish out of the way. But that is not how it is done.

The advantage was that the bar would meet their eyes and assuage whatever worries that they might have had concerning punch.

Edgar said, "Three couples are not going to dance. Three couples would feel like fools. You've got to have a lot of people before people dance."

Irma smiled. She said, "Don't be too sure."

Nine o'clock came and went. This is the hour when a happy man yawns and thinks of bed. If he enjoys a drink, he has had it. Tonight Edgar had not so much as set a lip to a sherry. As an escaped principal, no one knew better how cruel the young can be.

What if they did not come at all?

154

And Irma with her new hairdo? With the fruits of her efforts displayed upon her best tablecloth: the blushing ham, the paled turkey, the cranberry hot with anger in the cut-glass bowl?

But there she was ahead of him, for once.

"That's why I asked for nine o'clock," she said with a worldly assurance that he did not care for. "So that they'll come by ten."

In his part of the world people came at the hour for which they were asked and then they ate and then they went home. He wondered where Irma was getting her ideas.

But then he saw that, after all, she had not changed.

"I have a little surprise for you," she said.

He hoped it wasn't hats.

"Let's walk," Jessie said to Angus.

He was never sure when she was jesting. The barometer had held steady all the day but in the thermometer the mercury had tumbled. Walking there might be nice, but walking back?

"Suppose I should get drunk," he said.

She considered this. Then she said, "We won't be there that long."

Jessie was principled. Having accepted Irma's invitation, she meant to arrive sober and hungry. Both aims could only benefit by a walk through the woods, and as soon as they stepped ouside, bundled and booted, he saw that she was right. It was a winter's night to savor.

On the last night of that last year the waning moon hung in a vast bright sky. The Christmas snow was iced to incandescence and upon those shining sheets, weeds trembled in the cold. Over the wide silver beaches the muted water murmured, and as they walked they saw in the thickets small watching eyes, alight. The pure clustered stars swung slowly overhead.

"This is the only way to live," Jessie said flatly.

Well, it was one way to live. There are others.

Crow Point was pleasant, but there was a real world out there from which, Angus thought, Crow Point was in full retreat. The organism that does not advance atrophies and already his own talent, which had refused to accompany him from home, sulked. He had begun to feel that if he proved dilatory, he might get home to find his muse had flown the coop.

"S'matter?" Jessie asked. "Cat got your tongue?"

So he would drag her back to the real world, willy-nilly. If she did not want to marry, he would not marry her. If she wanted a child, he wouldn't mind one. He caught her mittened hand so abruptly that she skidded, swung her close to him and kissed her. After a moment, she began to kiss him back.

"Happy New Year," he said.

Irma's surprise was that she had asked Emma Lou and Harold Pepper down from China Falls and they accepted!

Naturally they would have to spend the night, which meant that in the morning there would be someone with whom to discuss how things had gone, which is the best part of any party and failed to hold Edgar's interest at any time.

Then the Elders called to ask if they might bring guests.

Now her party was beginning to feel like a party, because there was one place less to sit than there were guests. Even two places less if they did not want to sit three to the sofa, and it had been her experience that no one does.

What she had overlooked was that Edgar had never much liked Harold. It is one thing to encounter someone whom you do not like very much in the faculty lounge, and quite another to have him sleeping in your house. Edgar did not choose to know what mouthwash Harold Pepper preferred or to see his used dental floss.

And the very first thing Harold said and said fuming, was "That's some dangerous road. I don't suppose it's much better in the summertime."

However, they were almost properly attired. Emma Lou wore her good suit from Porteous Mitchell and Harold his pinstripe, with a nice tie and a blue shirt as a concession to the times. But they had not thought out their feet. One does not drive to Crow Point in midwinter without galoshes, but galoshes do not add much to style, and neither did the bedroom slippers — pink in her case, maroon in his — which were the best that Irma could supply.

And when the Elders arrived with their guests, Emma Lou shot Irma a glance of pure hatred. The female wore a large square of scarlet tissue silk and sandals so frail and inconsequential that they appeared to be an afterthought and he, a ruffled shirt. Though this excited Irma, she was not offended that Tom Elder was attired in cords — where in that little house would he keep evening clothes? In fact, where in that little house did he keep guests?

Which, among other things, Brigid was worrying about. Cornelia was an old and treacherous friend and a truth-teller. Your truth-tellers are all dangerous. Human relationships are explosive enough at the best, which is why society demands of us all a decent silence, over which with some care, we can skate. Through that brittle surface your compulsive truth-teller and your drunk crash as by accident: Cornelia was malicious and said nothing by accident.

This afternoon she had said to Brigid, "Why, honey — you invited us. Don't you remember?"

Fortunately at the moment Tom was outside, uncovering the extra gallon of gin that Crow Point finds it wise to hide from oneself.

No, Brigid did not remember. Yes, she did. She and Howard had run into Cornelia and her current companion at the Copley Plaza: late. The Copley has gone to hell. It was a great mistake to remove the Merry-Go-Round and a worse one to try to call it the Sheraton. One of those mistakes had been rectified but not the other and the best thing you can say for the big bare brown barren room that now passes for a bar is that you do not expect to meet anybody there. But no place in Boston is safe.

Boston is a very little city, and everyone, through a curious nexus, knows everybody else, so if illicit sex is what you have in mind, you will do better in New York.

If Brigid had invited Cornelia to visit them in Maine, and

she probably had — Cornelia had no need to resort to lies when the truth was so amusing — what she had probably had in mind was to establish that the Elders still kept house. Tom was a courteous person and would keep a good face as long as he thought this had come about by accident: for Brigid to have offered the intrusion meant either a callous lack of regard for his opinion or a drunken impulse. Neither was going to please.

Brigid began to blush and continued to do so through the rest of 1978. It was all beginning to come back: Cornelia had worn a hat and the new man, like all the others, was wide of hip.

"You said you were going to Antigua," she reproached.

"Ah," Cornelia said. "We thought this might be more fun. And since we've been skiing in the Laurentians, you might say we were passing by your door."

Hardly.

Cornelia had a head that was shaped like that of an attractive snake, and she had narrow, light, colorless eyes that at that moment flicked across the folding bed.

"I'm afraid you won't be comfortable," Brigid said.

"Honey," Cornelia said, "I wouldn't miss this for the world."

It seemed to Brigid and to Tom that there was nothing for it but to start drinking. By the time they got to the Pedersens' it showed, though just a little.

"This is my little friend," Irma told Emma Lou, and then, peering at her little friend, "Do you have fever, dear?"

The Peppers were not prepared to like Cornelia nor her husband whose name they never caught and for whom they had not been sufficiently prepared. As old inland people, they had trouble enough with those who deserted to the coast without coping with supercilious strangers who were not much interested in anything between Brookline and Quebec.

When Harold Pepper was uncomfortable he attacked, as many of us do.

He said to Edgar, "I must say that I think you were wise to stay in a cold climate," which implied that if Edgar had retired to Florida, he might have spoiled.

Edgar got up and made himself another drink.

Tom Elder drank because he was bored and because Brigid kept topping up his drinks; she had decided that vile as he might be tomorrow, it was better than letting Cornelia have at him tonight.

By the time that Angus and Jessie arrived, cold and wholesome as milk, everyone was offended. Except for Irma, who was under the impression that everything went well.

Cornelia said to Jessie, "Ah — we haven't met since the doctor's."

Since there are many reasons why you see your doctor, including the fact that it is that time of year again and no intelligent woman risks what she has been threatened with since she began her menses, it was not unnatural that they should have met in the office of the competent doctor. You can no longer tell what the woman sitting next to you is there for. If you wish to be aborted, that can be arranged. One understands that a very few of us would like to be the other sex; some are just naturally aggressive and some would prefer, if there is any hitting to be done, to be the one who hits.

Jessie was there because she was bleeding and wanted to keep the child. Since she had been insulted and affronted, she thought that it was only fair that she get something out of it. However, there was little that the good man could do. He told her to stay off her feet and wait and that Mother Nature had a way of cleaning up her own messes — though Jessie had not thought of her potential son as a mess — and that there would always be a next time. Jessie did not tell him that there was not going to be a next time.

Jessie of course confided nothing to Cornelia, but Cornelia was clever at sniffing out the distresses of her friends, and given the place and Jessie's demeanor, there were only so many things that could be wrong.

Now she looked speculatively at Jessie and then smiled.

Jessie saw that upon the occasion of that meeting, Cornelia thought her to have just arranged to have her child removed, and took it as a savage and ugly invasion upon her inmost privacies. Abstemious as she had been all evening, she was drunk with rage.

Brigid was watching her husband carefully and had begun to follow him around with ashtrays lest he drop ashes or even cigarettes on Irma Pedersen's new carpeting. Tom would have said, and would have been more or less right, that left to himself he had very little traffic with liquor, but that there was no way of supporting Cornelia's presence without it. She had looked at his paintings, which there had been no time to conceal, and had said only, "So that's what you've been up to."

By now, like Mr. Pickwick on another evening, Tom had undergone the ordinary transitions from the height of conviviality to the depth of misery and from the depth of misery to the height of conviviality; like a gas lamp he exhibited an unnatural brilliance — and now threatened to go out altogether, which was not what was worrying his wife nor his hostess. Irma had not anticipated uncoordinated guests; she was beginning to think she might have erred in not arranging to serve the cranberry sauce from the kitchen, where Edgar could supervise the serving — better yet, *do* the serving and thus protect both damask cloth and carpet.

With a gay little laugh meant to suggest that she recognized her behavior to be eccentric, Irma carefully lifted the great cut-glass bowl and carried it into the kitchen where, had she not been interrupted, she would have placed it safely on the stove. As it was, when someone as unexpected as Elijah rang the doorbell, she placed it on the bar, which was not altogether wise.

"Who could that be?" she asked.

They looked at one another. Since they were all accounted for, it could not very well be anyone in distress; therefore it might be someone who intended to inflict distress. The Peppers jumped easily to the conclusion that back in China Falls their house was afire. They looked reproachfully at Edgar.

However, it was only Howard Thorne, who was cold, inconvenienced, and looking for his wife.

Cornelia said, "Behold a witness, Brigid!"

Jessie had no idea to what Howard was witness, but she understood from the scarlet that rose beneath Brigid's brown satiny skin that it was she that Howard had been seeing all the fall. Having so recently been violated herself, she resented for both the Elders this public pillory and thought how pleasant it would be if Cornelia choked.

Howard spoke on, and every word self-serving, in Jessie's judgment, since the litany of small disasters he reported won first the sympathy of the women and then the empathy of the men. It had been lonely, with no one in town. He rubbed his dark curls ruefully in the way that he had always found effective. So he decided to join the gathering on Crow Point. He realized that it would have been more courteous to call the hostess, but it had been spur-of-the-moment.

Temporarily in cahoots, Brigid and Jessie looked at one another. Neither had mentioned any gathering.

"Besides," he said, "some people like surprises."

Jessie and Brigid were not among them.

Howard said that things had gone wrong from the first. He had a flat right between Howard Johnsons and though he had put the hood of the car up no one had stopped and no one had sent the patrol, and he had had to change the tire himself, which was dangerous enough in the daytime, let alone at night and let alone on New Year's Eve when half the drivers on the road were drunk.

There wasn't a man there who didn't agree with him, but Jessie also knew that Howard was proud of his hands as well as of his feet and hated even clean heavy work.

Then — and a new car, too — the plugs began to foul, and he coughed into Portsmouth to find, naturally, everything closed up tighter than a tick, and it had taken the police a dozen calls to find a young mechanic whose cupidity outweighed his pleasure in his friends. Then between Brunswick and New Bristol there was a roadblock, with the traffic backed up for what seemed to be forever.

It was the roadblock that did it. Jessie didn't believe a word of this tale any more than she had believed a mischievous friend who had told of starting her car in reverse by mistake and backing up at forty miles an hour. She thought he had probably stopped along the way for a dinner and some drinks. Something unpleasant occurred to her: thus ensuring that he would arrive at Crow Point late and unexpected. Jessie wondered if he had any moral nature at all. Audacity, betrayal and deceit came easily to him but none of it seemed to amount to much; certainly to no more than his affection and his promises had amounted. Of such as these it was said: *I would thou wert cold or hot.*

"And now," Howard said, "I would like to speak to Jessie. Privately."

Irma looked with concern at the clock. It was almost time for the hats and the singing.

"Certainly," Jessie said, and stepped into the kitchen.

The trouble was that the house wasn't shaped for privacy; while you could close the kitchen door it would be silly to do so, because it was a Dutch half-door, and since Irma had placed the radio in the kitchen, she couldn't get at it now to turn it up. Although she raised her voice and counted on Edgar to do the same, everyone heard Howard.

At what point does honest rage degenerate to malice?

"I found two cars in the yard and the house dark," he said. "What do you think I thought?"

"Excuse me," Angus said. He rose and headed toward the kitchen.

Jessie said, "Why would I give a damn about what you thought?"

Nothing is more exciting to civilized people than an uncivilized scene, unless you happen to be the host. Edgar did not like what was going on in his house; you might say, in his castle. He drained his drink, which was stronger than he remembered it as being.

"See here," he heard Angus say.

162

Cornelia in her scarlet silk rustled a bit closer to the kitchen. The wide-hipped husband edged after her.

"Who *are* these people, dear?" asked Emma Lou.

The clock came to Irma's assistance; the long arm clicked and nudged.

"Last round-up!" she cried gaily, before it occurred to her that there was no good way of getting to the bar. It occurred to Tom Elder, too. He looked reproachfully at Brigid, who had been neglecting him.

There had been a lot of careless thinking all along. Had Irma not drawn his attention to the dire fact that the evening shrank to its conclusion, Tom would not have been precipitate. Had Brigid been alert, she would have recognized his need. Had Edgar not wanted to divert Harold Pepper's interest from the unseemly scene: who knew what word was going to get around China Falls? he would not have yanked him out to admire the deck, and if he had not done that he would not have mistaken the source of the crash that followed.

It was only that the cut-glass bowl of cranberry sauce, as if it levitated, flew from Tom Elder's attempt to attain the bar and broke: the sauce spattered and the glass splinters rose and fell like fireworks. But Edgar took the noise for fisticuffs.

He burst back shouting.

"Out! Out of my house! Everyone!"

Meantime, over the birth of the new year, the cold stars presided silently.

18

IT WAS CHARLEY PRATT'S OPINION — and he took comfort from it — that all were mad and most, malevolent. Once you perceived this nothing could astonish you, not even your own vagaries. If your own vagaries do not astonish you, you are armed in triple brass against the shock to which the public and private behavior of everyone subjects you. Charley was the last person to be surprised at the failure of Irma's little party, and so he told Jessie Thorne.

"Least folks see of one another the better," Charley said.

He had come to this conclusion long ago when somebody at school told: somebody at school always tells. Malevolence begins early. Charley couldn't have been more than ten.

That was a gold and orange day drabbing to bronze: no reds were left except for the blueberry bushes, which still burned. After school Charley took the woman home a brittle bunch of blueberry leaves and when they snapped off and littered up her rug she picked them up every one and put them in her best bowl and that gave him courage although all she said was, "Neither of you remembered to take off your shoes."

So because he trusted her he came right out and asked. She said, "You are too mine." And then she slapped his face. Then his father slapped him, although not so hard.

"Don't ever sass your mother again," he said.

But when she was upstairs and crying this man who might not be his father but was good said, "Does it make a mite of difference?"

Yes, sure it makes a mite of difference, because if you don't know who you are you don't know who to trust or who is going to lie to you. Charley must have been more than ten, maybe about thirteen, because he decided to find out who lied. And this man whom he had always trusted proved that he could be trusted.

Because when Charley asked, "Do you love her more than you love me?" this man said, "Yes."

So after that they understood and liked each other very much and they both sassed her all the time but in no way that was hurtful, so all she did was turn pink and pleased and say to them, "Oh — you two!"

When he turned seventeen and eighteen, Charley still thought about these things once in a while, say when the two of them were out at night with their liver-spotted hounds. What is a father? When does fatherhood begin? Who nurtures and protects and loves, he is the father. But apart from his parents, Charley never trusted anyone again until he met the girl who turned out to be Mrs. Charley.

He was not embittered. Embittered men are not happy and Charley Pratt was a happy man. If men are fools, it is more a matter for merriment than for despair.

"I wouldn't vote for either fellow," Charley said. "Neither one knows enough to pound sand into a rathole."

Jessie Thorne sneezed. The first week in January was cold as a stepmother's kiss and Mrs. Charley thought Jessie inadequately clad.

"But Charley," Jessie said, "somebody's got to run things."

"I saw a picture of President Ford the other day," said Charley. "He was riding a camel."

"But Charley, if you think that way, you'd never vote."

"That's right," said Charley.

Though as a matter of fact he always voted, and always for the one he felt would do the least harm.

Now Charley snorted and slapped his big hand with the white curly hairs on the knuckles down on the New Bristol *Record*.

"What now?" asked Mrs. Charley. She liked a laugh well as the next.

What now was a picture of a resister resisting a resister. Kindly men both of them and honest enough, no doubt; devoted to their children and more often than not faithful to their wives; taxpayers, even educated as the world thinks of education, yet here they were lunging at one another like boys in a row at recess, each persuaded that upon his point of view depended not only his own well-being but the virtual survival of his family and race, and prepared to defend that point of view with sticks.

Charley said, "Fools."

Mrs. Charley swiped nervously at a table top with her apron. "But someone's got to take a stand. I read they found DDT in the Arctic."

Charley said, "Oh, I know."

Jessie said, "I don't want to go the way of the trilobite."

"You won't," he said. But having the vote wouldn't have helped the trilobite.

What the voter had going against him, to Charley's mind, was change: relentless, irrevocable and irreversible, and running around like chickens with their heads cut off was no answer because there was no answer.

He said, "Do you remember Snowy Beach?"

Did they not.

166

That year the United States Navy, having little else to do at the time, announced that it was going to invade Crow Point. Or more precisely, that it was going to simulate a landing at the state park adjacent to Crow Point in order, one assumes, to keep its hand in. There had been no true landings for some time and those for the most part in southern climes: suppose it became necessary to invade Hudson Bay?

All over the country people looked nervously at their maps. Canada had been huffy lately.

Paper forays prove nothing. But if thousands of men could be landed in the winter, in the Gulf of Maine, against the opposition of an imaginary enemy, and if these men could be fed, provided with latrines and after twenty-four hours safely whisked off again, why, that would be one up for the Navy.

An enemy: confused, splintered and impotent but not imaginary, immediately sprang up. There was a good deal of criticism, but the real opposition quickened within the State of Maine and reached hysteria as it reached the boundaries of New Bristol. Some felt it was expensive to have the military playing war, some that it was provocative to veritable enemies and some that unless those in high places proved traitorous, the young men engaged in such a farce would have long been civilians before they could be used. But the group that was most heated and vociferous was composed of conservationists, who saw in the maneuver a low blow at state lands: lands, mind you, that belong to you and me.

Were we not trying to keep the state parks inviolable for our progeny? Yes, we were, and for that purpose paying plenty. Even on the most benign summer day the number of cars that could enter the park was strictly limited and the beaches patrolled against beer-drinkers, litterers and dogs. Were we now meekly to surrender the wetlands and the dunes to thousands of booted feet, tons of heavy equipment, the remnants of field rations and a porous carpet of cigarette butts? The gulls and snowy owls and deer would suffer, gasoline and oil pollute the tidal plains; it was quite possible that the entire coastal ecology would not recover; not in our time. Were we supinely to accept?

It seemed so.

It is hard to get at the Navy, and the Secretary of the Interior is no help. Tempers rose and such hot words were bandied that the local authorities, alarmed, announced that not only would the park be sealed off from civilians but also Crow Point, since from the Point and at low tide hordes could charge with no danger greater than wet feet; the Navy, high-handed though it might be, would not repel them with real ammunition.

Therefore the sheriff and his man stood guard at the Crow Point road. No one was to pass except owners — the day has not yet come when you can prevent owners. It was this that determined Charley Pratt to be present. Any number of owners would have been happy to invite him, but Charley scorned to be invited anywhere on Jacataqua Island. He made his plans.

That was the year the teacher fellow started his house; the frame was up and the roof on and the carpenters in all likelihood were going to start coming down as soon as possible after mudding. The new house hung on the cliff that overlooked the basin and the beach and there should be plenty of lumber lying around to make a fire in the new fireplace. He would be comfortable as could be.

Mrs. Charley said he ought to remember there was no water and no toilet and he said there were forty acres of woodland across the way.

She said none but an old fool would crawl around the woodlands. Charley closed his eyes. When he started out she was still sleeping. She said she didn't want to go because it was trespassing, but he thought it was because of the toilet: it was just as well. Women get restless and are afraid you're going to burn up property. Even the nicest women.

Naturally at that hour the sheriff was not watching the Crow Point road — who would go down Crow Point at four o'clock in the morning? But Charley wasn't trying to avoid the sheriff, who was an old friend and wanted to get reelected, nor did he wish to enter the new house unseen: in his opinion at this stage he was as entitled as the next. He did want to be down before first light because he thought that was when the fun would start.

The morning was cold but had followed a three-day thaw; the road was bare but the ruts hard and the old Packard bounced easily along. Inside the Pedersens' it was black as the ace of spades and there was the good clean smell of new wood and shavings. He swung his flash around, but briefly. As a young man Charley had perfect night vision, but it was blunted now and he wouldn't force it with even a small fire until the flames flickered transparent in the new light.

From a dark corner he had missed, Jessie Thorne said, "Hi."

Charley didn't much like to be surprised. He said crossly, "You might have said."

"Didn't decide until last night."

"He with you?" Charley asked.

"He wouldn't come if it were real."

Then it was nice to have her company. "Too early for a hot toddy?" he asked.

She didn't feel it was too early. Besides their thermoses he had brought coon cheese and pilot bread and she, black bread and sausage, so when the time came they could make quite a good thing of it and meantime they wrapped up in their car robes and in companionable silence watched the black spaces where the windows were going to be.

And they were right. An hour before sunup and on signal, those spaces lit up like sparklers and the whole of the black bay dazzled with lights. The big lights lifted and fell slowly with the deep water and above and about them tiny ones darted like fireflies. Charley had never thought to see the day. He had watched a brief gam of lobstermen, and a regatta, with its sails flocked like butterflies, is a pretty thing to see. But as the pale sky leached with light and the gray monsters loomed everywhere, you could imagine it was real, and between the shipyard and the nuclear plant, who knows? It may yet be real.

Below them bystanders blackened the beach, clustered uneasily in little bunches. Charley Pratt sighed. The danger to which the globe is vulnerable is people. We swarm like bees, we hatch like flies, destructive everywhere and every one of us with his own fish to fry: no wonder there are wars.

Now the sun slid up fast behind thick clouds and left a narrow line of light on the horizon, bright as acetylene. Above, the skies were heavy and below, a sudden sheet of wind troubled the aluminum water.

Charley said, "Change of weather."

He hoped it would be a change for the worse; not enough to hurt anyone — just to remind them. Just enough to rock the barges that were crawling like sea-slugs to the shore and to wobble the confidence of the destroyers, angry and ugly with their mean profiles, and to give the big carrier from whose flat top the helicopters rose a second thought.

> Roll on, thou deep and dark blue Ocean — roll!
> Ten thousand fleets sweep over thee in vain. . . .

Every spring Mrs. Charley swooped on the big blue battered book and cried, "Here's something that the library could use!"

> Man marks the earth with ruin — his control
> Stops with the shore. . . .

Charley would find it hard to explain why he dipped often into the Romantic poets.

> . . . upon the watery plain
> The wrecks are all thy deed, nor doth remain
> A shadow of man's ravage, save his own.

Or why he felt he should not be caught dipping. A lot of decent people read and a lot of decent people don't. On the fly-leaf Miss Sturtevant had written in her flowing Spenserian hand, "For Charley Pratt — a good student." Privately, she had warned him that Byron was not a good man, and that there was some question about Wordsworth.

Miss Sturtevant was a good woman and had gone quietly in her sleep, the way we all would like to go.

Beside him, Jessie laughed. The first barges had bumped into shallow water, but the Navy erred. Operation Snowy Beach had assumed that the beach would be snowy. Someone had said so. Instead, these boys scrambling to shore in their white rompers were conspicuous as Stonehenge.

Down there the owners and their guests were easily routed as a long series of giant helicopters swung trucks as big as freight cars too close to their heads for comfort. And besides, mankind loses its capacity for astonishment, and presently the United States Navy in limited action was not so commanding as the picnic hampers.

Charley was right. The weather changed rapidly. The waves turned choppy and churly and slapped and shouldered one another and banged against the barges, one of which went down. When it had somersaulted, leaving orange life-jackets and silver flashlights and canteens proliferating upon the water like Japanese flower toys, apparently somebody talked it over. Because when the boys were rescued and redressed, they all went back to the base by Greyhound bus.

To Charley and Jessie, cold and sleepy and a little high, the funniest sight of the morning was the organized indignation of those who stalked the state highway with their cardboard signs: *Save Our Dunes.*

Because the Navy didn't do any harm. But two days after the invasion a northeaster gnawed out four feet of everything.

When Jessie coughed, the blade cleanly bisected the branches of her trachea. It hurt. There were a lot of viruses around that year and some said you should have shots and some said you shouldn't. In either case, the aged were to avoid.

Jessie looked at the friends whom, given the choice, she would in no way endanger.

"Look," she said, "it's been swell, but I really do have to get down home."

Charley Pratt's wicked old eyes laughed at her.

"Not before you have a cup of tea," he said.

19

THE NEXT MORNING a sulfurous sun ignited rags of clouds that
flared and fluttered and then, stamped on by a brisk wind, went
out and left a day as gray as ashes.

Jessie would not have wakened except that the beagle wanted
out. While she waited for the beagle to want in, she leaned
against the kitchen door and shivered. The air was sour with the
stench that follows the death of wood-fires. Angus had said she
would be better off with coal, which could be banked during the
night. But the question was academic now that coal is hard to
find and the trucks that used to dump it in your bin no longer
come and dump it. You have to go to Lewiston yourself; why,
she'd be up to Lewiston all the time.

Watching the livid sunrise, Jessie realized that she was sick
— and perhaps very sick. All night she had watched Ezekiel's
wheel spin and spark, and through that cascade of fire voices

had made disquieting demands. Howard wanted her to sell some land — he hadn't said so; she hadn't given him a chance to say so, but why else would he have showed up? Angus wanted her to desert the shore for the wrinkled old spine of the continent. Either way, she was to turn her back on what she loved. Oh, she was, was she? Once she remembered being sick, she was sicker. Her eyes swung upon wires. Her bones bumped over rapids. There were no caps in her knees.

Jessie had always rather liked being sick. One can be comfortable and is permitted, even encouraged, to be idle. There is no question of clearing out the cupboard or getting books back to the library; appointments can be canceled, and virtuously. Whoever is under the same roof brings icy orange juice and magazines, though one of the nice parts is not wanting magazines. And then he goes away, leaving quite a good sandwich carefully wrapped in the refrigerator. After which you get back to bed with that delicious feeling of stretching your feet into the clean and arctic sheets and then withdrawing them.

But this was different. This was *sick*. The thought of eating made her want to throw up; she envisioned stale hard bread clamping dried, buckled slices of processed cheese. This was unfair to Howard, who at these times had taken good care of her and once or twice had brought her Karmel-Korn. The house was cold and, leaning her hot forehead upon her glacial hand, Jessie knew that she could not start the fire again and tend it. If the pipes freeze they freeze.

The beagle scrabbled at the door but apparently merely for reassurance, because the moment she opened it he dashed with his tail high. Jessie turned on the tap in the old slate sink because it probably wasn't going to be cold enough to freeze dripping water. She would have abandoned the beast to the elements — beasts are designed to exist with the elements, are they not? But she was not at all sure she could weave back and forth again and the beagle was indefatigable and capable of scratching all day long. The next time his claws scarified the paint she flung the door wide, lunged for the beagle's collar and dragged it through. It was quite willing.

Back in her bed with the blanket turned high as it would go, she shivered and sweated. What she should do was to call someone. But who did she know well enough to ask them to let the dog in and out all day? The Pratts. But she wouldn't let the Pratts near her with a twenty-foot pole if it was going to hurt them — and only hoped to God the damage wasn't already done. Edgar and Irma would come, but Irma would feel she had to cook and Jessie would feel she had to be cooked for, when all she wanted was to lie here in silence until in the fullness of time, she was either better or worse.

Angus. Angus would come and would not obligate her.

But overnight her hair had dankened and greased, her eyes looked like prunes punched in dough and she felt that she smelled of fever and of sheets. It occurred to her that she would not mind at all if Howard saw her in such shape, which she hoped meant that she was now indifferent to him. She was pretty sure Howard would be glad to come, if only to insinuate that she had fared better in his care. But it would take him hours to get here.

And meantime, the beagle dangled its chin upon her and stared steadily and reproachfully. It was no time of day to be lolling around in bed. Jessie closed her eyes against that thoughtful gaze — this was the animal that was supposed to bring her comfort. His tail tapped like a metronome. Impossible: she thirsted for sleep as one who drowns thirsts for air, but who can sleep with patient, critical eyes upon him? Twisting around while the cold air gripped her shoulders, she grappled for the wall phone.

The moment her fingers touched the phone, it rang.

Bless Angus.

Except that it was Howard.

Instantly and with no volition, her treacherous body responded to the comfort of his voice because it was the voice she knew. The sound of a bitter voice is better than a stranger's voice. At the same time, she raged like a child whose parent has vamoosed. Jessie curled on her side, drew up her chill knees and cradled the receiver.

"Yes?" she asked coldly.

The instant that she spoke she realized that her words, muffled by the electric blanket as they were, might sound as if she had been crying.

"Are you all right?" he asked.

She thrashed up through the bed-covers and surfaced like a fish.

"Why wouldn't I be all right?" she asked.

"I don't know. Something unpleasant might have come up." Anything could happen, he implied, up in those winter woods.

Attack, as the world knows, is intelligent defense. "Are you all right?" she demanded. "It isn't like you to call during business hours."

"It's Saturday," he said. That put him ahead. But one of the nicest things about Crow Point was that you never knew what day it was, nor cared to: if you had to know, somebody at the post office always knew and would tell.

"Why are you calling?"

"First, because I want to apologize for New Year's."

To this she was probably to respond, "Oh, that's all right," but because it had not been all right, she said nothing.

"Well, Jessie, you know how I am."

Yes, indeedy.

"And it's the second time I came to talk to you."

So?

"Both times you were with that same fellow."

Drowning people are supposed to relive their whole lives, though if they drown, who can tell? For a warm instant Jessie lived her whole future: Howard wanted her back and was ready to offer inducements — she would no longer be treated as a child nor chided nor guided in any way, and she would never mention what she had suffered but would again sleep cupped against his back. . . .

176

Howard said, "Did you get my letter?"

"Probably," Jessie said. "I get a lot of business mail."

Howard said, "Jessie, don't play games."

She could imagine Howard in his new apartment with his new life, but she couldn't see him. In her fever it seemed impossible to talk to a husband that she couldn't see.

"Where are you sitting?" Jessie asked. "What are you sitting on?"

"I'm sitting on the sofa. Sort of late Grand Rapids."

"What color?"

"Blue."

Now she could see him. He was wearing his old Pendleton robe. Most women don't like to be disturbed, displaced, uprooted, driven like beasts into new burrows: maybe most men don't like it either. She knew Howard didn't like blue; that cold and grudging color.

Jessie giggled.

His silence was a sufficient reproach. Then he said, "I understand that you see quite a lot of What's-his-name."

"You have spies?"

"No," he said, hotly. "Brigid mentioned it."

But perhaps that was all over now.

"Jessie? Are you still there?"

"I'm here." There was no reason why they should ever see the Elders again.

"Both times I came it was to talk over something that's important."

"I'm listening."

Now he would say that the whole thing had been a damn-fool mistake and she'd admit that she'd been childish.

He said, "I have a client interested in your land."

So much for your delirium. At first she thought that she would just hang up, but huddled as she was the best she could do was to fumble the receiver, which would rob her of her proper slam and all the satisfaction. He would assume that they had been cut off.

"I'm not interested."

Through the small square window the day was stern and pewter-colored and the damp mist thickening; the foghorn was moaning on Seguin.

"Do I hear the foghorn?" Howard asked, interested.

"You hear me say that I'm not interested."

His voice held the cool reason that infuriates the unreasonable. "The value of shore properties has appreciated a lot faster than your income has," he said. "Don't forget I know what your income is."

New people with the right to be on her own beach? Driving upon her road? Knocking upon her door for two eggs and the heel of a bottle of vermouth?

"No."

"Taxes are going up."

"No."

"Damn it, Jessie, I'm just suggesting that you let these people look at it. Offer an offer."

"What's your concern in this?" she asked, knowing her question was insulting and unfair.

He was as hurt as she could wish. "It's nothing to me!"

She didn't for a moment believe that Howard Thorne had, upon two occasions, driven all the way to Maine to discuss real estate.

"Why are you doing this?" she asked. "Why do you keep doing this?"

He said, "Part of our trouble was that you need as much care as a child." But his voice gentled. "Jessie, I care. Just because we're not married now . . ."

Her nose filled at once. She said, "We're not married now?"

"Good God," he said. "You've got a lawyer!"

Yes, but she certainly hadn't told her lawyer that she had a phone. And she certainly hadn't read his letters, of which there were quite a little clutch poked in behind the flour cannister. Knowing that one day you will not be married is quite different from knowing that now you're not. A great longing for sleep came over Jessie.

"I'm going to hang up now," she said.

The beagle yelped and flung itself against the door in a hysteria of desire. Jessie dragged from her bed, pushing the wet cold hairs from her forehead. The beagle pranced into the fog, indomitable and growling.

"You stay out this time," she said. "Go chase something."

Alone in the old cold empty house she lay convulsed and shivering before the warmth of the blanket began to lap around her, but sleep was elusive. When you are lonely and frightened, sometimes you can woo sleep. For some time Jessie had given up sexual fantasies.

"I should hope so," Angus had said.

Lately she had substituted another wakeful dream that was soft, sensuous, infinitely comforting: death will come. Death came with no pain and no fear and no disorder, but gently as an angel to a white marble maiden. Jessie drew the soiled sheet smooth and turned on her back and stretched straight; she clasped her hands below her breasts and closed her eyes. She felt the room's cold anoint her hot brow.

That for the world and the world's woes; there are some who escape. Now she would slip away into the little death of sleep.

However, the beagle wanted in.

20

ON CROW POINT the winterers were well into the new year and living precisely as they chose to live. Wouldn't you think that they'd be happy?

Well, they weren't.

And yet they had much for which to congratulate themselves; not one of the town's dire predictions had yet come true. For one thing, they had asked no special favors. Not one of them had pleaded that the road crew fill potholes or widen corners where one could not pass, especially since after the first deep snow the road commissioner had erred and sent the small plow down; now the big one could not negotiate the ice-rimmed alley. Had they complained or dropped remarks at the post office? They had not!

Nor, though it is one thing to dissipate a summer chill and quite another to heat when the wind shakes the shingles and the temperature plummets and hovers in the single numbers, had they misjudged a woodstove or a fireplace and set fire to a chimney or a wall, which according to the town was just as well. The fellows do a bang-up job but they are all employed, and unless you have your fire at a decent hour they are not going to be able to gather and get down.

Nor, though they contributed generously to its expense, had they desired the ambulance.

There had been no interruption in the telephone service, except for that one time when the squirrel got into the transformer. Not that it mattered. They had come for privacy and after the failure of Irma's festivities avoided speech with one another except, as now, when they met by chance.

"I hate to see footprints," Jessie said to Angus. "Even mine." During the night four inches of fresh snow had fallen; now a gold sky arched over it. The shadows were blue as paint. The new snow was light as dust and had you had to, you could have swept the road. Her capped head bobbed at his shoulder and as they marred the perfect page of the snow, the needles of the firs shook and let down errors.

Where the lane branched they met the Pedersens.

Not quite enough time had elapsed since their last meeting and the men were a little more silent than they should have been; the women, more effusive. Each couple scuffed the snow and assured the other that they were just turning back.

Irma did want to know if Jessie was quite sure she should be out? Because she still looked a little pale.

Jessie was utterly recovered and didn't believe, anyway, in giving in to small indispositions.

Irma was dubious. "When Edgar's sick I try to keep him down after he thinks he's well," she said.

Edgar said, "I am never sick."

Irma's mouth made a little O. She said, "What a whopper!"

Edgar scowled. "Come along," he said. "Nice to see you." And he had turned away when Irma tugged him back.

"Wait," she said. "I want to show them."

She took her mitten off and plunged into her pocket. The clipping was much folded and from somewhere else.

Folklorist Predicts a Rough Winter

Did you know that misty mornings
in August are a sure sign of heavy snows?

"I don't remember," Irma said. "In August, were the mornings misty?"

And that in the South in 1977 the doves and teal migrated early and the cypress trees yellowed before their time? The squirrels ate voraciously. The fur of the woolly caterpillar was thick and black. Dogs' coats were heavy. Bears were fat. Mrs. Sven Ireson of Sheboygan, Wisconsin, aged eighty-six, had giggled.

"Cackled," said Edgar.

"That," Irma read, "was to drive home her point."

Mrs. Sven Ireson's point was that the worst Atlantic storm of the century could be expected after Christmas.

"Here it is after Christmas," Irma said. "Couldn't be nicer!"

Jessie was interested. Everyone knew about the woolly bears but she who was supposed to know everything had not known about the cypress trees. And because beagles shed all the time, you can't tell much by the coats of beagles.

Angus was skeptical. Sheboygan was a long way from the Atlantic.

Edgar was sour.

"Our son sent it for a laugh," Irma said, uneasily, because no one had laughed.

The sun had left the green corridor of the conifers and the wind stirred. Angus said, "It sounds different here in the pines." In the long needles of the pines, the wind laments.

Edgar said, "I for one am going home." And then he went.

"He took it wrong," Irma said, troubled. "Our son just sent it for a laugh." Then she went after him.

Jessie narrowed her smoky eyes. "She's sore," she said.

182

"Irma?"

"Yes," Jessie said. "She's pissed off."

And turning home, she tried to balance in her own footprints, so as not to mess up the snow.

Jessie was right, though Irma would have said that she was miffed.

Look at him. He knew perfectly well that she couldn't keep up with his long strides, and though there was no one there to see but a chipmunk, she felt it very deeply that she was left to trudge alone through the steep fluff of snow.

It was a reprimand, was what it was, and Irma didn't feel she had one coming. By the time she got to the turn at the broken tree, he was just rounding the corner by the Bombing Gate. He had no idea how hard it is to live pinched between the rising and the setting sun. Balancing between her men, Irma felt used by both. She was sick to death of having them reproach one another on her account. Let them have at one another openly.

Why don't you write your mother? You know she worries.
You should remember these are my mother's golden years.
I thought I had taught you to avoid clichés.
I thought you were in a position to teach.

What had happened?

When she first brought the baby home, Edgar had looked at him as at a miracle. Before she thought that it was wise, he opened the window and laid the infant in the sun; three minutes at a time by his watch because sunlight is better than cod-liver oil. First he heaped pillows around him to prevent drafts, and in the unlikely event that he should take off.

"Irma!" Edgar had cried. "He raised his head!"

Later there were times when she would have liked to be the one who read, but Edgar said, "Not that pap." And skipping nursery rhymes and Pooh he drove straight into *Treasure Island*. Once in a while the child was sick, and then she caught up.

183

Even the softest snow turns wet and hard when it has sifted over the tops of your boots. Before her the whole hill lifted slowly, looking gradual enough until you climb it on foot and alone. Edgar said that she didn't walk enough, but Irma would like to know why one should walk when due to some inexplicable geographical mistake, the entire road went uphill all the way?

Irma used to get her feelings hurt because in the first years father and son were indivisible and because Edgar taught him early to laugh at Mama. It does not matter how loving is the laughter: no one likes to be the butt of the joke. And besides, being by nature a person who preferred to please, she found herself assuming the role of the willing clown — which was not Irma Pedersen at all. Irma *Wright* Pedersen.

But even as she pranced and postured, she saw trouble coming.

When he was four Edgar bought him a small bicycle when what he wanted was a trike because everyone else on the block had trikes.

"Yes you can," Edgar had said.

Her son, like every other mother's son, was precocious, but not precocious enough to express in words what Irma read in his fists. *This present is for you and not for me.*

Edgar said, "I am going to show you how."

After he had "skun" one knee and then the other, the boy said, "I am too little for this machine."

"I guess you are," Edgar said.

Then he returned the bicycle and brought back a scooter, which solved nothing for either one of them.

Why did they have to vie, why did they have to clash, when they were going to get over it and when it was her years that were spent in hurting?

Down by the Bombing Gate there was a very nasty bit of ice that fooled you even though you knew that it was there. If you were going to get one wheel into the ditch that's where you did it. No skill was sufficient to cross that patch and at the same time accelerate enough to take the right-angle bend and get up the short sharp hill. If Edgar had stomped on home and was not there to take her hand and help her up the hill, then nothing that he said or did could compensate her for a wasted life.

At this moment, because she was worrying about the ice that was ahead, she slipped on the ice that was here. For a split second and quite accidentally, she performed an incredibly graceful action — with no one there to see; as a result of which she found herself still upon her feet and madder than a wet hen.

Of course Edgar was waiting for her. He had brushed off a nice little place on a cold boulder, but was on his feet with his hand outstretched before she turned the bend.

"You didn't think I wouldn't be here," he said.

That is all very well.

But if they lived forever she would never be able to explain to him why she still felt deserted.

Or why she was wild with him, and at the same moment if his comfort required it — *really* required it; Irma was not a martyr — she would have walked right past the Bombing Gate and into Inner River. Didn't he know that?

Apparently he did. He took her mitten tenderly and said, "There. You didn't mean anything."

Did she not?

So it became absolutely necessary that she hurl at him the freshest phrase she could come up with. Certainly he had degrees. But the Wrights were not unsophisticated folk. Irma stretched to her every inch and her pink little face got pinker.

She said, "Go fly a kite!"

But that was your true, caustic and annealing anger, and not the petulance that nibbled at the Elders.

Women don't really like men to work: it robs them of attention. But Brigid was not a stupid woman and she knew very well that part of her distress sprang from the fact that she was not working. There was more to her than blushes. But these are vertiginous times for women. Who was she? She had a sharp little mind and when she exercised it a whole lot of people breathed easier about money and maybe even got to take that trip. On the other hand, since as a couple they had elected not to reproduce, what did it all amount to? Crisp in her cubicle with her telephones at hand, she had a function and could stay out of mischief. Well, out of much mischief.

But you can only cook three meals a day. While she cleaned up she recognized that what annoyed her was that she had nothing to do but clean up. Where there he was, totally absorbed and confident.

She could only compel his attention by complaints and by suggestions.

So she would say, "We really ought to turn the mattress."

Or clean the refrigerator. Or shovel a path up to the Pedersens'; that would be thoughtful.

His indignant glance said, *we!*

Or knowing that he didn't like to talk about money, never having made much money, she would wait until his brush was raised and then say, "How much have you got left of what your aunt left?"

This did not please.

She said, "I only thought that I might invest a bit for you. A little coming in is better than everything going out."

He would put by his brush and, later, try again.

She couldn't see why he couldn't talk while he painted. It wasn't as if he had to think.

Had she been able to disturb his euphoria she would not have; she was not that mean. And she honestly thought that his paintings were very pretty. But the State of Maine is knee-deep in pretty pictures; driftwood, dunes and dories. True, Tom's were different: but were they fine, were they permanent, were they pathmakers, or only different? She was beginning to feel that if you had seen one you had seen them all — but then, she felt the same way about Renoir.

Small things began to be annoying.

When her pot was bubbling, Tom stood looking thoughtfully at the spice rack and then added things she had not deemed appropriate. Invariably, he put the dripping spoon upon the counter top. She placed a saucer and explained the purpose of it, but to no avail. The next time he tasted, down went the spoon. Tight-lipped, Brigid took up the sponge.

Moreover, he left the seat of the toilet up and more than once Brigid, flouncing into the bathroom in the dark, sat upon cold porcelain. She did not find this as funny as he found it.

The volume at which he played his records physically distressed her, but he assumed that she didn't mean it. "How could it distress you?" he asked.

Oh, ye of little faith. Since he would not take her word for it, all she could do was fume.

But except when he was actually at his easel, Tom too grew sullen and quiet and drew her attention to what was not conducive to his comfort. He had stopped smoking and she had not. Tobacco was discoloring her teeth; her breath was unpleasant. Cigarettes were an unreasonable expense.

"I buy my own cigarettes," she reminded him.

That did not excuse her from endangering her health, which in the long run was going to be his problem. And there was always the chance that her stray ash would land upon his palette.

She said, "The stove's more likely to do that."

She loathed the stove. She hated the gray drift that sifted out when he stoked and merely flew about before her broom. She would prefer not to go to bed roasted and wake up shivering.

Except for fun, Brigid had always been a light drinker; it is best that those who handle other people's money be known as light drinkers. But now she had begun to match him drink for drink. He pointed out that this, too, was an unnecessary expense.

"At least it passes time," she said.

He was appalled that anyone should want to pass the time.

On the seventh of January they went to bed under a sky as clear as glass and a sugar of high bright stars. When they woke the sun bubbled coldly among curdled clouds. Drafts rattled the newspapers by the dead stove; when Brigid swung her feet from the bed the boards shocked her soles. Unshaven and shivering, Tom shrugged into his jacket. Under his knitted cap, one ear stuck out at an unlikely angle. How could she ever have thought he was attractive?

"We're out of wood," he said crossly. "Where did you put my gloves?"

She wrapped a blanket around her robed shoulders. "I said we needed wood."

His nose was pink. "I have to split some kindling."

Then it would be some time before the fire snapped and crackled. She said, "I said we needed kindling."

His mouth was harsh as the stiff boots he was lacing.

"When you do one damn thing around here but beef," he told her, "you can refer to yourself as *we.*"

Startled and unkempt and cold, they stared at one another.

"I'll leave today," she said.

"Do that."

He slammed the door and she began to pack.

21

HOWEVER, it began to snow.

The radio spoke quite seriously about the weather: something was going on south of Boston, a wild storm was expected and factories and offices were already sending people home. Here in Maine it had just started to cloud up, but by the time Brigid's bags were packed it was snowing, though in a purposeless sort of way. The flakes were light and aimless and blew this way and that; you could still see quite far out to sea. The branches of the firs moved sluggishly and then were still again.

Tom said doubtfully, "You'd probably better not start out in this."

Later he would claim prescience, but the fact was that conscience, only, compelled him to speak up. The thought of being alone again was too attractive and he might be punished for it. Nor was he inhumane. He didn't want her to have a slow, uncomfortable drive, as she might well have if the roads turned greasy and the visibility contracted. But these things are unpredictable. If she left right away the snow might peter out by Portland. If she stayed it might thicken and they be trapped here together.

Surreptitiously, Tom looked again at the *Old Farmer's Almanac*. The ninth of January still threatened a bad moon and an impossible tide but the conjunction of these things is not important unless it is accompanied by storm and even then, it depends upon what you mean by storm. The Old Farmer can predict moons and tides because they are predictable, but about storms he can only guess. The *Almanac* still said bright and clear.

But Tom thought Brigid a bad driver, one of those who do well enough as long as they steer straight ahead but go all to pieces if they have to rock a car out of a drift, and though he yearned to be rid of her he did not want her to get into trouble. The snow still flew in false starts and stops and in circles, but it was heavier now; he could no longer see the water, nor whether the slate-colored waves were chopping in from the north or south. It might be that if she left right now she could beat the storm to Boston. Or she might not.

"You'd beter wait for the noon news," he said.

Jessie could not have been more pleased.

She had always wanted to see a real coastal storm and the radio kept telling her that this might be one. The entire coast as far south as New Jersey was involved and Boston already had high winds and driving snow. Power lines were snapping, there were accidents on the Southeast Expressway and on the Turnpike the speed limit had been lowered. The storm was moving at eight miles an hour and was expected to go out to sea. But who knows? Maine still might get it.

As a child she had been disappointed that New England had not had a proper storm since the hurricane of '38, which had long ago receded into legend. That shattering wind had not reached Maine, or not in any force, but all along the southern coast the sea had slopped over its shores and whole beaches had gone, along with the cottages that perched precariously on them. Lives had been lost. Of course Jessie did not want anyone to lose his life or even his boat, but the child in her would like to see those walls of water and the sky-mounting spray. From her house she would have a ringside seat.

That storm had been so devastating because no one knew that it was coming; you could go into the subway at Harvard Square and come up again at Ashmont in quite a different clime, with the poles crashing and the signboards airborne. But nowadays the Weather Bureau knows all and everyone has time to prepare. And besides, that was September and the torrential rains at least were warm, though to those caught in their cottages on the Cape it probably hadn't mattered whether they drowned in cold water or in warm. Her point was that you don't have hurricanes in winter. This storm, the radio assured her, was just a good old Southeaster.

And she so well prepared!

Jessie had never felt more efficient. Her shelves were heavy with canned goods, most of which could be eaten cold, and she had laid in Calo for the beagle. Because her can-opener was electric she had even thought to pick up one of those bad ones that you jab into the can and then saw back and forth. She had apples and cheese and raisins. There was wood stacked in the house and mountains more out in the yard. She had candles and kerosene and new batteries in all her flashlights. There were new batteries in the radio, too. She had gin.

With the aid of the new batteries the radio told her that the winds in Boston had been clocked at fifty miles an hour and showed no sign of abating. So there was a real chance that Jacataqua might at least get high winds. That meant that the surf would be worth watching and that the power, which even in summer went out at the drop of a hat, would go out. And with it, the pump.

That made no difference to Jessie, who could haul water from her well, which would be good exercise and fun. It would not be fun to use the outhouse, so she filled the bathtub and flushed the toilet with a bucket. It worked fine. She filled old bottles with fresh drinking water.

Then she ran out of things to do and felt let down. She was not fool enough to have a freezer, but from the refrigerator she took everything that might be noisome if it spoiled, though nothing was likely to spoil in that cold kitchen. Then she made a meat-loaf sandwich and chewed it at the front window, looking out. The snow had stopped but the wind was rising; behind the offshore ledges the surf was kicking and the spray burst tall and white. The sky looked odd. Beyond low canopies of cloud a small sun must be burning fiercely because the air was suffused with color as if past Southport, a city flamed.

Emergencies are more fun if they are shared, but in order to share you have to admit there is an emergency. However, she could call Irma Pedersen under the guise of concern: they might not have thought of filling their own tub. But no matter how she denied it, they might think that she was frightened. When her own phone rang she assumed that it was Angus, who would be frightened for her; she was prepared for his importunate commands.

But it was Mrs. Charley Pratt.

She was the last person on the island that Jessie thought to hear from. Mrs. Charley knew Jessie knew that she was welcome; to suggest that their home was open to her would be to question her common sense.

But Mrs. Charley said nothing about the storm except to mention that the Women's League had postponed. In fact, they talked for minutes before Jessie fathomed the purpose of her call. What about? Well, Mrs. Charley reported that her own begonia was doing well — when she gave that slip to Jessie, had she mentioned that begonias like the south light? And the Pelletiers who had the lobster pound were off to Florida again. "It used to be that we stayed put," Mrs. Charley said, "and it was the summer people who moved around. Well, lobster's high enough, God knows."

Jessie knew Mrs. Charley wasn't calling about her begonia. But because people are proud, it is profitless to probe. One thing one may ask because it is common usage and does not indicate curiosity.

Jessie said, "How've you been?"

Mrs. Charley made a false little laugh.

"You know that bug you had? Well, I believe Charley has the self-same thing."

The Pratts were not in the habit of discussing their health. They were aware of other folks' bursitis and emphysema and knew who had cancer before the doctor did, but they avoided any mention of their own bodies as they would avoid any indecent exposure.

So when Jessie asked, "Does he have fever?" and Mrs. Charley said, "A mite," she meant that Charley Pratt was very sick.

She meant that she was frightened and that she couldn't deal with Charley and that no doctor would come way down here and that they had no way of getting way up there. She meant she needed Jessie.

"You didn't plan to come out for your mail?"

"I certainly did," Jessie lied. "I'll drop by, shall I?"

"Only if you planned anyway," Mrs. Charley said.

This put a whole new complexion on Jessie's storm. If Mrs. Charley proved to need only reassurance, Jessie could get back in time to be snowed in, but if the Pratts needed help, she would just have to skip the fun. In any case, you don't leave your house without considering alternatives.

The blackened wood in the stove was bedded on dull coals, the stovepipe cooling and the floor about the asbestos mat was cold, so that was all right. If she left the lights on, early thieves would know she was away; late thieves wouldn't be out on a night such as this promised to be, so she left them off. She could leave the begonia to freeze but not the beagle, so she whistled and it ran jauntily to her, pleased to be wanted.

There was very little else she could do except to lock the door against the Atlantic Ocean.

When she stopped to drop off the dog because Mrs. Charley had enough without the beagle, Jessie saw why Angus had not been badgering her: he hadn't even heard about the weather. He had not left the house, listened to the news, or even shaved. But she doubted that his day had been so profitable that he had not had time for these rites. He had once made the mistake of confiding to her those devices to which he resorted, as he said, to prime the pump.

"I never had to do that before," he admitted.

Now like a pole vaulter, he needed poles to vault. One of them was research. Whole days could be spent reading and in keeping a bibliography of what you read. Then you could go back and take notes and then those notes must be arranged and finally, typed. Oh, there are many ways to put off writing.

First Jessie tried to frighten him, but since he was not familiar with coastal storms, he was not very frightened.

"I tell you what," he said. "I'll go back with you, shall I?"

It had begun to snow again but this time, the flakes were mean and fast.

"If we can get back," she said.

"If we can't, you can stay here."

She would never understand the intricacies of his moral code, but assumed that perhaps the West lagged behind. Why should tongues wag the less because she was now divorced? Are the legally unentangled never maligned?

She said, "I really hate to miss the show."

Angus put his arms around her and although it was hard to be sure, she thought he kissed the top of her thick cap. Then he said something that amazed her.

"You're a good person," he said.

Good? *She?*

The beagle, perceiving that it was to be abandoned, followed her anxiously to the door. It was much colder and the snow skidded in fast thin sheets across the road, but Jessie did not mind the wind. Why, if she were *good!* Then all that Howard found inadequate in her did not matter, because it is not required of anyone to be everything. She parked in the Pratts' driveway, checked the car robe (present) and left the motor idling so the car would stay warm.

She was good. Why was it that Howard had not noticed that?

In the Pratts' big sprawling house the small parlor was tight as a box and hot as the tall stove they had used since they began to housekeep. Open grates in the ceiling released some heat to the bedchambers up above: enough. Charley said nothing would freeze up there anyway, not unless it was something wet.

Even Charley saw that you couldn't be sick up there; not at this time of year. He lay on a one-armed sofa, his big spare body covered with an afghan colored like Joseph's coat. Beneath it Jessie could see the hard bump of his shoes. Charley Pratt had never been seen without his shoes and wasn't about to start. He wore a baggy old cap with a visor against drafts. Charley's eyes had sunk. When he coughed it sounded as if someone rattled a jar of nuts and bolts.

Jessie said, "How long has this been going on?"

"Two days," said Mrs. Charley. And two nights.

Jessie knew well enough how he felt, but when you are young all you did was stay put and eventually you felt better. At least when she was sick she was good-natured. Charley snapped at her.

"Out of the way, girl."

She jumped and swung and saw against the television screen a ribbon of letters snaking out of sight.

"He's watched that thing all day," Mrs. Charley said.

Jessie thought she knew pretty well what it had probably said. The Weather Bureau did this from time to time and it was always exciting; certainly if you were laid up it would help pass the time, if all it said was SMALL CRAFT WARNING or GALES ALONG THE COAST. You could tell that by looking out the window, where the telephone wires had begun to swing.

Or perhaps it had said ACCUMULATION UP TO TWELVE INCHES . . . in which case and with that driving wind she had better get to cutting while the roads were still clear into New Bristol. Already a car was having trouble on the hill. Jessie heard the protesting screech of tires and the whine of a motor.

"All right," she said, "where's your thermometer?"

"Haven't got one," Charley said smugly.

"We have so," Mrs. Charley said.

While she waited for a full three minutes and decided to make it four (Charley was having trouble breathing and kept opening his mouth) Jessie indulged her disappointment, which was, she found, severe. At the least, she would have to get up to the drugstore. You could get up and back from New Bristol in forty minutes but only if you didn't stop for anything, which, unless you had your first license and wanted to make it up and back in thirty-eight, didn't make much sense. But that was under normal road conditions. Today it would be creep and crawl, and by the time she got back she was pretty sure the road to Crow Point would be corked with drifts.

The center of the island was no place to spend a storm. Between the stone palisades on one side and the wooded hills on the other, the narrow waters of the cove ran deep; it would be some storm that would more than ruffle the cove. You couldn't even be snowed in long with the state highway right at the door, not after the big plows came coughing back and forth. Still, what can't be cured must be endured. If you are good.

Jessie tipped the thermometer to the light. Then she whistled.

"OK," she said. "Who's your doctor?"

The line was bad but the doctor free to talk; sensible souls no doubt had canceled their appointments. The man was young, or young as doctors can be by the time they practice; his voice was confident and stern. Jessie told him what it looked like to her, though she supposed he got impatient with how it looks to friends.

"He's ninety," she told him.

"I'll meet you at the hospital," the doctor said.

Jessie was surprised to meet with no opposition, but not after

196

she looked into Mrs. Charley's tired eyes. It is pneumonia, mostly, that takes off the old.

There was no time to waste; already under the deep eaves of the tall old house the wind snarled and rocked.

"His coat's already warming," Mrs. Charley said.

Nobody ages in two days, and yet as Charley sat up with difficulty, Jessie was startled at his bent back and the thin wrists that dangled from the old coat-sweater. But under the bristle of his brows the sunken eyes gleamed with triumph.

"There it goes again!"

Jessie whirled. The letters marched rapidly off the screen. But this time, here it came again.

ALL RESIDENTS OF LOW-LYING AREAS
SHOULD NOW EVACUATE.

22

HOW?

How can a man turn his back upon his hi-fi and his life's work? His records alone were worth thousands of dollars; Tom Elder couldn't believe the sea was going to get them, but looting often followed this sort of thing.

SEVERE COASTAL FLOODING ACCOMPANIED BY EROSION . . .

"That doesn't mean us," he said firmly.

Why not? By shore properties they meant shore properties, didn't they? It seemed to Brigid that theirs was a shore property.

"But we're on rock," he reminded her.

What the advisory meant was places like Old Orchard Beach and, closer home, Popham. Where cottages, as you might say, skidded on sand, there was bound to be trouble; already had been. Last winter the Portland *Press-Herald* had pictured porches tilted crazily, and there had been some agitation for seawalls.

Brigid looked dubiously out into the too-early dusk. It was already wild out there and the foam seemed to be breaking at the level of her eyes. What was happening, she had seen once or twice before; the waves were running against one another and, where they clapped, sent the spray geysering.

"We're forty feet up," Tom said.

Yes, but even in summer she had seen salt water boil up that belt of broken rock. Once, its force spent, it had washed gently over the long ledge that topped the rise, and in the morning there had been a sea urchin in the grass.

She said, "If I had left right away, I could be home."

Steam heat and thermostats instead of this thin shed, through the board walls of which the wind was beginning to whistle. Her eyrie on the fourth floor from which she could look safely down on traffic in the streets. For since the storm was mounting here, presumably at home the worst was over. Cars would be grinding through the narrowed passages with their chains clanking; she might have to garage her car under the Common and scuff home, but there would be voices and neighbors opening their doors.

Tom said, "Or else you might be stranded on the road. Have you been listening at all?"

Not really. She had hoped to distract herself by watching the actor with the weak chin — very attractive, none the less — at last strike his wife: but the picture bounced and streaked and perforce, she joined Tom at the radio.

The wee voice of WEEI kept fading and all that emanated from the oracle was bulletins: highways were closed and cars abandoned between exits. Plows and the State Police were trying to get through. Those in such difficulty were reminded to remain with their vehicles and, periodically, to get out and breathe. If you have something red it is wise to attach it to your antenna, because of heavy drifting.

Brigid, who suffered a mild claustrophobia, shuddered. So far, by avoiding subways and all ladies' rooms where you cannot see your neighbor's feet, she had managed, but she felt a vicarious distress as the voice continued: then you should turn your engine off and wrap yourself in any cloth you have; if there are passengers, body heat will help. *While the snow inches up the windows toward the roof.*

Throughout the metropolitan area those without power were now advised that churches and municipal buildings were open for temporary shelter. Hotels made lobbies available. (Unfortunate he who got stranded at the Ritz — that best of hotels has no true lobby; how long can you stay drinking at The Bar, even if you are known there?) Nobody caught in the inner city should try to get home. Anyone attempting to drive in from the suburbs would be arrested.

They looked at one another, cold with shock. Arrested? Citizens? In *Boston?*

Now the tinny voice said, "What's that, Joe?" And then, "Folks, the power just failed in Mattapan. Up until now, that makes . . ."

His words were, for the moment, lost.

Tom's smile was evil. He said, "Somebody's stuck between floors in Mattapan."

There was no excuse for that. That was mean. He knew that she always expected to be stuck in an elevator and would prefer not to think about it. The one in their building, in spite of the good address, was a decrepit and open cage through which you saw all too clearly the black and ugly cables snaking up and down. Brigid was too sensible to walk up if she were carrying packages, but she never made that uncertain ascent without fear that she would be jammed between floors with the neighbors gone to Scituate, the janitor drunk, and a fire crawling through the walls.

Here on Crow Point the wind punished these walls and a picture she had never liked leaped from its hook and fell to the cold floor. At least if this shack collapsed one could scramble out. But to what? Already both cars were drifted in above the wheels, which was of little moment, since had they been mobile there was no road upon which to move.

But on Crow Point the telephone still rang.

Tom seemed to feel that Edgar Pedersen, acting from hubris and self-congratulatory malice, meant to commiserate with him. He lifted his voice against the war-cry of the wind.

Yes, they had seen the warning. No, he thought not. Kind of them, but the Elders were fine where they were.

Maybe he was. To Brigid the sea sounded close. She had not married in order to be drowned. At Radcliffe they used to ask, would you not give your life for the beloved? No. At least, not for a whim on the part of the beloved. The Pedersens were perched much higher up.

"It might be wise," Brigid said.

"Have you looked out?" His tone accused her of desertion. "Go if you like. I'll tell them to expect you and then when you don't get there they can call back and I'll go out looking for you."

She had read of those who fall and freeze between the barn and the back door. Scrambling and struggling, she would be up to her crotch in snow and would have to lug along dry clothing as well as her toothbrush and her makeup kit. It did sound hard.

The windows shook and shivered in their frames.

Brigid subsided sullenly. He had secured his canvases quickly enough, roping them overhead on the rafters. Did he expect the floor to be flooded? She thought of the tons of displaced water that would be required to raise the ocean to the level of the floor; was it not his first duty to see that she was secured?

Then the Pedersens' lights that had beaconed hospitality went out and with them their own lights and the last semblance of normality.

"Stay where you are," Tom said. "I'll get the lamp."

A gust of wind shook the shack; the door of the stove jarred open and gaped in the blackness like the gate to a little hell.

"Damn," he said. "There's no oil."

She wailed. "I told you!"

She would have said that she was one who was not afraid of the dark; she would have said her terrors were more contemporary than that. But she saw now that she had never before been in the dark except by choice. This numbing fear was vestigial as caves: while Tom grappled for candles, Brigid crouched and heard the tiger prowl and howl below — and not far enough below — she felt the cold and clammy breath of the sabertooth.

Just then she had an unpleasant insight. Most physical harm comes silently these days and falls, impersonal as acid rain, upon the just and the unjust. But these beasts that battered and screamed were emissaries and were punitive, and she felt the voice that directed from the swirling depths of the Atlantic was that of Urizen who judges: you have not done well. What blinded her like the last light was William Blake's god hunched above his terrible compass — and who squirmed and wriggled on the central foot?

Brigid Elder, who had not done well and would now be punished.

Though it did seem unfair that the whole seaboard should suffer.

Tom said, "Where did you put them?"

Her integrity? Her promises?

"Look in the second drawer," she said.

How had she thought that she could get away with it?

"Good girl," Tom said. "Got a match?"

Now the room was alive with drafts in which the thin candles flickered feebly. The wind screamed, trying to get in, and threw snow against the window panes until the glass was masked with white: then the whole mass slipped and collapsed and again the panes glittered black.

He stood listening.

She heard it too: An animal gnawed at the concrete squares in which their security was positioned. The waves that smashed against their ledge and should have broken there and toppled came on, hurling broken rock.

She was not a good woman; it had not occurred to her before.

Tom raced for the back door. It made a lot of difference where, once it had flung its ammunition, the water went. If it sheared and slipped off where it belonged, that was one thing. If it came on . . .

The wind leaped like a leopard, clawing the screened door from his hands; it ripped from its hinges. Brigid grabbed his belt. They leaned and looked.

In the wavering circle of his flashlight and on the dark and choppy water, the door rocked like a raft. The snow hissed. A line of white foam curled its lip and smirked, and then withdrew to its stern purpose.

Tom said uneasily, "I hope Jessie's all right."

The very name she didn't want to hear.

But following him back along the hall where the flashlight fractured the dark, Brigid defended herself. Jessie had not parted with Howard because of her; she had done Jessie no injury. Unless the eyes that met, the hands that brushed and the private laughter had proved to be an injury.

While the shadows pranced in the weak light, Brigid brooded. One is not supposed to give a thought to it these days and when she first went to bed with Howard she had not given a thought to it.

But that was in another country; and besides, the wench is dead.

For a moment, in the face of that cynicism, she forgave herself.

But it was she, was it not, who was in that other country at the time, and had not had the grace to be dead. For the itch of an ego, the tickle of a groin.

What appalled her now was the irretrievability of the act.

She had meant no harm; but for a square little woman she liked men and knew that she had hot eyes. She liked the game and Howard played it well and was amusing, which is the purpose of the game. He knew how to move and she knew how to move and it was perfectly all right because they both knew that the aim of the game is ephemeral and the prize shabby. Since they meant nothing by it, how could it damage anyone?

Besides, such slight behavior is but contemporary manners, is it not?

She could not divide the boom of the water from the boom of the wind.

No, it is not. It is adultery.

"Maybe Jessie's at the Pedersens'," she said.

"If she were, they would have said. Now it's too late."

She hoped he joked. He didn't. "It will be flooded now from beach to bay."

Then toward town it would be flooded, too, and on the marsh the small grassed hummocks that looked so like porcupines would be drowned. In that case they were cut off from the mainland — no; islanded from the island. She welcomed back the fear of physical danger, which is so much easier to put up with than fearing the essence of yourself. Her throat tightened: trapped. Surely all is forgiven to one who is trapped.

In that black holocaust she could not see the waves mounting but could only strain for the thunder of their retreat. In the instant before their long grumbling, the wind racketed. If she could attack him, she would be in a way vindicated.

"Has Maine ever had a tidal wave?" she asked.

"Oh, I don't think so." However, his brows drew together. "Not that I ever heard."

It seemed to Brigid that no one had the right to live in a place he knew so little about.

She said, "When I was at Radcliffe I was told there's a serious fault up here."

"Yes," he said absently. "I've heard that, too."

She was feeling better. It was pretty silly to worry about your soul when your brittle bones were endangered. A sense of proportion is a wholesome thing.

"This friend of mine," she said. "She took geology? She said if this fault let go Maine would be inundated as far as Waterville?"

Tom said, "For that you'd need an earthquake. Maine doesn't have earthquakes."

Oooh — what a lie. There is no place where the earth does not quake. Even she knew that much. When the earth quakes, then comes the tidal wave.

As she understood it, tidal waves come like walls of water, silent, gigantic and inexorable. If one were rearing up out there, say the equivalent of sixty stories high, they wouldn't even know it was coming. First it would snap the lighthouse on the Cuckolds like a match and then it would keep coming. It might be right out there now, and not enough time left to quarrel about it, although it did seem to her that Tom had played fast and loose with her well-being. If your husband plays fast and loose with your well-being, who owes him anything?

Tom said, "You have an earthquake or you have a north or a southeaster. This is a southeaster. We'll be all right if we get by high tide."

She asked with anguish, "How long till high tide?"

Brigid had never been able to read the tide-clock. She knew the single hand fell to low tide or climbed to high, but she couldn't remember how long it took to fall or climb. To her it looked like ten minutes until noon.

But Tom said that high tide was still an hour away.

If you stop to think of it, you can forgive yourself your childish errors: Good Lord, we are children, all. But as the sad little house shook beneath her, she recognized her own sophistry. God was after her. But why should this good man suffer? Oh dear God, if the house should stand, from now on what an honest wife she would be.

The ratty old Oriental that had been his mother's levitated as the wind scoured the inadequate boards of the bad floor, and then the water chuckled and lay low. Brigid moaned.

Tom said, "Are you all right?"

"Of course I'm not all right," she snapped. "How could I be all right?"

The telephone jingled faintly. Brigid rushed for the receiver: others were alive. But she heard only the muffled sound of space, cold and convulsed.

"No use," Tom said.

No use. The universe gone stark out of its mind and Brigid, who had been rescued all her life by janitors, cabdrivers, beaux, and by her own Daddy, had no one left to rescue her.

And what had she expected. Helicopters?

In the meager candlelight the hand of the tide-clock seemed to have affixed itself forever. Shuddering, Brigid pressed her knees together; she must retreat.

Uneasy in the little bathroom, it occurred to her that the drab cubicle unpleasantly resembled an elevator. She was about to rise and was anxiously clutching at her slacks when things began to happen. There was a roaring and a resounding crash that shook the bowl under her; then her small cage shuddered and began to move. Shooting forth, she collided with her husband by the door from which he again hung with his flashlight.

"It's an ice floe," he said, awed.

The screened door had long since vanished. The brutal ice nuzzled against one of the shack's frail spindles and waited for the next collusive wave to use it as a hammer. Husband and wife for a moment clung together the way husband and wife are supposed to cling.

Be thou then perfect.

Oh, I will, I will.

Somehow the tide-clock had raced ahead, tottered at its apogee and started its slow tumble down.

Tom said, "That's it. The worst is over."

That's what he thought.

Now that we pride ourselves upon a Faustian knowledge of our sphere and can predict everything, Somebody's laughing. It was a full hour after what should have been high tide when the sea bit the last soil from the rock, licked out the grass and tongued away the quaking-aspen tree.

And with a loud, metallic sound, their septic tank went bouncing down the boulders.

Tom Elder cried aloud. Septic tanks cost.

But to Brigid it seemed a sign of grace. Their lives were spared and for the most part their property, which meant that under threat of unimaginable penalty, she must redeem her promises. But now she could go back to Boston and be good in comfort, since it is not required of any woman to be good without a septic tank.

No God would expect it.

23

THERE EXISTS between Brunswick and New Bristol the kind of smiling rivalry that exists often between sisters; on the whole, Brunswick seems to have coped better with the ravages of time. Each of the little cities started with advantages: each was situated upon a handsome river, each was roofed by tall and branching elms, and if Brunswick boasted Bowdoin College — a college is a nice trait in a town — New Bristol had the shipyard, where, at one time, the high white sails must have been good to see.

However, in each place the elms are gone or going. Astonished in the new flat light, the wide mall in Brunswick still sports geraniums, but the main street in New Bristol is cramped between decaying buildings in which small shops have failed or from which they have fled and a bare and neglected waterfront. And each has erred. The college, about which the ancient pines still whisper, constructs broad-shouldered buildings out of glass that shoulder the walks where Hawthorne lingered and Long-fellow thought long thoughts, and over the smutty shipyard the tallest crane on earth, like an angry giraffe, threatens the highway and the quivering old iron drawbridge. The outskirts of each are measled with fast-food stands, gas stations and, in summertime, trucks with open beds in which clams and crabs simmer suspiciously.

Such custom as comes along is whipped past both towns by the highway and deposited in the maws of shopping centers. In a hysterical attempt to reverse this process, New Bristol tore up cement sidewalks and replaced them with uneven brick, in-stalled iron hitching posts for long-dead horses, planted upon the sandy riverbank some thin grass and encouraged to be built there a group of those contemporary buildings which resemble nothing so much as abandoned mining shacks.

It was opposite these curious structures of unpainted wood, so much more appropriate to the steep flanks of Colorado than to the wide flowing river from which the ships once went out to the China trade, that the old Emerson House made a desperate last stand, and from a window of the Emerson House that Jessie Thorne, on the morning of January tenth, gazed out upon a scene that looked as if an enraged giant had bucketed up the river in an attempt to slosh away those misconceived improve-ments. Before the night ended the great gales had turned warm; far inland the ice broke up and was now grinding down the river. Commercial Street was flooded; huge cubes of ice were tumbled there as if ejected from some faulty, vast refrigerator. Smelt shacks went bobbing by, red and blue toys against the gray chop of the channel. But it was not the painted playhouses in which men crouched gleefully with their bottles and their lines that Jessie regretted most (although she did regret them) but the visible signs of somebody's real loss. The fish factory still stood, but what the city planners with blandishment and bait had not been able to do the storm had accomplished, and Henry Hinckley's Boat Supply was gone. His wharf looked like jackstraws and the building, listing on its side, swung loosely in the river. If this were true in town, how had the island fared? Impatiently she put aside the thought of her own home: her home would be all right. It always had been. But others would have lost gear, traps and trap-sheds, the very boats themselves; years of husbandry negated by one night of wind and water.

Mrs. Charley said, "Can we get up to see Charley?"

"Oh, sure," Jessie said, although she was not sure.

The sun was struggling through a bright, heavy mist. Her car was probably all right because she had parked on high ground behind the Emerson House, but the city plows were slow at the best, the melting snow weighty and the hospital on the far side of town. Below, at least one car was not all right; a flying sheet of metal had collapsed its roof.

While Mrs. Charley dressed, Jessie kept her back turned. She who had never been embarrassed by nakedness in her life, found that age hurt her. She thought too much of Mrs. Charley to witness her thin legs, the loose flesh falling underneath her arms, or even her shining scalp before the harsh curls were pinned in place. She had thought of the Charleys' many years in terms of wit and wisdom, and did not wish to see in a partial plate the intimations of mortality.

There are no telephones in the rooms at the Emerson House. It wouldn't look right. Anyway, hospitals won't tell you anything. To her at the desk, everyone not in crisis is resting comfortably and those in crisis are always stable. But your own loved one wants you to make the effort, so though you very much doubt that anyone will tell him that you tried, you try. When Mrs. Charley had stepped down the hall, Jessie looked critically about her. She was not much of a one for atmosphere.

The new owners of the old Emerson House, in the heat of their desire to beguile the infrequent traveler, had kept the upstairs as unchanged as possible: ceilings were low, floors sloped and in the shallow closets ropes were coiled; more, one hoped, for the fun of it than for security. The fairly new fire escapes depended from the rear of the building, where they did not show. Each room contained a small fireplace with a basket crate where no cannel coal glowed. In one of these very rooms a long-dead lady had written an incendiary book.

Most people, once they had looked around and got the good of it, preferred to stay in the annex. Jessie and Mrs. Charley would have preferred that, too, but last night there had been no heat out there. Downstairs, in the small dark lobby that consisted of a narrow hall and an ill-lit desk, the clerk was much excited to have guests. In the empty dining room, the girls were not.

As long as your own limbs are sound and your goods, such as they are, intact, disaster's fun. Doris and Dorcas had borrowed the television from the blackened bar and were pleasurably glued to the devastation that sifted across the screen. Once in a while they giggled with wonder and excitement; hashing day after day is dull. But Doris would sing another tune when she discovered that she would not, after all, get married in the spring, and Dorcas when she found that Pa and Ma would be moving in with her until the roof could be fixed.

The coffee was pale and the bacon cold; it would be captious to expect more at such a time. On the screen the storm again savaged the New England coast. Mountains of water filled the frame with spume; when it withdrew it left overturned cars, boats broken back to boards and sheets of water seething over roads and railings, while beyond, the next mass heaved and moved in upon the delicate debris. Cottages were splintered into kindling. A young woman and an old man wept. But that was Massachusetts.

Maine had to wait its turn, since there had not been time to process films, but meantime, here were bulletins: historic landmarks had disappeared and piers had exploded under flood water and fifty-knot winds. No deaths had been recorded but at least one bridge was closed because of the ice battering at its buttresses.

"Fishing men," said the platitudinous voice, "watched, helpless, while the sea destroyed their livelihoods."

"I'll see if I can get the car out," Jessie said.

In winter Maine towns are drawn in chalk and charcoal: white spires and widows' walks and fanlights are slashed by the black intact strokes of poles and the broken black strokes of branches. Jessie drove slowly, her tires sheeting up gray water to pock the sooty snowbanks. She let Mrs. Charley out at the door of the New Bristol Regional and watched with concern as her friend tested the slush with a cautious foot. The end so often starts with hips.

"Stay there," she called. "I'm coming."

Mrs. Charley had been a substantial woman. Overnight she had dwindled and the arm that Jessie grasped felt brittle as a stick. She was abashed at her own strong bones in their cushion of firm flesh and startled to perceive how abruptly we move from season to season: she herself had been a child one day and a woman the next and might yet be old.

"Oh, he's in geriatrics," said the thick-skinned person at the desk.

What the person had said was in no way insulting and yet they both felt insulted, although they did not, naturally, acknowledge this to one another. From the broad hall hung with photographs of the fine old men who had first made this hostel possible, they rose in silence and were much cheered to find that the nurse on the floor disapproved of Charley Pratt. One does not disapprove of the dying.

"He's no worse," this woman said. "Maybe a mite better. But he's sure filled with — vinegar."

Since they had not expected him to be better, that was fine news. So was the fact that though he might be filled with vinegar, they didn't have to cope with it. Mrs. Charley had never been much good at bullying and was quite ready to let a professional do it. Meantime, Charley certainly couldn't blame her.

But in geriatrics the corridors always smell faintly of urine, which is disheartening, and Jessie shrank when she saw Charley Pratt. It is not easy for the young to love the old, because it is dangerous. If you can keep your distance you look upon the aging as a different race, but to love them is not only to be wrung with pity for the drawing-in of their days but to walk beside them on that inexorable path knowing that you must walk it once again: it is to approach death twice. What distressed Jessie was not so much the stubble of white beard nor even the petulance that had replaced his pride, but the metal bars that changed his bed into an obscene crib in which he lay caged and diminished.

"Is this necessary?" Jessie asked the nurse, who, accustomed to attack, said only, "We're required by law."

No wonder Charley Pratt was cranky.

And women fare better in hospitals than men. They lie in foamy robes of pink or baby blue with a comfortable clutter of Kleenex and of magazines and no matter what her age, it is a sick woman who does not get her lipstick on. And then, they are resigned to indignity and have been since the first time that they were poked.

But there is that about a hospital that robs a man of sovereignty. Whether he strolls the halls in that thin borrowed robe and in disposable slippers or, mute and rebellious, is displayed upon a bed he is, as he had always feared, under the thumb of women. One is reminded that he defecates.

Besides, Charley was missing all the fun. The worst storm since the *City of Portland* went down, and he not there to guide and to advise. His sunken eyes were still light with fever.

"Would a TV help?" Mrs. Charley asked. "Shall I see if the Hardware's got one?"

Bitterly pleased that he knew something they didn't know, he said, "The Hardware's flooded."

No one knows how this is, but such things are known simultaneously all over town. Before the Hardware had had a chance to call his wife, the fact had been observed and, with many other interesting facts too small to warrant formal coverage, had spread like a brush fire. That pretty little Perkins ninny had been in with her mop.

But Charley was not dependent on word of mouth. Knowing how stubborn doctors are, he'd had a good idea he wouldn't be let home. "They're all afraid of being sued," said Charley. So he had taken the precaution of bringing along the small transistor radio that Jessie had given him last year. He took it out from underneath the sheet. The mouse-voice of the local station squeaked.

Flood waters showed no sign of abating and shop owners not yet inundated had sandbagged their shops. All schools were closed. The Methodists had postponed their Bean Supper and the Elks their Bingo Game. The ramp to the bridge was three feet under water.

"You won't get home today," Charley said, pleased.

"Oh, yes I will," said Jessie. She would, too, if she had to go upriver to another bridge.

Furious, she glared at her friend. Having been hale, he had no more right to lie there ill and helpless than had the Kennebec to burst from its banks. A spasm of coughing shook the spare shoulders that she should never have seen exposed in a coarse gown. Can one depend on nothing?

Mrs. Charley's hand in its tight shiny skin covered the bony hand of her husband. He turned his palm to hers and for a moment their fingers gripped. Then Charley drew away.

"Now, if you girls don't mind," he said, and turned the radio higher. On Land's End the Old Bottle Shop, sturdy as a ship, had sailed out to sea. In Harpswell Chester Wallace had watched his own seawall bounce apart. On Jacataqua the town wharf was weakened, and the shrimp shed had collapsed. There was no power on the island; those pressing woodstoves into service were warned that the fire department couldn't be everywhere at once.

Charley could have told them the shrimp shed wouldn't stand. In fact, he had. He wasn't the type to crassly say, "I told you so." But it would be inhuman, wouldn't it, not to cluck sympathetically. And smile.

"Never mind," Jessie told him. "Soon as you're out, I'll give you the grand tour."

He said, "It'll all be cleaned up by then."

The doctor, a brisk young man, flew on his appointed rounds. When he saw Jessie waiting in the hall, he stopped.

He said, "Are you the daughter?"

She nodded. For all intents and purposes, she was.

"Good," he said. "Step in here."

In here was a small family room without ashtrays where the anxious and the committed could wait for the information with which the staff parts so reluctantly. At this hour of the day it was dark and empty and the better for it; the doctor snapped on a bald light and made no motion to sit upon either the plastic sofa or the metal chair.

"Tough old man," he said. "Mr. Pratt."

"Yes," she said proudly. But he had not taken her aside to speak of the old man's toughness. So she said, "What's wrong?"

By the harsh light he examined her for signs that she was the daughter. She saw his eyes evaluate her smooth throat and the blue veins running strongly at her satin wrists: unlikely. But what counted was that she acknowledge some relationship.

"We can handle the virus," he said.

Then there was something that we couldn't handle. What?

He told her, not ungently, how it is with the old. One thing triggers another. "You or I would bounce back," he said.

Why shouldn't Charley?

He said, "It's the old ticker."

That sounded like something that her father might have said and because of that made her furious.

"Just tell me what you mean," she said.

Congestive heart failure. No, there was nothing to be done. You could repair a damaged valve or a valve weakening and about

215

to blow. His pale eyes lit with enthusiasm. In that case, there could be surgery.

But not when the old ticker's quietly running down.

No reason it should happen this week or next, and he could give the old man medication if the old man would take medication. And apart from that, Charley Pratt was in sterling shape. The young doctor had seldom seen a finer muscle tone, better bladder control nor such a liver. But where you've got your congestive heart failure . . .

"Don't tell his wife," said Jessie.

Only a scattering of cars was parked before the hospital where usually there was no room for anyone to park. A last late gust of wind shook the steel water in the gutter. Jessie looked down upon Mrs. Charley who had once been taller and she raged at the thieving years.

Those who have spent long lives in lovingkindness are not much to be envied, since the price is parting. Jessie herself had thought to have such a life with such a good companion. Now she was not sure she wanted any part of it. There are worse things than being lonely.

Here at the high point of the town only broken branches, silence and emptiness and a street sign askew marked the storm's passage.

Mrs. Charley said, "He'll be all right?"

"He'll be all right," said Jessie. And he would, too. This time.

24

"OH, MY GAWD," Parker Redlon said. "Ain't that something!"

It was never easy to get hold of Parker. Sometimes you could reach his wife; she always said he had just left but would probably be home sometime for lunch. There were those who believed that Parker was sitting right there, and that they both had a good laugh after you hung up.

Tom Elder was too old a hand to be taken in by Parker's tricks; he started out to find for himself Parker's truck. It looked like a big year for Parker. There was hardly a house on the island that did not need new shingles or new glass. Tom wanted to head the list. After Town Meeting you could say good-bye, Parker, but Parker wasn't going to start on the town wharf without something in writing (. . . to see whether the town will repair the wharf). Of course the town would repair the wharf. It had to.

Meantime, Parker always kept a meticulous list. This did not mean that he followed it; he skipped around depending on how he felt and how his crew felt. His crew was going to like working at the Landing. All their friends were there. People can get along without shingles; you can put a bucket out. As for that broken window, why don't you board it up? Just for now. But Tom's need was dire. A man without a septic tank is in dire need. Surely even Parker Redlon considered diredom.

Parker could be anywhere on the island, but Tom was willing to bet he was on Crow Point. The rest of the island knew what damage it had sustained but the Crow Pointers, in agony and suspense, would be calling from Boston and Baltimore and Bridgeport; that is, if they could get through. The new people would try and try and ask the operator to confirm that there was nothing wrong with Parker's line. Those who had been around longer sent letters. Registered.

At the post office they made Parker sign.

This has happened before: first you get your storm and then you get your January thaw. That was a big storm and this was a big thaw. Four feet of snow was scooting to the sea; on its impetuous way it scooped and channeled canyons across the roads. On Crow Point you had to watch your tailpipe, but you could ease down.

Tom's interest in his own situation was so acute that it had not until now occurred to him to wonder what had happened to his right and left. Now he was stricken with awe. First he found his septic tank, folded like an accordion and caught between the rocks. Nuzzled close to it a set of steps had somehow hung together and now, like Jacob's ladder, went nowhere. He thought it looked like Edgar Pedersen's steps, but since one set of steps looks very much like another, who can tell? The young Raffertys had been grumbling about their lawn but had no reason to grumble anymore. There was no lawn.

At the Bombing Gate the chain that prevented was raveled like yarn. Thirty feet farther he had to get out and move a tree; it was mostly a hysteria of branches and the trunk wasn't all that heavy. On the bay side the usually docile water like a too-obedient child

218

had had a tantrum. One of the new houses was no longer a new house. He couldn't get past Gin Beach because the road that threaded past Gin Beach was still under water. From it one sign leaned lazily. It urged PROTECT OUR DUNES.

Tom backed and turned and found it was like being in another country and without a map. Lydia Pullen's house was without a hat. The walls leaned. He was interested to see that Lydia's closets were a mess. That was all right. If Lydia had to rebuild she could afford to bring someone in from Bridgeport.

But the next place gave him pause.

The pleasant little academic gutsy woman who owned it had already had enough. She had been happy with her husband, who had died. Now the sea had bashed her cottage through from one side to the other; through the rear wall and through the front, the false sea smiled. Who was going to tell her?

Tom found himself saying like a litany, "It is the land. It is the land that counts."

Wouldn't you know that when he had circled the whole Point, he found Parker Redlon at the Pedersens'?

They were having words.

Parker didn't intend to do anything about it, not right now. He said, "You folks insured?"

For fire and wind but not, as Parker knew full well, for flood. Nobody on Jacataqua was insured for flood. Insurance hadn't been available and then when the federal government made it available, one of the selectmen had blundered and before the new forms came back, the storm arrived.

Edgar pinned Parker with his look. He said, "This was wind damage."

Parker laughed.

Edgar's obduracy came not so much from his desire to avoid expense, though any sensible man prefers to avoid expense, as from his reluctance to admit to Parker or to Irma or to anyone or to himself that the water had come up that high.

Parker sank down upon his heels and ran his palms along the

tarpaper where, just above the foundation, so many shingles were gone. He pushed back the painter's cap he always wore and rubbed his scalp. Then he touched the darkened shingles that were left.

He said, "I can tack on some shingles for you. Bye and bye. But that there were water."

"Well now, Tom," Parker said, "I don't know's I can help you out."

Sometimes beyond Parker Redlon's bland and pleasant look you felt he totted up your bank account.

"Why not?" Tom asked. "There's not much to it."

Parker said, "Oh, there's a lot to it."

What?

Well, you take in your old days. A septic tank was just a big old can and you could put it anywheres. But not now.

"No siree-bob," Parker said. "Not now."

Tom had been pleased as the next when they all stopped hurling their bottles on the rocks and throwing their corncobs over. But that was when his septic tank was working.

"These days," Parker said, "You got to ask Augusta."

Why, in the name of God?

Because these days the fellow has to come down from Augusta to see if you can bury your tank deep enough and your big filter tank and your chlorinated one. If there's not enough dirt over your rock to bury deep, maybe you can't have your tank at all.

Tom said, shocked, "That tank's been there forever. What about the grandfather clause?"

Oh, *that*. Well, probably if you had a septic tank before, they wouldn't say you couldn't have one now, not if the fellow thought you had enough dirt. But first you got to get your license from Augusta. Augusta's pretty busy these days because a whole lot of folks lost their septic tanks. They probably have a list.

Tom thought of his aunt's dwindling hoard. He said, "What's all this going to cost?"

Your septic tank used to run about five hundred, but everything's gone up. Parker shifted on his haunches; you'd think it was his fault. He said, "Well, the last one I did, seven thousand and seven-o-six. Might as well call it eight."

When he had caught his breath Tom said, "That's ridiculous."

"Sure is," Parker agreed. "I think I could do you for five." And then he proved he was a friend. "Was I you, I'd just go on using her."

They exchanged a long, conspiratorial look.

Parker said, "Of course come spring, she's going to smell."

It was a long time until spring.

"And anyways, we can't dig her up before thaw."

So that was how they left it.

"I'll be down about April Fool's," Parker said. "Probably. Give a day or two."

Angus insisted on going home with Jessie. "You don't know what you're going to run into down there," he said.

It was all right with her. It was all right with the beagle, too. The beagle liked Angus well enough though he stayed close to Jessie, who had proved that she was not completely to be trusted.

The woods were deep in debris and the water, salt and fresh mixed, was still receding from the marsh. Angus crept through, hoping he wasn't going to short the wires. From Gin Beach on they had to walk, which none of them minded though the beagle, bewildered by the unfamiliar look of things, kept close to their heels. They passed cottages underneath which there had been grass and where there now was drifted sand, and cottages underneath which there had been sand and where there now was stripped and naked rock.

Jessie was quiet. But at one point, opposite the sphagnum bog, she said, "If I went west with you, I'd still want to be here summers."

She had never gone so far as "if" before. Angus, a bird-watcher who feared to frighten the winged thing away, said only, "Sure."

Jessie's big house stood sturdy and unmolested. But the waves had visited. Sand circled the whole and lay rippled about the back door. For a moment her gray eyes were wide with surprise. "Maybe the Captain's House is gone," she said.

It wasn't. It stood as it had stood for a hundred years, just high enough to have escaped the long seas that had dropped boulders — big ones — all the way up the lawn. Jessie leaned suddenly against one of the great white pillars. The little hairs curled around the margin of her cap and the tears sprang.

"Don't cry," Angus said, agitated. "It can be cleaned up."

"It isn't that," she said. "But it won't happen again in a lifetime. And I missed it."

25

THE REAL DAMAGE was to the psyche.

That had happened which should not have happened, and the Crow Pointers were not the only owners of low-lying properties to be aghast. Wherever they looked they were reminded that they were fortune's playthings: on shore, buildings and woods and beaches had been breached; when they looked out to sea, they saw big rafts of turf float by. It made them ill at ease; they were exposed to calamity.

And January in Maine is a rotten month that brings out chilblains and animosities. Day drags beyond gray day, the cold hovers, the gulls rain like soot; nothing changes except when the sky spits. February is not much better.

During the month that followed the big storm, the winterers went through predictable phases of psychic shock. In the first phase they turned to one another with zeal and offers of aid: could they pick up anything in town, bring the mail, share the results of a new recipe? While this stage lasted they displayed a tendency to meet together — indeed, to cling together — and to rehearse every detail that they remembered. Each of them had almost complete recall. During this period their friends and their acquaintances showed an increasing desire to avoid them.

"We've heard this all before," they were told.

In the second stage they began to snarl and to withdraw. Tom Elder felt the Pedersens forgot that while they might be retired, he himself was a working artist. He began to take his phone off the hook, which hurt Irma's feelings. Edgar felt that Tom's hearty offers to relieve him of anything that involved physical effort was an unnecessary emphasis of his age. Jessie sulked. She felt the others were condescending because she alone had spent the historic night in the relative comfort and complete safety of New Bristol.

At last they hid, not so much from one another as from their own unshaped anxieties. Irma said two could play that game, and took her own phone off the hook. Tom wouldn't leave his house until he had seen the Pedersens drive away. On every day when there was not precipitation, Jessie rolled those of the boulders that were manageable back to the beach.

"Sorry," she said to Angus. "Not today."

Edgar paced — endlessly, it seemed to Irma — up and down before the great windows.

"I don't want you to discuss this with the boy," he warned. "It would just distress him."

"Oh, I won't!" Irma vowed, understanding more than she admitted to understanding. She herself had begun to knit again and spent silent hours over a yellow rabbit.

Tom painted as if his life depended upon it, which it did. He was pleased with his coloring, his composition, his chiaroscuro and his concepts and was more than once tempted to take a few to Boston. Who but he could wrest so much from a stalk of grass, a gull's feather? So he decided to wait and burst upon the best galleries with a completed series.

He might be able to afford a septic tank.

Then on the fifth of February the radio told them to watch out for heavy snows. Their initial enthusiasm for being snowed in had moderated but no one really minded, although no one had planned to go to town that day. Tom Elder waited until the last minute before he decided that he did not, after all, have enough drink, because so often the radio changes its mind.

By the morning of the sixth the television had joined the radio and had added that one might also expect heavy gales. So far this information was only proffered at normal news times; still, it had an unpleasantly familiar ring. Irma began to listen to both the radio and the television in case one of them knew something that the other didn't. She became absorbed in a variety of game shows, and Edgar could hear her calling out answers. She was surprisingly adept at evaluating various objects the very purpose of which Edgar did not know she knew.

So it was Irma who first saw the electrifying letters snaking again from right to left.

ALL RESIDENTS OF LOW-LYING AREAS
SHOULD NOW EVACUATE . . . .

26

"Mene, mene, tekel upharsin," Howard said bitterly. "You have been weighed in the balance and found wanting."

Jessie said, "Me?"

"This one's going to knock the spots off the last one. Get your things. We're getting out of here."

"You mean you're getting out of here," Jessie said, but absently. She was so elated to think that the new storm might knock the spots off the last one that she didn't even mind his showing up again.

"Why are you here this time?" she asked.

"I worry about you," he said, wounded. "Although I did think Whosis might be here."

226

"He's on his way," she said.

The storm was hours away but in the early dusk a few flakes loitered lazily; not enough to even faintly veil the sea, which ran dully.

"I bet it won't peak before daylight," Jessie said.

If she could see and savor this one, she didn't care whether the men were there or not. Let them stay if they wanted. It was immaterial. What counted was that there might never be a storm like this. Not in her lifetime.

But then Howard said something material.

Glancing over his shoulder he said, "Jessie. About that baby."

Don't spoil my storm. I have forgotten about the baby as far as I will ever forget.

"What do you know about that?" she demanded.

"Nothing except what I pieced together. With a little help." Cornelia.

If he claims that loss, Jessie thought, I will never speak to him. If he thinks I created that loss, I will not forgive him. If he shares that loss . . . and she began to tremble like the aspen tree.

Howard said, "I should have been with you."

Outside, the sad-colored day began to weep.

He said, "I would have been with you. Jessie, come back to me."

An intimacy between old enemies cannot be easily replaced. Old quarrels rob new quarrels of their potency. If it prove true that those who for their own purposes have created life are linked, it is unfair.

The wind clawe! Cape Cod and kept on prowling. Its tail switched inland. If the first storm had played like a kitten with a mouse, this was a tiger, hunting. Marblehead and Pride's Crossing cringed and squeaked. Portsmouth cowered. Ogunquit went to ground. Where the wind went the water followed, scavenging.

There is this to be said about having been here before: you lived through it. Irma was not much fussed when the wind began to shake Crow Point as the big cats break the necks of prey.

"Isn't it lucky," she said, "that Parker didn't get the shingles on?"

It was way past their bedtime. Who could sleep, at high tide and with a bigger one coming on?

"Oh, Eddie, don't miss this!" Irma cried, flattered. "We're on the national news!"

It wasn't ten minutes later when the telephone rang.

Wouldn't you think that at such a time a man would be safe from his son?

But Irma said, "He doesn't want to talk to me. He wants to talk to you."

The son proved right and the father, wrong.

Everyone knows sons love their mother better. Mothers read aloud and when you are feverish they bring you gingerale. And where is Father all this time?

Father is there.

And Mother is not much help when you become a man. Edgar's boy said, "Pa?"

"Yes?" Edgar challenged. A man does not have to be attacked. A man who has tried should be given credit. Even if he has done some things that were ill advised.

His son said to him, "I have a son."

Here it comes round again: the panic and the pride.

"That's all right, boy," Edgar said. "Don't panic."

Here is an elation that comes only twice.

The little boy will probably look like his father and he will not wander off into the woods because we all will watch him, and this time Edgar is not going to make the same mistake and will buy him a trike. They will be very good friends because it is easy for grandparents and grandchildren to be friends and Edgar will never again raise his voice to the child's father. Probably.

"And now," his son said, "may I speak to Mother?"

And while Edgar turned, dazed and delighted, the deck went

228

down and the Atlantic Ocean climbed the cliff and as if in a trough rushed up and banged the big window out and swung the couch where Edgar had been sitting six feet into the living room. Where his throat had been the air was filled with shards of glass that sliced everything it could slice, but not his jugular.

The new carpeting was under and the salt water splashed up the walls and over the desk and the coffee table and casually destroyed every one of Irma's trinkets. The wind screamed in behind the water.

"Oh, shoot," Irma said happily.

What does it matter? When your son has a son.

Nevertheless, the boy had been right. Crow Point was an expensive and a dangerous place to live.

However, Edgar felt better and younger and more competent and ingenious than he had felt for a long time. Right now the thing to do was to nail up blankets, which would not keep out the cold but would break the fury of the wind. Then to retreat to the bedroom, which did have a door. Tomorrow he would board that window up and in the spring he would have shutters made all around, against the next time.

They would hold onto the property, because it was a way of leaving something. But from now on Edgar and Irma were going to rent, because they had to live closer to Seattle. And in the meantime he felt that he was not going to die for a long time. There was too much to do.

The son must be protected from the father and later on, the father from the son.

Below them, Tom Elder spent a bad night. He was not a brave man. Had you asked he would have said this was a century that did not encourage, or even permit, bravery. Never has the individual been more at the mercy of society nor society more at the mercy of the natural world. The rivers sicken. The seas' bounty is burdened with mercury and lead. The earth gives up its poisoned treasures. Brigid had left him and it now appeared that he had never understood the ocean.

During the night, sleep had been out of the question. He had done what he could; again he piled his canvases upon the rafters, remembering bitterly that Brigid had taken the last of the rope to reinforce a suitcase. The last one — and the best one — had to stay upon the easel: it was wet. He flirted with the notion of retreating to the Pedersens' but could not face Edgar's complacent hospitality. When the first high tide had passed without the rogue wave, the devastator, the deviant, he had stretched fully dressed upon the bed and had lain picturing the long black rollers moving in upon the land.

Miles above, the winds were spinning toward Maine like the hands of a demented clock, so that the gusts that shook the camp sprang from the south but moved in from the north and east. For a while he left the radio on, but it made him nervous not to hear the full crash of the water, the creak of the walls, the rattle of sleet across the roof.

And so Tom tossed and thrashed and probably for a few minutes slept and wakened to wonder why marriage didn't work. Or at least his marriage, which he now saw as a matter of mutual inconvenience and a long series of petty tricks. Presumably marriages exist between adults; Brigid and Tom and brought to the difficult estate only the tantrums and rancors of children.

Toward morning the sound of the sleet stopped and the sound of the wind rose. Tom swayed his flashlight out of doors and found the air white with snow that the wind swung and fountained. He couldn't hear the water now above the howling frenzy of the wind but in the tunnel of the flash he could see it, black, bad and dangerous and already, at half-tide, battering the ledge below the house. Tom put his coat and cap and gloves and boots within easy reach and then stood by the window, waiting.

That morning the sun didn't rise. The only thing that happened at 7:30 was that a sick and livid light began to seep into chaos. Gradually out of the sound and fury Tom saw the white spray lift and tower. Then he saw something he had never thought to see. All night the blacksmith waves had pounded the long protective ledge below the house that had been his father's pride, his father's comfort; now as Tom watched, that ledge broke up and tons of ragged rock jumped like popcorn.

This is supposed to take millenniums. As the gneiss thaws and freezes and splits in laminated layers, hairlines of mist and rain invade. The hungry water is supposed to wait. But perhaps the land suffered a wee frisson and a new passage opened; then the greedy salt sea from which everything came and which intends to take everything back — takes everything back.

Tom turned and fled.

Halfway up the hill and waist-deep in snow, he was still struggling into his coat when he heard the next giant coming and swung and saw it, more than a wave, a flood racing fast and venomous; as he watched and without pausing, it picked up pieces of the broken ledge and roaring, hurled them between and against the camp's slender props. Silent as film, the little house sank to its knees and went over. The triumphant water carried away a table, a broken chair, portions of roof, firewood and pots and pans and all Tom's canvases. They bobbed and floated like the bright petals of a rain-ruined flower.

For a moment he felt nothing at all except the snow in his unlaced boots. Then what he felt astonished him. He felt: all right, to hell with it. He felt, that's that.

A new plan rose in his mind so instantly that he knew it for an old plan that had been lurking there. He would sell the land, every inch, and let someone else worry about the septic tank. He would take every dollar from every inch and go to Spain, where, as he understood it, a man could paint in comfort and afford a maid. Brigid could come or not as she chose and he thought she wouldn't. He rather hoped she wouldn't.

Then he trudged up the hill and before he could smell it, he thought he smelled Irma's hot and heady coffee.

27

JESSIE HAD PLANNED her storm carefully.

With distances, the radio reports and the tides in mind, she had figured out a kind of timetable, and according to that timetable she might as well sleep between midnight and, say, four. The men glared at her. Sleep? When through her stubbornness they were all placed in mortal danger?

She told them scornfully that they were jumpity as drops on a hot griddle.

By the first high tide branches were whipping and bushes bowed like dancers. The sea was unusually full. Her grandmother had always said they were protected by the offshore islands: Fox, Salters and Seguin, but already the waves covered the dry beach and lapsed upon her lawn. The men had turned the cars around and headed them toward the road.

"You won't get by Gin Beach," she said.

And by low tide the cars would be mired in snow.

And so she fell asleep serenely and awakened fresh and rested to the timpani of the wind and the long roll of the kettledrums of the surf. Candle in hand, she bent as quietly as Psyche over Cupid to where Howard and Angus lay crumpled, one in a chair and one upon the couch. Men with beards do come out of this sort of thing better. Already Angus's chin was feathered with blond fuzz.

In the kitchen Jessie stoked the stove, put on a pot of coffee and muffled from head to toe, opened the door prepared to slip into the maelstrom. There was water all around the house. It was wind-ruffled and wind-shaken but had lost all force of its own and must have lapped gently on from where it had broken, halfway up the lawn. That had to have been a big one. They say every seventh is a big one. In the swung light of her Coleman lantern and through swirling snow, her shingles flew like blackbirds.

Contented, she settled with her cup to wait for light, and she thought about human relationships and how — on the whole — unsatisfactory they are, since the human animal does not get along with his kind. Perhaps like sea lions we should meet at stated periods and for the purpose of reproduction and then go our ways. Howard could be Beachmaster. Howard would like that. Though as she understood it, the bulls scattered and the cows stuck together and helped out, which now that she thought of it seemed to be what women were now about.

And yet when she had been married to a man, she had been happy.

For a moment a deep pang struck her for those days that Howard wanted back again and could not have because he had never really had them. She had thought him happy when he had been bored and restless and she had thought him honest when, in and out of bed, he had been lying to her.

The light leaked loosely into a battered sky; the snow began to stop, though the wind still drove the drifts into swift dunes and valleys. The men woke rumpled and apprehensive of the waves crawling on the lawn.

"It won't come up much further," she said, though she knew it would.

Howard pointed out that the wind had torn the screens from the Captain's House and had toppled the tall thin chimney; Angus, that on its hill the little house was still knee-deep in snow, while everywhere below there was now salt slime where the brown grass lay like a sick beaver's pelt.

"Maybe we better move up there," Angus said. "While we can."

Jessie said that was silly. Jessie said there was plenty of time. Then she thought she had phrased that badly since it implied that she thought it only a matter of time before it would be wise to move up, and she didn't. If she was worried about anything it wasn't about the big house but about the big pillars, which were set on but not in concrete. And they still had two hours before high tide.

Jessie said, "Everyone ought to eat."

While the two men who wished to marry her devoured cold beans, Jessie considered marriage, which is a treaty drawn up by two for mutual comfort and support against a world in which there is much to fear: poverty, illness, boredom, loneliness. Others. The betrayed spouse feels less like a wounded individual than like a nation whose ally has made a unilateral agreement with the enemy.

Most marriages. She still thought the Charleys had married in a wild delight. Nothing else explained the residue of sweetness that remained between them.

Part of the roof lifted like the lid of a box, ripped off and blew away.

Howard looked up from his beans and said, "What was that?"

Jessie looked in to where it was storming in the living room. The last flakes of snow circled around the room and the wind that drove them made the curtains fly like flags and swept her grandmother's mementos to the floor; the lobsters and the pouncing china dog crashed and splintered. But what interested Jessie more than that was that the front windows were suddenly half-blind with green water.

From the doorway she said, "When you're quite finished, perhaps we'll go."

Nothing is worth fretting about that can eventually be repaired. But for once the fellows were right and the waves were hammering across the porch; no one would choose to be in a house when a wall goes down. Jessie and Angus and Howard tried the back door first, but the sea was running strong between the big house and the little and the water swirling above the wheels of the cars, so they stood at the front windows calculating their chances. The little house still beckoned from its mound of snow.

The wind was lessening; now it was busily parting the clouds and blowing them away as a housekeeper blows away dust. Scraps of blue sky appeared and then the sun burned through and began to help. Snow and sea dazzled, but the waves came on. Far out beyond Seguin the spray rose higher than the lighthouse, and the great combers took a second breath and glittered toward the land.

"We'll have to run between them," Howard said.

"I want to speak to Jessie first," said Angus.

Howard, she thought, seemed to be regressing. He told her like a petulant child, "I asked you first."

But his desire for her she knew for a velleity, composed of vanity and spite and the disappointment of not finding himself, without her, as comfortable as he had thought.

A minute later she thought Angus's proposal — if that was what it was — the strangest a woman ever had. His eyes shone with a strange excitement; had she not known, she would have suspected that he had been smoking. He guided her into the bedroom and clamped her shoulders with his hands.

Then he said, "Just a moment." And he took out his pocket notebook and made several notes. Then in tones low with awe he said, "I've got a book!"

He put the notebook back in his pants pocket and then on second thought, he placed it higher. When it was safe against the flood he put his hand beneath her chin and tipped her eyes to his.

"Coming along?" he asked.

Jessie thought not. She did not doubt that he was fond of her and deeply fond of her and that he would be faithful as far as women were concerned. But this book and the next one and the next one would come first.

"What are you doing?" Howard wailed.

Then they stood hand-in-hand and waited for the big one and when it had burst against the door Howard said, "Now!" and they ran between one wave and the next.

It was a bit more dangerous than getting wet. The sea that was tossing up logs and furniture and portions of other persons' wharves was, like a pack rat, eager to trade for anything it could wrest away, including people. And beneath its boiling surface there were still all those old rocks that Jessie had not been able, by herself, to move. If you were sprawled against one of them you could break a wrist. Or a skull.

Yanked along between two of them and with the water pulling at her knees, Jessie thought Howard had miscounted. The wave that towered toward them had to be the seventh. It shouted up the lawn tumbling and exulting as love should exult. Her ankle turned beneath her and it took two of them to tug her on. And she knew she wanted no arrangement that took two of them.

No. She would wait for the love that shouts and exults.

Meantime she had the big house and the beagle.

Jessie whirled, and beyond the scalding froth, the beagle waited on the porch. The next wave was gathering. The door had slammed behind him. The beagle whined and wriggled.

"Here!" Jessie called and slapped her knee.

The beagle's paws danced and drew back.

Jessie cried, "Come!"

He waved his tail apologetically.

So she went after him.

The ninth wave crested leisurely and crashed. She had one arm around a pillar and one arm around the beagle and she hung hard and was salt-blinded and gasping and the beagle and the pillar slipped and she clung harder and felt the gigantic suck as if the whole sea were intent on plucking them. Then it slid back silver in the sun and she was running with the dog heavy in her arms and slippery as if he had been greased. And while she ran the ocean rose and took the great white pillars down like tenpins.

So then because thou art lukewarm I will spew thee out.

But Jessie was not lukewarm.

Like Eve, she stood outside the ruined gates of Eden, dispossessed. Well, the two Adams could wander where they would and find in another vale a place of rest.

But unlike Eve, she purposed to be back.

Mrs. Charley sat all the night by Charley's side and all through the cacophonous morning, and she held his hand. Then she sighed and rose and went to the telephone and spoke to the post office.

"Charley's gone," she said.

And the town grieved with her for much that was valued and was good and now was gone. Except that what was good is never wholly gone, and it would be a long, long time before the town stopped quoting Charley Pratt.

But Parker Redlon shook his head. "Pity," he said. "He missed the first one, too."